D1268921

Blind Love and Other Stories

BOOKS BY V. S. PRITCHETT

SHORT STORIES

Sailor, Sense of Humor and Other Stories
When My Girl Comes Home
Collected Stories
It May Never Happen
You Make Your Own Life
The Spanish Virgin
Blind Love and Other Stories

NOVELS

Mr. Beluncle
Dead Man Leading
Nothing Like Leather
Shirley Sans
Claire Drummer
The Key to My Heart

MEMOIRS

A Cab at the Door

LITERARY CRITICISM

Books in General
The Living Novel and Later Appreciations
In My Good Books

TRAVEL

The Spanish Temper
Marching Spain
London Perceived
(With photographs by Evelyn Hofer)
The Offensive Traveller
Dublin: A Portrait
(With photographs by Evelyn Hofer)
New York Proclaimed
(With photographs by Evelyn Hofer)

BLIND LOVE

and Other Stories

V.S. PRITCHETT

Random House · New York

MOUNT UNION COLLEGE
LIBRARY

823
P961b

135208

First Printing
Copyright © 1969 by Random House

All rights reserved under International and Pan-American Copyright Conventions. Published in the United States by Random House, Inc., New York, and simultaneously in Canada by Random House of Canada Limited, Toronto.

Library of Congress Catalog Card Number: 70-85570
Manufactured in the United States of America
by American Book-Stratford Press

Of the stories in this collection,
the following appeared originally in *The New Yorker:*
Debt of Honor, The Liars, The Nest Builder,
and *The Skeleton. The Speech* originally appeared in
Harper's Magazine.
The Cage Birds was first
published in *Queen* Magazine.

2 3 4 5 6 7 8 9

To Dorothy

Contents

Blind Love

"I'M BEGINNING to be worried about Mr. 'Wolverhampton' Smith," said Mr. Armitage to Mrs. Johnson, who was sitting in his study with her notebook on her knee and glancing from time to time at the window. She was watching the gardener's dog rooting in a flower bed. "Would you read his letter again: the second paragraph about the question of a partnership?"

Since Mr. Armitage was blind it was one of Mrs. Johnson's duties to read his correspondence.

"He had the money—that is certain; but I can't make out on what conditions," he said.

"I'd say he helped himself. He didn't put it into the business at Ealing—he used it to pay off the arrears on the place at Wolverhampton," she said in her cheerful manner.

"I'm afraid you're right. It's his character I'm worried about," said Mr. Armitage.

"There isn't a single full stop in his letter—a full page on both sides. None. And all his words are joined together. It's like one word two pages long," said Mrs. Johnson.

"Is that so?" said Mr. Armitage. "I'm afraid he has an unpunctuated moral sense."

Coming from a blind man whose open eyes and face had the fixed gleam of expression you might have seen on a piece of rock, the word "unpunctuated" had a sarcasm unlike an ordinary sarcasm. It seemed, quite delusively, to come from a clearer knowledge than any available to the sighted.

"I think I'll go and smell out what he's like. Where is Leverton Grove? Isn't it on the way to the station? I'll drop in when I go up to London tomorrow morning," said Mr. Armitage.

The next morning he was driven in his Rolls-Royce to Mr. Smith's house, one of two or three little villas that were part of a building speculation that had come to nothing fifty years before. The yellow-brick place was darkened by the firs that were thick in this district. Mrs. Johnson, who had been brought up in London houses like this, winced at the sight of them. (Afterwards she said to Mr. Armitage, "It brings it back." They were talking about her earlier life.) The chauffeur opened the car door, Mrs. Johnson got out, saying "No curb," but Armitage waving her aside, stepped out unhelped and stood stiff with the sainted upward gaze of the blind; then, like an army detail, the party made a sharp right turn, walked two paces, then a sharp left to the wooden gate, which the chauffeur opened, and went forward in step.

"Daffodils," said Mrs. Johnson, noting a flower bed. She was wearing blue to match her bold, practical eyes, and led the way up the short path to the door. It was opened before she rang by an elderly, sick-looking woman with swollen knuckles who half-hid behind the door as she held it, to expose Smith standing with his gray jacket open, his hands in his pockets—the whole man an arrangement of soft smiles from his snowball head to his waistcoat, from his fly to his knees, sixteen stone of modest welcome with nothing to hide.

"It is good of you to come," he said. He had a reverent voice.

"On my way to the station," said Armitage.

Smith was not quite so welcoming to Mrs. Johnson. He gave her a dismissive frown and glanced peremptorily at his wife.

"In here?" said Mrs. Johnson, briskly taking Armitage's arm in the narrow hall.

"Yes," he said.

They all stood just inside the doorway of the front room. A fir tree darkened it. It had, Mrs. Johnson recorded at once, two fenders in the fireplace, and two sets of fire-irons; then she saw two of everything—two clocks on the fireplace, two small sofas, a dining table folded up, even two carpets on the floor, for underneath the red one, there was the fringe of a worn yellow one.

Mr. Smith saw that she noted this and raising a grand chin and now unsmiling, said, "We're sharing the 'ouse, the house, until we get into something bigger."

And at this, Mrs. Smith looked with the searching look of an agony in her eyes, begging Mrs. Johnson for a word.

"Bigger," echoed Mrs. Smith and watched to see the word sink in. And then, putting her fingers over her face, she said, "Much bigger," and laughed.

"Perhaps," said Mr. Smith, who did not care for his wife's laugh, "while we talk—er . . ."

"I'll wait outside in the car," said the decisive Mrs. Johnson, and when she was in the car she saw Mrs. Smith's gaze of appeal from the step.

A half an hour later, the door opened and Mrs. Johnson went to fetch Mr. Armitage.

"At this time of the year the daffodils are wonderful round here," said Armitage as he shook hands with Smith, to show that if he could not see there were a lot of things he knew. Mr. Smith took the point and replaced his smiling voice with one of sportive yet friendly rebuke, putting Mr. Armitage in his place.

"There is only one eye," he stated as if reading aloud. "The eye of God."

Softly the Rolls drove off, with Mrs. Smith looking at it fearfully from the edge of the window curtain.

"Very rum fellow," said Armitage in the car. "I'm afraid he's in a mess. The Inland Revenue are after him as well. He's quite happy because there's nothing to be got out of him. Remarkable. I'm afraid his friends have lost their money."

Mrs. Johnson was indignant.

"What's he going to do down here? He can't open up again."

"He's come here," Armitage said, "because of the chalk in London water. The chalk, he says, gets into the system with the result that the whole of London is riddled with arthritis and nervous diseases. Or rather the whole of London is riddled with arthritis and nervous diseases because it believes in the reality of chalk. Now, chalk has no reality. We are not living on chalk nor even on gravel: we dwell in God. Mr. Smith explains that God led him to manage a chemist's shop in Wolverhampton, and to open one of his own in Ealing without capital. He now realizes that he was following his own will, not the will of God. He is now doing God's work. Yesterday he had a cable from California. He showed it to me. 'Mary's cancer cured gratitude check follows.' He's a faith healer."

"He ought to be in jail," said Mrs. Johnson.

"Oh, no. He's in heaven," said Armitage. "I'm glad I went to see him. I didn't know about his religion, but it's perfect: you get witnesses like him in court every day, always moving on to higher things."

The Rolls arrived at the station and Mr. Armitage picked up his white stick.

"Cancer today. Why not blindness tomorrow? Eh?" he said. Armitage gave one low laugh from a wide mouth. And though she enjoyed his dryness, his rare laugh gave a dangerous animal expression to a face that was usually closed. He got out of the car and she watched him walk into the booking hall and saw knots of people divide to make way for him on the platform.

* * *

In the damp town at the bottom of the hills, in the shops, at the railway station where twice a week the Rolls waited for him to come back from London, it was agreed that Armitage was a wonder. A gentleman, of course, they said; he's well-off, that helps. And there is that secretary-housekeeper, Mrs. Johnson. That's how he can keep up his legal business. He takes his stick to London, but down here he never uses it. In London he has his lunch in his office or in his club, and can manage the club stairs which worry some of the members when they come out of the bar. He knows what's in the papers—ever had an argument with him?—of course Mrs. Johnson reads them to him.

All true. His house stood, with a sudden flash of Edwardian prosperity, between two larch coppices on a hill five miles out and he could walk out on to the brick terrace and smell the lavender in its season and the grass of the lawns that went steeply down to his rose garden and the blue tiles of his swimming pool boxed in by yew.

"Fabian Tudor. Bernard Shaw used to come here—before our time, of course," he would say, disparaging the high, paneled hall. He was really referring to his wife, who had left him when he was going blind twenty-two years ago. She had chosen and furnished the house. She liked leaded windows, brass, plain velvet curtains, Persian carpets, brick fireplaces and the expensive smell of wood smoke.

"All fake," he would say, "like me."

You could see that pride made him like to embarrass. He seemed to know the effect of jokes from a dead face. But, in fact, if he had no animation—Mrs. Johnson had soon perceived in her commonsensical way—this was because he was not affected, as people are, by the movements on other faces. Our faces, she had learned from Armitage, threw their lives away every minute. He stored his. She knew this because she stored hers. She did not put it like this, in fact what she said appeared to contradict it. She liked a joke.

"It's no good brooding. As mother used to say, as long as you've got your legs you can give yourself an airing."

Mrs. Johnson had done this. She had fair hair, a good figure and active legs, but usually turned her head aside when she was talking, as if to an imaginary friend. Mrs. Johnson had needed an airing very badly when she came to work for Mr. Armitage.

At their first interview—he met her in the paneled hall: "You do realize, don't you, that I am totally blind. I have been blind for more than twenty years," he said.

"Yes," she said. "I was told by Dr. James." She had been working for a doctor in London.

He held out his hand and she did not take it at once. It was not her habit to shake hands with people; now, as always, when she gave in she turned her head away. He held her hand for a long time and she knew he was feeling the bones. She had heard that the blind do this, and she took a breath as if to prevent her bones or her skin passing any knowledge of herself to him. But she could feel her dry hand coming to life and she drew it away. She was surprised that, at the touch, her nervousness had gone.

To her, Armitage's house was a wonderful place. The space, the light made friendly by the small panes of the tall leaded windows, charmed her.

"Not a bit like Peckham," she said cheerfully.

Mr. Armitage took her through the long sitting room, where there were yellow roses in a bowl, into his study. He had been playing a record and put it off.

"Do you like music?" he said. "That was Mozart."

"I like a bit of a sing-song," she said. "I can't honestly say I like the classical stuff."

He took her round the house, stopped to point to a picture or two and, once more down in the long room, took her to a window and said, "This is a bad day for it. The haze hasn't lifted. On a clear day you can see Sevenham Cathedral. It's twelve miles away. Do you like the country?"

"Frankly I've never tried it."

"Are you a widow, Mrs. Johnson?"

"No. I changed my name from Thompson to Johnson and not for the better. I divorced my husband," said Mrs. Johnson crisply.

"Will you read something to me—out of the paper?" he said. "A court case."

She read and read.

"Go on," he said. "Pick out something livelier."

"Lonely monkeys at the zoo?"

"That will do."

She read again and she laughed.

"Good," he said.

"As Father used to say, 'Speak up . . .' " she began, but stopped. Mr. Armitage did not want to hear what Father said.

"Will you allow me," Armitage said, getting up from his desk, "would you allow me to touch your face?"

Mrs. Johnson had forgotten that the blind sometimes asked this.

She did not answer at once. She had been piqued from the beginning because he could not see her. She had been to the hairdresser's. She had bought a blouse with a high frilled neck which was meant to set off the look of boyish impudence and frankness of her face. She had forgotten about touch. She feared he would have a pleading look, but she saw that the wish was part of an exercise for him. He clearly expected her to make no difficulty about it.

"All right," she said, but she meant him to notice the pause, "if you want to."

She faced him and did not flinch as his hand lightly touched her brow and cheek and chin. He was, she thought, "after her bones," not her skin, and that, though she stiffened with resistance, was "O.K. by her." But when, for a second, the hand seemed about to rest on her jaw, she turned her head.

"I weigh eight stone," she said in her bright way.

"I would have thought less," he said. That was the nearest he came to a compliment. "It was the first time," she said afterwards to her friend Marge in the town, "that I ever heard of a secretary being bought by weight."

She had been his secretary and housekeeper for a long time now. She had understood him at once. The saintly look was nonsense. He was neither a saint nor a martyr. He was very vain; especially he was vain of never being deceived, though in fact his earlier secretaries had not been a success. There had been three or four before her. One of them—the cook told her—imagined him to be a martyr because she had a taste for martyrdom and drank to gratify it; another yearned to offer the compassion he hated, and muddled everything. One reckoning widow lasted only a month. Blatantly she had added up his property and wanted to marry him. The last, a "lady," helped herself to the household money, behind a screen of wheezing grandeur and name-dropping.

Remembering the widow, the people who came to visit Mr. Armitage when he gave a party were relieved after their meeting with Mrs. Johnson.

"A good honest-to-God Cockney" or "Such a cheery soul." "Down to earth," they said. She said she had "knocked about a bit." "Yes, sounds as if she had": they supposed they were denigrating. She was obviously not the kind of woman who would have any dangerous appeal to an injured man. And she, for her part, would go to the pictures when she had time off or simply flop down in a chair at the house of her friend Marge and say, "Whew, Marge. His nibs has gone to London. Give me a strong cuppa. Let's relax."

"You're too conscientious."

"Oh, I don't mind the work. I like it. It occupies your mind. He has interesting cases. But sometimes I get keyed up."

Mrs. Johnson could not herself describe what keyed her up—perhaps, being on the watch? Her mind was stretched. She found herself translating the world to him and it took her time to realize that it did not matter that she was not "educated up to it." He obviously liked her version of the world but it was a strain having versions. In the mornings she had to read his letters. This bothered her. She was very moral about privacy. She had to invent an impersonal, uninterested voice. His lack of privacy irked her; she liked gossip and news as much as any woman, but here it lacked the salt of the secret, the whispered, the found out. It was all information and statement. Armitage's life was an abstraction for him. He had to know what he could not see. What she liked best was reading legal documents to him.

He dressed very well and it was her duty to see that his clothes were right. For an orderly, practical mind like hers, the order in which he lived was a new pleasure. They lived under fixed laws: no chair or table, even no ashtray must be moved. Everything must be in its place. There must be no hazards. This was understandable: the ease with which he moved without accident in the house or garden depended on it. She did not believe when he said, "I can hear things before I get to them. A wall can shout, you know." When visitors came she noticed he stood in a fixed spot: he did not turn his head when people spoke to him and among all the head-turning and gesturing he was the still figure, the lawgiver. But he was very cunning. If someone described a film they had seen, he was soon talking as if he had been there. Mrs. Johnson, who had duties when he had visitors, would smile to herself, at the surprise on the faces of people who had not noticed the quickness with which he collected every image or scene or character described. Sometimes, a lady would say to her, "I do think he's absolutely marvelous," and, if he overheard this—and his hearing was acute—Mrs. Johnson would notice a look of ugly boredom on his face. He was, she noted, particularly vain of his care of money and accounts. This pleased Mrs. Johnson because she was quick to understand that here a blind man who had servants might be swindled. She was indignant about the delinquency of her predecessor. He must have known he was being swindled.

Once a month Mrs. Johnson would go through the accounts with him. She would make out the checks and take them to his study and put them on his desk.

The scene that followed always impressed her. She really admired him for this. How efficient and devious he was! He placed the check at a known point on his blotter. The blunt fingers of his hairless hands had the art of gliding and never groping, knowing the inches of distance; and then, as accurately as a geometrician, he signed. There might be a pause as the fingers secretly measured, a pause alarming to her in the early days, but now no longer alarming; sometimes she detected a shade of cruelty in this pause. He was listening for a small gasp of anxiety as she watched.

There was one experience which was decisive for her. It occurred in the first month of her employment and had the lasting stamp of a revelation. (Later on, she thought he had staged the incident in order to show her what his life was like and to fix in her mind the nature of his peculiar authority.) She came into the sitting room one evening in the winter to find a newspaper and heard sharp, unbelievable sounds coming from his study. The door was open and the room was in darkness. She went to it, switched on the light, and saw he was sitting there typing in the darkness. Well, she could have done that if she had been put to it—but now she *saw* that for him there was no difference between darkness and light.

"Overtime, I see," she said, careful not to show surprise.

This was when she saw that his mind was a store of maps and measured things; a store of sounds and touches and smells that became an enormous translated paraphernalia.

"You'd feel sorry for a man like that," her friend Marge said.

"He'd half kill you if you showed you were sorry," Mrs. Johnson said. "I don't feel sorry. I really don't."

"Does he ever talk about his wife?"

"No."

"A terrible thing to do to leave a man because he's blind."

"She had a right to her life, hadn't she?" said Mrs. Johnson flatly. "Who would want to marry a blind man?"

"You are hard," Marge said.

"It's not my business," said Mrs. Johnson. "If you start pitying people you end up by hating them. I've seen it. I've been married, don't forget."

"I just wish you had a more normal life, dear."

"It suits me," said Mrs. Johnson.

"He ought to be very grateful to you."

"Why should he be? I do my job. Gratitude doesn't come into it. Let's go and play tennis."

The two women went out and played tennis in the park and Mrs. Johnson kept her friend running from court to court.

"I smell tennis balls and grass," said Mr. Armitage when she returned.

* * *

In the March of her third year a bad thing happened. The winter was late. There was a long spell of hard frost and you could see the cathedral tower clearly over the low-lying woods on most days. The frost coppered the lawns and scarcely faded in the middle of the day. The hedges were spiked and white. She had moved her typing table into the sitting room close to the window to be near a radiator and when she changed a page she would glance out at the garden. Mr. Armitage was out there somewhere and she had got into the habit of being on the watch. Now she saw him walk down the three lawns and find the brick steps that led to the swimming pool. It was enclosed by a yew hedge and was frozen over. She could see Armitage at the far side of it pulling at a small fallen branch that had been caught by the ice. His foot had struck it. On the other side of the hedge, the gardener was cutting cabbage in the kitchen garden and his dog was snuffling about. Suddenly a rabbit ran out, ears down, and the dog was yelping after it. The rabbit ran through the hedge and almost over Armitage's feet with the dog nearly on it. The gardener shouted. The next moment Armitage, who was squatting, had the dog under his legs, lost his balance and fell full length through the ice into the pool. Mrs. Johnson saw this. She saw the gardener drop his knife and run to the gap in the hedge to help Armitage out. He was clambering over the side. She saw him wave the gardener's hand away and shout at him and the gardener step away as Armitage got out. He stood clawing weed off his face, out of his hair, wringing his sleeves and brushing ice off his shirt as he marched back fast up the garden. He banged the garden door in a rage as he came in.

"That bloody man. I'll have that dog shot," shouted Armitage. She hurried to meet him. He had pulled off his jacket and thrown it on a chair. Water ran off his trousers and sucked in his shoes. Mrs. Johnson was appalled.

"Go and change your things quickly," she said. And she easily raced him to the stairs to the landing and to his room. By the time he got there she had opened several drawers, looking for underclothes, and had pulled out a suit from his cupboard. Which suit? She pulled out another. He came squelching after her into the room.

"Towel," she cried. "Get it all off. You'll get pneumonia."

"Get out. Leave me alone," shouted Armitage, who had been tugging his shirt over his head as he came upstairs.

She saw, then, that she had done a terrible thing. By opening drawers and putting clothes on the bed, she had destroyed one of his systems. She saw him grope. She had never seen him do this before. His bare white arms stretched out in a helpless way and his brown hands pitiably closed on air. The action was slow and his fingers frightened her.

"I told you to leave me alone," he shouted.

She saw she had humiliated him. She had broken one of the laws. For the first time she had been incompetent.

Mrs. Johnson went out and quietly shut the door. She walked across the landing to the passage in the wing where her own room was, looking at the wet marks of his muddy shoes on the carpet, each one accusing her. She sat down on the edge of her bed. How could she have been such a fool! How could she have forgotten his rule? Half naked to the waist, hairy on the chest and arms, he shocked because the rage seemed to be not in his mind but in his body like an animal's. The rage had the pathos of an animal's. Perhaps when he was alone he often groped; perhaps the drilled man she was used to, who came out of his bedroom or his study, was the expert survival of a dozen concealed disasters?

Mrs. Johnson sat on her bed listening. She had never known Armitage to be angry; he was a monotonously considerate man. The shout abashed her and there was a strange pleasure in being abashed; but her mistake was not a mere mistake. She saw that it struck at the foundation of his life and was so gross that the surface of her own confidence was cracked. She was a woman who could reckon on herself, but now her mind was scattered. Useless to say to herself, "What a fuss about nothing," or "Keep calm." Or, about him, "Nasty temper." His shout, "Get out. I told you to leave me alone," had, without reason (except that a trivial shame is a spark that sets fire to a long string of greater shames), burned out all the security of her present life.

She had heard those words, almost exactly those words, before. Her husband had said them. A week after their wedding.

Well, *he* had had something to shout about, poor devil. She admitted it. Something a lot more serious than falling into a pond and having someone commit the crime of being kind to you and hurting your silly little pride.

She got up from the bed and turned on the tap of the washbasin to cool down her hot face and wash her hands of the dirt of the jacket she had brought upstairs. She took off her blouse and as she sluiced her face she looked through the water at herself in the mirror. There was a small birthmark, the size of a red leaf which many people noticed and which, as it showed over the neck of the high blouses she usually wore, had the enticement of some signal or fancy of the blood; but under it, and invisible to them, were two smaller ones and then a great spreading ragged liver-colored island of skin which spread under the tape of her slip and crossed her breast and seemed to end in a curdle of skin below it. She was stamped with an ineradicable bloody insult. It might have been an attempt to impose another woman on her. She was used to seeing it, but she carried it about with her under her clothes, hiding it and yet vaunting.

Now she was reaching for a towel and inside the towel, as she dried herself, she was talking to Armitage.

"If you want to know what shame and pride are, what about marrying a man who goes plain sick at the sight of your body and who says 'You deceived me. You didn't tell me.' "

She finished drying her face and put the towel on the warm rail and went to her dressing table. The hairbrush she picked up had been a wedding present and at each hard stroke of the brush on her lively fair hair, her face put up a fight, but it exhausted her. She brushed the image of Armitage away and she was left staring at the half-forgotten but never-forgotten self she had been.

How could she have been such a fool as to deceive her husband? It was not through wickedness. She had been blinded too—blinded by love; in a way, love had made her so full of herself that, perhaps, she had never seen *him*. And her deceptions: she could not stop herself smiling at them, but they were really pitiable because she was so afraid of losing him and to lose him would be to lose this new beautifully deluded self. She ought to have told him. There were chances. For example, in his flat with the gray sofa with the spring that bit your bottom going clang, clang at every kiss, when he used to carry on about her wearing dresses that a man couldn't get a hand into. He knew very well she had had affairs with men, but why, when they were both "worked up," wouldn't she undress and go to the bedroom? The sofa was too short. She remembered how shocked his face looked when she pulled up her skirts and lay on the floor. She said she believed in sex before marriage, but she thought some things ought to wait: it would be wrong for him to see her naked before their wedding day. And to show him she was no prude—there was that time they pretended to be looking out of the window at a cricket match; or Fridays in his office when the staff was gone and the cleaners were only at the end of the passage.

"You've got a mole on your neck," he said one day.

"Mother went mad with wanting plums when she was carrying me. It's a birthmark."

"It's pretty," he said and kissed it.

He kissed it. He kissed it. She clung to that when after the wedding they got to the hotel and she hid her face in his shoulder and let him pull down the zip of her dress. She stepped away, and pretending to be shy she undressed under her slip. At last the slip came off over her head. They both looked at each other, she with brazen fear and he—she couldn't forget the shocked blank disgust on his face. From the neck over the left shoulder down to the breast and below, and spreading like a red tongue to the back was this ugly blob—dark as blood, like a ragged liver on a butcher's window, or some obscene island with ragged edges. It was as if a bucket of paint had been thrown over her.

"You didn't tell me," he said. If only she had told him, but how could she have done? She knew she had been cursed.

"That's why you wouldn't undress, you little hypocrite."

He himself was in his underpants with his trousers on the bed and with his cuff links in his hand, which made his words absurd and awful. His ridiculous look made him tragic and his hatred frightening. It was terrible that for two hours while they talked he did not undress and worse that he gave her a dressing gown to cover herself. She heard him going through the catalogue of her tricks.

"When . . ." he began in a pathetic voice. And then she screamed at him.

"What do you think? Do you think I got it done, that I got myself tattooed in the Waterloo Road? I was born like it."

"Ssh," he said, "You'll wake the people in the next room."

"Let them hear. I'll go and show them," she screamed. It was kind of him to put his arm around her. When she had recovered, she put on her fatal, sporty manner. "Some men like it," she said.

He hit her across the face. It was not then but in the following weeks when pity followed and pity turned to cruelty he had said, "Get out. Leave me alone."

* * *

Mrs. Johnson went to her drawer and got out a clean blouse.

Her bedroom in Armitage's house was a pretty one, far prettier than any she had ever had. Up till now she had been used to bed-sitters since her marriage. But was it really the luxury of the house and the power she would have in it that had weighed with her when she had decided to take on this strange job? She understood now something else had moved her in the low state she had been in when she came. As a punished and self-hating person she was drawn to work with a punished man. It was a return to her girlhood: injury had led her to injury.

She looked out of the window at the garden. The diamond panes chopped up the sight of the frozen lawns and the firs that were frost-whiskered. She was used to the view. It was a view of the real world; that, after all, was her world, not his. She saw that gradually in three years she had drifted out of it and had taken to living in Armitage's filed memory. If he said, for example, "That rambler is getting wild. It must be cut back," because a thorn caught his jacket, or if he made his famous remark about seeing the cathedral on a clear day, the landscape limited itself to these things and, in general, reduced itself to the imposed topographical sketch in his mind. She had allowed him, as a matter of abnegation and duty, to impose his world on hers. Now this shock brought back a lost sense of the right to her own landscape; and then to the protest, that this country was not hers at all. The country bored her. The fir trees bored her. The lanes bored her. The view from this window or the tame protected view of the country from the Rolls-Royce window bored her. She wanted to go back to London, to the streets, the buses and the crowds, to crowds of people with eyes in their heads. And—her spirits rising —"To hell with it, I want people who can *see* me."

She went downstairs to give orders for the carpet to be brushed.

In the sitting room she saw the top of Armitage's dark head. She had not heard him go down. He was sitting in what she called the cathedral chair facing the window and she was forced to smile when she saw a bit of green weed sticking to his hair. She also saw a heavy glass ashtray had fallen off the table beside him. "Clumsy," she said. She picked it up and lightly pulled off the piece of weed from his hair. He did not notice this.

"Mr. Armitage," she said in her decisive manner, "I lost my head. I'm sorry."

He was silent.

"I understand how you feel," she said. For this (she had decided in her room) was the time for honesty and for having things out. The impersonality could not go on, as it had done for three years.

"I want to go back to London," she said.

"Don't be a damn fool," he said.

Well, she was not going to be sworn at. "I'm not a damn fool," she said. "I understand your situation." And then, before she could stop herself, her voice shaking and loud, she broke out with: "I know what humiliation is."

"Who is humiliated?" said Armitage. "Sit down."

"I am not speaking about you," she said stiffly.

That surprised him, she saw, for he turned his head.

"I'm sorry, I lost my temper," he said. "But that stupid fellow and his dog . . ."

"I am speaking about myself," she said. "We have our pride, too."

"Who is *we?*" he said, without curiosity.

"Women," she said.

He got up from his chair, and she stepped back. He did not move and she saw that he really had not recovered from the fall in the pool, for he was uncertain. He was not sure where the table was.

"Here," he said roughly, putting out a hand. "Give me a hand out of this."

She obediently took him by the arm and stood him clear of the table.

"Listen to me. You couldn't help what happened and neither could I. There's nothing to apologize for. You're not leaving. We get on very well. Take my advice. Don't be hard on yourself."

"It is better to be hard," she said. "Where would you have been if you had not been hard? I'm not a girl. I'm thirty-nine." He moved towards her and put his hand on her right shoulder and she quickly turned her head. He laughed and said, "You've brushed your hair back." He knew. He always knew.

She watched him make for his study and saw him take the wrong course, brush against the sofa by the fireplace, and then a yard or two further, he shouldered the wall.

"Damn," he said.

At dinner, conversation was difficult. He offered her a

glass of wine which she refused. He poured himself a second glass and as he sat down he grimaced with pain.

"Did you hurt your back this afternoon?" she asked.

"No," he said. "I was thinking about my wife."

Mrs. Johnson blushed. He had scarcely ever mentioned his wife. She knew only what Marge Brook had told her of the town gossip: how his wife could not stand his blindness and had gone off with someone and that he had given her a lot of money. Someone said, ten thousand pounds. What madness! In the dining room Mrs. Johnson often thought of all those notes flying about over the table and out of the window. He was too rich. Ten thousand pounds of hatred and rage, or love, or madness. In the first place, she wouldn't have touched it.

"She made me build the pool," he said.

"A good idea," she said.

"I don't know why. I never thought of throwing her into it," he said.

Mrs. Johnson said, "Shall I read the paper?" She did not want to hear more about his wife.

Mrs. Johnson went off to bed early. Switching on the radio in her room and then switching it off because it was playing classical music, she said to herself, "Well, funny things bring things back. What a day!" and stepped yawning out of her skirt. Soon she was in bed and asleep.

* * *

An hour later, she woke up, hearing her name.

"Mrs. Johnson. The water got into my watch, would you set it for me?" He was standing there in his dressing gown.

"Yes," she said. She was a woman who woke up alert and clearheaded.

"I'm sorry. I thought you were listening to a program. I didn't know you were in bed," he said. He was holding the watch to his ear.

"Would you set it for me and put my alarm right?" He had the habit of giving orders. They were orders spoken into space—and she was the space, nonexistent. He gave her the watch and went off. She put on her dressing gown and followed him to his room. He had switched on the light for her. She went to the bedside table and bent down to wind the clock. Suddenly she felt his arms round her, pulling her upright, and he was kissing her head. The alarm went off suddenly and she dropped the clock. It went on screeching on the floor at her feet.

"Mr. Armitage," she said in a low angry voice, but not struggling. He turned her round and he was trying to kiss her on the lips. At this she did struggle. She twisted her head this way and that to stop him, so that it was her head rather than her body that was resisting him. Her blue eyes fought with all their light, but his eyes were dead as stone.

"Really, Mr. Armitage. Stop it," she managed to mutter. "The door is open. Cook will hear."

She was angry at being kissed by a man who could not see her face, but she felt the shamed insulted woman in her, that blotched inhabitant, blaze up in her skin.

The bell of the alarm clock was weakening and then choked to a stop and in her pettish struggle she stepped on it; her slipper had come off.

"I've hurt my foot." Distracted by the pain she stopped struggling and Armitage took his opportunity and kissed her on the lips. She looked with pain into his sightless eyes. There was no help there. She was terrified of being drawn into the dark where he lived. And then the kiss seemed to go down her throat and spread into her shoulders, into her breasts and branch into all the veins and arteries of her body and it was the tongue of the shamed woman who had sprung up in her that touched his.

"What are you doing?" she was trying to say, but could

only groan the words. When he touched the stained breast she struck back violently, saying, "No, no."

"Come to bed with me," he said.

"Please let me go. I've hurt my foot."

The surprising thing was that he did let her go, and as she sat panting and white in the face on the bed to look at her foot, she looked mockingly at him. She forgot that he could not see her mockery. He sat beside her but did not touch her and he was silent. There was no scratch on her foot. She picked up the clock and put it back on the table.

Mrs. Johnson was proud of the adroitness with which she had kept men away from her since her marriage. It was a war with the inhabitant of the ragged island on her body. That creature craved for the furtive, for the hand that slipped under a skirt, for the scuffle in the back seat of a car, for a five-minute disappearance into a locked office.

But the other Mrs. Johnson, the cheerful one, was virtuous. She took advantage of his silence and got quickly up to get away; she dodged past him, but he was quick too. He was at the closed door. For a moment she was wily. It would be easy for her to dodge him in the room. And, then, she saw once more the sight she could not bear that melted her more certainly than the kisses which had filled her mouth and throat: she saw his hands begin to open and search and grope in the air as he came towards the sound of her breathing. She could not move. His hand caught her. The woman inside her seemed to shout, "Why not? You're all right. He cannot see." In her struggle she had not thought of that. In three years he had made her forget that blindness meant not seeing.

"All right," she said and the virtue in Mrs. Johnson pouted. She gently tapped his chest with her fingers and said with the sullenness of desire, "I'll be back in a minute."

* * *

It was a revenge: that was the pleasure.

"Dick," she called to her husband, "look at this," when the man was on top of her. Revenge was the only pleasure and his excitement was soon over. To please him she patted him on the head as he lay beside her and said, "You've got long legs." And she nearly said, "You are a naughty boy" and "Do you feel better?" but she stopped herself and her mind went off on to what she had to do in the morning; she listened and wondered how long it would be before he would fall asleep and she could stealthily get away. Revenge astonished by its quickness.

She slyly moved. He knew at once and held her. She waited. She wondered where Dick was now. She wished she could tell him. But presently this blind man in the bed leaned up and put both his hands on her face and head and carefully followed the round of her forehead, the line of her brow, her nose and lips and chin, to the line of her throat and then to her nape and shoulders. She trembled, for after his hands had passed, what had been touched seemed to be new. She winced as his hand passed over the stained shoulder and breast and he paused, knowing that she winced, and she gave a groan of pleasure to deceive him; but he went on, as if he were modeling her, feeling the pit under the arms, the space of ribs and belly and the waist of which she was proud, measuring them, feeling their depth, the roundness of her legs, the bone in her knees until, throwing all clothes back he was holding her ankle, the arch of her foot and her toes. Her skin and her bones became alive. His hands knew her body as she had never known it. In her brief love affairs which had excited her because of the risk of being caught, the first touch of a man stirred her at once, and afterwards, left her looking demurely at him; but she had let no one know her with a pedantry like his. She suddenly sat up and put her arms around him and now she went wild. It was not a revenge now; it was a triumph. She lifted the sad breast to his lips. And when they lay back she kissed his chest and then—with daring—she kissed his eyes.

It was six o'clock before she left him, and when she got to her room the stained woman seemed to bloom like a flower. It was only after she had slept and saw her room in daylight again that she realized that once more she had deceived a man.

It was late. She looked out of the window and saw Armitage in his city clothes talking to the chauffeur in the garden. She watched them walk to the garage.

"O.K." she said dryly to defend herself. "It was a rape." During the day there would be moments when she could feel his hands moving over her skin. Her legs tingled. She posed as if she were a new-made statue. But as the day went on she hardened and instead of waiting for him to return she went into the town to see Marge.

"You've put your hair up," Marge said.

"Do you like it?"

"I don't know. It's different. It makes you look severe. No, not severe. Something. Restless."

"I am not going back to dinner this evening," she said. "I want a change. Leonard's gone to London."

"Leonard!" said Marge.

Mrs. Johnson wanted to confide in Marge, but Marge bored her. They ate a meal together and she ate fast. To Marge's astonishment she said, "I must fly."

"You *are* in a mood," Marge said.

Mrs. Johnson was unable to control a longing to see Armitage. When she got back to the house and saw him sitting by the fire she wanted him to get up and at least put his arms round her; but he did not move, he was listening to music. It was always the signal that he wanted to be alone.

"It is just ending," said Armitage.

The music ended in a roll of drums.

"Do you want something, Helen?" he said.

She tried to be mocking, but her voice could not mock and she said seriously, "About last night. It must not happen again. I don't want to be in a false position. I could not go on living in the house."

She did not intend to say this; her voice, between rebuke and tenderness, betrayed this.

"Sit down."

She did not move.

"I have been very happy here," she said. "I don't want to spoil it."

"You are angry," he said.

"No, I'm not," she said.

"Yes, you are; that is why you were not here when I got back," he said.

"You did not wait for me this morning," she said. "I was glad you didn't. I don't want it to go on."

He came nearer to her and put his hand on her hair.

"I like the way your hair shows your ears," he said. And he kissed them.

"Now, please," she said.

"I love you," he said and kissed her on the forehead and she did not turn her head.

"Do you? I'm glad you said that. I don't think you do. When something has been good, don't spoil it. I don't like love affairs," she said.

And then she changed. "It was a party. Good night."

"You made me happy," he said, holding on to her hand.

"Were you thinking about it a long time?" she said in another voice, lingering for one more word.

"Yes," he said.

"It is very nice of you to say that. It is what you ought to say. But I mean what I said. Now, really, good night. And," giving a pat to his arm, she said, "Keep your watch wound up.

Two nights later he called to her loudly and curtly from the stairs: "Mrs. Johnson, where are you?" and when she came into the hall he said quietly, "Helen."

She liked that. They slept together again. They did not talk.

* * *

Their life went on as if nothing had happened. She began to be vain of the stain on her body and could not resist silently displaying, almost taunting him, when she undressed, with what he could not see. She liked the play of deceiving him like this; she was paying him out for not being able to see her; and when she was ashamed of doing this the shame itself would rouse her desire: two women uniting in her. And fear roused her too; she was afraid of his blindness. Sometimes the fear was that the blind can see into the mind. It often terrified her at the height of her pleasure that she was being carried into the dark where he lived. She knew she was not but she could not resist the excitement of imagining it. Afterwards she would turn her back to him, ashamed of her fancies, and as his finger followed the bow of her spine she would drive away the cynical thought that he was just filing this affair away in one of the systems of his memory.

Yet she liked these doubts. How dead her life had been in its practical certainties. She liked the tenderness and violence of sexual love, the simple kindness of the skin. She once said to him, "My skin is your skin." But she stuck to it that she did not love him and that he did not love her. She wanted to be simply a body: a woman like Marge who was always talking about love seemed to her a fool. She liked it that she and Armitage were linked to each other only by signs. And she became vain of her disfigurement, and looking at it, even thought of it as the lure.

I know what would happen to me if I got drunk, she thought at one of Armitage's cocktail parties, I'm the sort of woman who would start taking her clothes off. When she was a young woman she had once started doing so, and someone, thank God, stopped her.

But these fancies were bravado.

They were intended to stop her from telling him.

* * *

On Sundays Mrs. Johnson went to church in the village near the house. She had made a habit of it from the beginning, because she thought it the proper thing to do: to go to church had made her feel she need not reproach herself for impropriety in living in the same house as a man. It was a practical matter: before her love affair the tragic words of the service had spoken to her evil. If God had done this to her, He must put up with the sight of her in His house. She was not a religious woman; going to church was an assertion that she had as much right to fair play as anyone else. It also stopped her from being "such a fool" as to fall to the temptation of destroying her new wholeness by telling him. It was "normal" to go to church and normality had been her craving ever since her girlhood. She had always taken her body, not her mind, to church.

Armitage teased her about her churchgoing when she first came to work for him; but lately his teasing became sharper: "Going to listen to Dearly Beloved Brethren?" he would say.

"Oh, leave him alone," she said.

He had made up a tale about her being in love with the vicar; at first it was a joke, but now there was a sharp edge to it. "A very respectable man," he said.

When the church bells rang on Sunday evening he said, "He's calling to you." She began to see that this joke had the grit of jealousy in it; not of the vicar, of course, but a jealousy of many things in her life.

"Why do you go there? I'd like to understand, seriously," he said.

"I like to get out," she said.

She saw pain on his face. There was never much movement in it beyond the deepening of two lines at the corners of his mouth; but when his face went really dead, it was as sullen as earth in the garden. In her sense, she knew, he never went out. He lived in a system of tunnels. She had to admit that when she saw the gray church she was glad, because it was not his house. She knew from gossip that neither he nor his wife had ever been to it.

There was something else in this new life; now he had freed her they were both more watchful of each other. One Sunday in April she saw his jealousy in the open. She had come in from church and she was telling him about the people who were there. She was sitting on the sofa beside him.

"How many lovers have you had?" he said. "That doctor you worked for, now?"

"Indeed not," she said. "I was married."

"I know you were married. But when you were working for those people in Manchester? And in Canada after the war?"

"No one else. That was just a trip."

"I don't believe you."

"Honestly, it's true."

"In Court I never believe a witness who says 'Honestly.' "

She blushed for she had had three or four lovers, but she was defending herself. They were no business of his.

The subject became darker.

"Your husband," he said. "He saw you. They all saw you."

She knew what he meant, and this scared her.

"My husband. Of course he saw me. Only my husband."

"Ah, so there were others."

"Only my husband saw me," she said. "I told you about it. How he walked out of the hotel after a week."

This was a moment when she could have told him, but to see his jealousy destroy the happiness he had restored to her made her indignant.

"He couldn't bear the sight of me. He had wanted," she invented, "to marry another woman. He told me on the first night of our marriage. In the hotel. Please don't talk about it."

"Which hotel was this?" he said.

The triviality of the question confused her. "In Kensington."

"What was the name?"

"Oh, I forget, the something Royal . . ."

"You don't forget."

"I do honestly . . ."

"Honestly!" he said.

He was in a rage of jealousy. He kept questioning her about the hotel, the length of their marriage. He pestered for addresses, for dates and tried to confuse her by putting his questions again and again.

"So he didn't leave you at the hotel!" he said.

"Look," she said. "I can't stand jealous men and I'm not going to be questioned like one of your clients."

He did not move or shout. Her husband had shouted and paced up and down, waving his arms. This man sat bolt upright and still, and spoke in a dry exacting voice.

"I'm sorry," he said.

She took his hand, the hand that groped like a helpless tentacle and that had modeled her; it was the most disturbing and living thing about him.

"Are you still in love with your husband?"

"Certainly not."

"He saw you and I have never seen you." He circled again to his obsession.

"It is just as well. I'm not a beautiful woman," she laughed. "My legs are too short, my bottom is too big. You be grateful—my husband couldn't stand the sight of me."

"You have a skin like an apple," he said.

She pushed his hand away and said, "Your hands know too much."

"*He* had hands. And he had eyes," he said in a voice grinding with violence.

"I'm very tired. I am going to bed," she said. "Good night."

"You see," he said. "There is no answer."

He picked up a Braille book and his hand moved fast over the sheets.

She went to her room and kicked off her shoes and stepped out of her dress.

I've been living in a dream, she thought. Just like Marge, who always thinks her husband's coming back every time the gate goes. It is a mistake, she thought, living in the same house.

The jealous fit seemed to pass. It was a fire, she understood, that flared up just as her shame used to flare, but two Sundays later the fit came on again. He must hate God, she thought and pitied him. Perhaps the music that usually consoled him had tormented him. At any rate, he stopped it when she came in and put her prayer book on the table. There was a red begonia, which came from the greenhouse, on the table beside the sofa where he was sitting very upright, as if he had been waiting impatiently for her to come back.

"Come and sit down," he said and began kindly enough. "What was Church like? Did they tell you what to do?"

"I was nearly asleep," she said. "After last night. Do you know what time it was?" She took his hand and laughed.

He thought about this for a while. Then he said, "Give me your hands. No. Both of them. That's right. Now spit on them."

"Spit!"

"Yes, that is what the Church tells you."

"What *are* you talking about?" she said, trying to get her hands away.

"Spit on them." And he forced her hands, though not roughly, to her lips.

"What are you doing?" she laughed nervously and spat on her fingers.

"Now—rub the spittle on my eyes."

"Oh, no," she said.

He let go of her wrist.

"Do as I tell you. It's what your Jesus Christ did when he cured the blind man."

He sat there waiting and she waited.

"He put dust or earth or something on them," he said. "Get some."

"No," she said.

"There's some here. Put your fingers in it," he said shortly. She was frightened of him.

"In the pot," he insisted as he held one of her wrists so that she could not get away. She dabbed her wet fingers in the earth of the begonia pot.

"Put it on my eyes."

"I can't do that. I really can't," she said.

"Put it on my eyes," he said.

"It will hurt them."

"They are hurt already," he said. "Do as I tell you." She bent to him and, with disgust, she put her dirty fingers on the wet eyeballs. The sensation was horrible and when she saw the dirty patches on his eyes, like two filthy smudges, she thought he looked like an ape.

"That is what you are supposed to do," he said. Jealousy had made him mad.

I can't stay with a mad man, she thought. He's malicious. She did not know what to do, but he solved that for her. He reached for his Braille book. She got up and left him there. The next day he went to London.

* * *

His habits changed. He went several times into the nearby town on his own and she was relieved that he came back in a silent mood which seemed happy. The horrible scene went out of her mind. She had gone so far as to lock her bedroom door for several nights after that scene, but now she unlocked it. He had brought her a bracelet from London; she drifted into unguarded happiness. She knew so well how torment comes and goes.

It was full undreaming June, the leaves in the garden still undarkened, and for several days people were surprised when day after day the sun was up and hot and unclouded. Mrs. Johnson went down to the pool. Armitage and his guests often tried to persuade her to go in but she always refused.

"They once tried to get me to go down to Peckham Baths when I was a kid, but I screamed," she said.

The guests left her alone. They were snobbish about Peckham Baths.

But Mrs. Johnson decided to become a secret bather. One afternoon when Armitage was in London and the cook and gardener had their day off, she went down with the gardener's dog. She wore a black bathing suit that covered her body and lowered herself by the steps into the water. Then she splashed at the shallow end of the pool and hung on to the rail while the dog barked at her. He stopped barking when she got out and sniffed round the hedge where she pulled down her bathing dress to her waist and lay down to get sun-drunk on her towel.

She was displaying herself to the sun, the sky and the trees. The air was like hands that played on her as Armitage did and she lay listening to the snuffles of the dog and the humming of the bees in the yew hedge. She had been there an hour when the dog barked at the hedge. She quickly picked up a towel and covered herself and called to the dog: "What is it?"

He went on barking and then gave up and came to her. She sat down. Suddenly the dog barked again. Mrs. Johnson stood up and tried to look through one of the thinner places in the hedge. A man who must have been close to the pool and who must have passed along the footpath from the lane, a path used only by the gardener, was walking up the lawns towards the house carrying a trilby hat in his hand. He was not the gardener. He stopped twice to get his breath and turned to look at the view. She recognized the smiling gray suit, the wide figure and snowball head: it was "Wolverhampton" Smith. She waited and saw him go on to the house and ring a bell. Then he disappeared round the corner and went to the front of the house. Mrs. Johnson quickly dressed. Presently he came back to look into the windows of the sitting room. He found the door and for a minute or two went into the house and then came out.

"The cheek," she said. She finished dressing and went up the lawn to him.

"Ah, there you are," he said. "What a sweet place this is. I was looking for Mr. Armitage."

"He's in London."

"I thought he might be in the pool," he said. Mr. Smith looked rich with arch, smiling insinuation.

"When will he be back?"

"About six. Is there anything I can do?"

"No, no, no," said Mr. Smith in a variety of genial notes, waving a hand. "I was out for a walk."

"A long walk—seven miles."

"I came," said Mr. Smith modestly lowering his eyes in financial confession, "by bus."

"The best way. Can I give you a drink?"

"I never touch it," Mr. Smith said, putting up an austere hand. "Well, a glass of water perhaps. As the Americans say, 'I'm mighty thirsty.' My wife and I came down here for the water, you know. London water is chalky. It was very bad for my wife's arthritis. It's bad for everyone really. There's a significant increase in neuralgia, neuritis, arthritis in a city like London. The chalky water does it. People don't realize it"—and here Mr. Smith stopped smiling and put on a stern excommunicating air—"If you believe that man's life is ruled by water. I personally don't."

"Not by water only, anyway," said Mrs. Johnson.

"I mean," said Mr. Smith gravely, "if you believe that the material body exists." And when he said this, the whole sixteen stone of him looked scornfully at the landscape which, no doubt, concealed thousands of people who believed they had bodies. He expanded: he seemed to threaten to vanish.

Mrs. Johnson fetched a glass of water. "I'm glad to see you're still there," she laughed when she came back.

Mr. Smith was resting on the garden seat. "I was just thinking—thank you—there's a lot of upkeep in a place like this," he said.

"There is."

"And yet—what is upkeep? Money—so it seems. And if we believe in the body, we believe in money, we believe in upkeep and so it goes on," said Mr. Smith sunnily, waving his glass at the garden. And then sharply and loftily, free of this evil: "It gives employment." Firmly telling her she was employed. "But," he added, in warm contemplation, putting down his glass and opening his arms, gathering in the landscape, "but there is only one employer."

"There are a hell of a lot of employers."

Mr. Smith raised an eyebrow at the word "hell" and said, "Let me correct you there. I happen to believe that God is the only employer."

"I'm employed by Mr. Armitage," she said. "Mr. Armitage loves this place. You don't have to see to love a garden."

"It's a sweet place," said Mr. Smith. He got up and took a deep breath. "Pine trees. Wonderful. The smell! My wife doesn't like pine trees. She is depressed by them. It's all in the mind," said Mr. Smith. "As Shakespeare says. By the way, I suppose the water's warming up in the pool? June—it would be. That's what I should like—a swim."

He *did* see me! thought Mrs. Johnson.

"You should ask Mr. Armitage," she said coldly.

"Oh, no, no," said Mr. Smith. "I just *feel* that to swim and have a sun bathe would be the right idea. I should like a place with a swimming pool. And a view like this. I feel it would suit me. And, by the way," he became stern again, "don't let me hear you say again that Mr. Armitage enjoys this place although he doesn't see it. Don't tie his blindness on him. You'll hold him back. He *does* see it. He reflects all-seeing God. I told him so on Wednesday."

"On Wednesday?"

"Yes," he said. "When he came for treatment. I managed to fit him in. Good godfathers, look at the time! I've to get the bus back. I'm sorry to miss Mr. Armitage. Just tell him I called. I just had a thought to give him, that's all. He'll appreciate it."

"And now," Mr. Smith said sportively, "I must try and avoid taking a dive into that pool as I go by, mustn't I?"

She watched his stout marching figure go off down the path.

For treatment! What on earth did Mr. Smith mean? She knew the rest when Armitage came home.

"He came for his check," he said. "Would you make out a check for a hundred and twenty pounds—"

"A hundred and twenty pounds!" she exclaimed.

"For Mr. Smith," he repeated. "He is treating my eyes."

"Your eyes! He's not an ophthalmic surgeon."

"No," said Armitage coldly. "I have tried those."

"You're not going to a faith healer!"

"I am."

* * *

And so they moved into their second quarrel. It was baffling to quarrel with Armitage. He could hear the firm ring of your voice but he could not see your eyes blooming wider and bluer with obstinacy; for her, her eyes were herself. It was like quarreling with a man who had no self or, perhaps, with one that was always hidden.

"Your church goes in for it," he said.

"Proper faith healing," she said.

"What is proper?" he said.

She had a strong belief in propriety.

"A hundred and twenty pounds! You told me yourself Smith is a fraud. I mean, you refused his case. How can you go to a fraud?"

"I don't think I said fraud," he said.

"You didn't like the way he got five thousand pounds out of that silly young man."

"Two thousand," he said.

"He's after your money," she said. "He's a swindler."

In her heart, having been brought up poor, she thought it was a scandal that Armitage was well-off; it was even more scandalous to throw money away.

"Probably. At the end of his tether," he said. He was conveying, she knew, that he was at the end of his tether too.

"And you fall for that? You can't possibly believe the nonsense he talks."

"Don't you think God was a crook? When you think of what He's done?"

"No, I don't." (But, in fact, the stained woman thought He was.)

"What did Smith talk about?"

"I was in the pool. I think he was spying on me. I forget what he was talking about—water, chalky water, was it?"

"He's odd about chalk!" Armitage laughed. Then he became grim again: "You see—even Smith can see *you*. You see people, you see Smith, everyone sees everything and so they can afford to throw away what they see and forget. But I have to remember everything. You know what it is like trying to remember a dream. Smith is right, I'm dreaming a dream," Armitage added sardonically. "He says that I'm only dreaming I cannot see."

She could not make out whether Armitage was serious.

"All right. I don't understand, but all right. What happens next?"

"You can wake up."

Mr. Armitage gave one of his cruel smiles. "I told you. When I used to go to the Courts I often listened to witnesses like Smith. They were always bringing "God is my witness" into it. I never knew a more religious lot of men than dishonest witnesses. They were always bringing in a Higher Power. Perhaps they were in contact with it."

"You don't mean that. You are making fun of me," she said. And then vehemently: "I hate to see you going to an ignorant man like that. I thought you were too proud. What has happened to you?"

She had never spoken her mind so forcibly to him before.

"If a man can't see," he said, "if *you* couldn't see, humiliation is what you'd fear most. I thought I ought to accept it."

He had never been so open with her.

"You couldn't go lower than Mr. Smith," she said.

"We're proud. That is our vice," he said. "Proud in the dark. Everyone else has to put up with humiliation. You said you knew what it was—I always remember that. Millions of people are humiliated: perhaps it makes them stronger because they forget it. I want to join them."

"No, you don't," she said.

They were lying in bed and leaning over him she put her breast to his lips, but he lay lifeless. She could not bear it that he had changed her and that she had stirred this profound wretchedness in him. She hated confession: to her it was the male weakness—self-love. She got out of bed.

"Come to that," she said. "It's you who are humiliating me. You are going to this quack man because we've slept together. I don't like the compliment."

"And you say you don't love me," he said.

"I admire you," she said. She dreaded the word "love." She picked up her clothes and left the room. She hadn't the courage to say she hadn't the courage. She stuck to what she had felt since she was a child: that she was a body. He had healed it with his body.

Once more she thought, I shall have to go. I ought to have stuck to it and gone before. If I'd been living in the town and just been coming up for the day it would have been O.K. Living in the house was your mistake, my girl. You'll have to go and get another job. But, of course, when she calmed down, she realized that all this was self-deception: she was afraid to tell him. She brusquely drove off the thought, and her mind went to the practical.

* * *

That hundred and twenty pounds! She was determined not to see him swindled. She went with him to Mr. Smith's next time. The roof of the Rolls-Royce gleamed over the shrubbery of the uncut hedge of Mr. Smith's house. A cat was sitting on the window sill. Waiting on the doorstep was the little man, wide-waisted and with his hands in his optimistic pockets, and changing his smile of welcome to a reminder of secret knowledge when he saw her. Behind the undressing smile of Mr. Smith stood the kind, cringing figure of his wife, looking as they all walked into the narrow hall.

"Straight through?" said Mrs. Johnson in her managing voice. "And leave them to themselves, I suppose?"

"The back gets the sun. At the front it's all these trees," said Mrs. Smith, encouraged by Mrs. Johnson's presence to speak out in a weak voice, as if it was all she did get. "I was a London girl."

"So am I," said Mrs. Johnson.

"But you've got a beautiful place up there. Have you got these pine trees too?"

"A few."

"They give me the pip," said Mrs. Smith. "Coffee? Shall I take your coat? My husband said you'd got pines."

"No, thank you, I'll keep it," said Mrs. Johnson. "Yes, we've got pines. I can't say they're my favorite trees. I like to see leaves come off. And I like a bit of traffic myself. I like to see a shop."

"Oh, you would," said Mrs. Smith.

The two women looked with the shrewd London look at each other.

"I'm so busy up there I couldn't come before. I don't like Mr. Armitage coming alone. I like to keep an eye on him," said Mrs. Johnson, set for attack.

"Oh yes, an eye."

"Frankly, I didn't know he was coming to see Mr. Smith."

But Mrs. Johnson got nothing out of Mrs. Smith. They were both half listening to the rumble of men's voices next door. Then the meeting was over and they went out to meet the men. In his jolly way Mr. Smith said to Mrs. Johnson as they left, "Don't forget about that swim!"

Ostentatiously to show her command and to annoy Armitage, she armed him down the path.

"I hope you haven't invited that man to swim in the pool," said Mrs. Johnson to Mr. Armitage on the way home.

"You've made an impression on Smith," said Armitage.

"No, *I* haven't."

"Poor Mrs. Smith," said Mrs. Johnson.

Otherwise they were silent.

* * *

She went a second, then a third, time to the Smiths' house. She sat each time in the kitchen talking and listening to the men's voices in the next room. Sometimes there were long silences.

"Is Mr. Smith praying?" Mrs. Johnson asked.

"I expect so," said Mrs. Smith. "Or reading."

"Because it *is* prayer, isn't it?" said Mrs. Johnson.

Mrs. Smith was afraid of this healthy downright woman and it was an effort for her to make a stand on what evidently for most of her married life had been poor ground.

"I suppose it is. Prayer, yes, that is what it would be. Dad—" she changed her mind—"my husband has always had faith." And with this, Mrs. Smith looked nervously at being able loyally to put forward the incomprehensible.

"But what does he actually *do?* I thought he had a chemist's shop," pursued Mrs. Johnson.

Mrs. Smith was a timid woman who wavered now between the relics of dignity and a secretive craving to impart.

"He has retired," said Mrs. Smith. "When we closed the shop he took this up." She said this, hoping to clutch a certainty.

Mrs. Johnson gave a bustling laugh. "No, you misunderstand me. What I mean is, what does he actually *do?* What is the treatment?"

Mrs. Smith was lost. She nodded, as it were, to nothingness several times.

"Yes," she said. "I suppose you'd call it prayer. I don't really understand it."

"Nor do I," said Mrs. Johnson. "I expect you've got enough to do keeping house. I have my work cut out too."

They still heard the men talking. Mrs. Johnson nodded to the wall.

"Still at it," said Mrs. Johnson. "I'll be frank with you, Mrs. Smith. I am sure your husband does whatever he does do for the best . . ."

"Oh, yes, for the best," nodded Mrs. Smith. "It's saved us. He had a writ out against him when Mr. Armitage's check came in. I know he's grateful."

"But I believe in being open . . ."

"Open," nodded Mrs. Smith.

"I've told him and I've told Mr. Armitage that I just don't believe a man who has been blind for twenty-two years—"

"Terrible," said Mrs. Smith.

"—can be cured. Certainly not by—whatever this is. Do you believe it, Mrs. Smith?"

Mrs. Smith was cornered.

"Our Lord did it," she said desperately. "That is what my husband says . . ."

"I was a nurse during the war and I have worked for doctors," said Mrs. Johnson. "I am sure it is impossible. I've knocked about a lot. You're a sensible woman, Mrs. Smith. I don't want to offend you, but you don't believe it yourself, do you?"

Mrs. Johnson's eyes grew larger and Mrs. Smith's older eyes were helpless and small. She longed for a friend. She was hypnotized by Mrs. Johnson, whose face and pretty neck grew firmly out of her frilled and high-necked blouse.

"I try to have faith . . ." said Mrs. Smith, rallying to her husband. "He says I hold him back. I don't know."

"Some men need to be held back," said Mrs. Johnson and she gave a fighting shake to her healthy head. All Mrs. Smith could do in her panic was to watch every move of Mrs. Johnson's, study her expensive shoes and stockings, her capable skirt, her painted nails. Now, at the shake of Mrs. Johnson's head, she saw on the right side of the neck the small petal of the birthmark just above the frill of the collar.

"None of us are perfect," said Mrs. Smith slyly.

"I have been with Mr. Armitage four years," Mrs. Johnson said.

"It is a lovely place up there," said Mrs. Smith, eager to change the subject. "It must be terrible to live in such a lovely place and never see it . . ."

"Don't you believe it," said Mrs. Johnson. "He knows that place better than any of us, better than me."

"No," groaned Mrs. Smith. "We had a blind dog when I was a girl. It used to nip hold of my dress to hold me back if it heard a car coming when I was going to cross the road.

It belonged to my aunt and she said 'That dog can see. It's a miracle.' "

"He heard the car coming," said Mrs. Johnson. "It's common sense."

The words struck Mrs. Smith.

"Yes, it is, really," she said. "If you come to think of it."

She got up and went to the gas stove to make more coffee and new courage came to her. We know why she doesn't want Mr. Armitage to see again! She was thinking: the frightening Mrs. Johnson was really weak. Housekeeper and secretary to a rich man, sitting very pretty up there, the best of everything. Plenty of money, staff, cook, gardener, chaffeur, Rolls-Royce—if he was cured where would her job be? Oh, she looks full of herself now, but she is afraid. I expect she's got round him to leave her a bit.

The coffee began to bubble up in the pot and that urgent noise put excitement into her and her old skin blushed.

"Up there with a man alone. As I said to Dad, a woman can tell! Where would she get another man with that spot spreading all over? She's artful. She's picked the right one." She was telling the tale to herself.

The coffee boiled over and hissed on the stove and a sudden forgotten jealousy hissed up in Mrs. Smith's uncertain mind. She took the pot to the table and poured out a boiling hot cup and as the steam clouded up from it, screening her daring stare at the figure of Mrs. Johnson, Mrs. Smith wanted to say: "Lying there stark naked by that swimming pool right in the face of my husband. What was he doing up there anyway?"

She could not say it. There was not much pleasure in Mrs. Smith's life; jealousy was the only one that enlivened her years with Mr. Smith. She had flown at him when he came home and had told her that God had guided him, that prayer always uncovered evil and brought it to the surface; it had revealed to him that the Devil had put his mark on Mrs. Johnson, and that he wouldn't be surprised if that was what was holding up the healing of Mr. Armitage.

"What were you doing," she screamed at him, "looking at a woman?"

The steam cleared and Mrs. Smith's nervousness returned as she saw that composed face. She was frightened now of her own imagination and of her husband's. She knew him. He was always up to something.

"Don't you dare say anything to Mr. Armitage about this!" she had shouted at him.

But now she fell back on admiring Mrs. Johnson again. Settled for life, she sighed. She's young. She is only fighting for her own. She's a woman.

And Mrs. Smith's pride was stirred. Her courage was fitful and weakened by what she had lived through. She had heard Mrs. Johnson was divorced and it gave Mrs. Smith strength as a woman who had "stuck to her husband." She had not gone round taking up with men as she guessed Mrs. Johnson might have done. She was a respectable married woman.

Her voice trembled at first but became stronger.

"Dad wanted to be a doctor when he was a boy," Mrs. Smith was saying, "but there wasn't the money so he worked in a chemist's but it was always Church on Sundays. I wasn't much of a one for Church myself. But you must have capital and being just behind the counter doesn't lead anywhere. Of course I tried to egg him on to get his diploma and he got the papers—but I used to watch him. He'd start his studying and then he'd get impatient. He's a very impatient man and he'd say 'Amy, I'll try the Ministry'—he's got a good voice—'Church people have money.' "

"And did he?"

"No, he always wanted to, but he couldn't seem to settle

to a church—I mean a religion. I'll say this for him, he's a fighter. Nixon, his first guv'nor, thought the world of him: quick with the sales. Nixon's Cough Mixture—well, he didn't invent it, but he changed the bottles and the labels, made it look—fashionable, dear—you know? A lot of Wesleyans took it."

Mrs. Smith spread her hands over her face and laughed through her fingers.

"When Nixon died someone in the church put up some money, a very religious, good man. One day Dad said to me—I always remember it—'It's not medicine. It's faith does it.' He's got faith. Faith is—well, faith."

"In himself?" suggested Mrs. Johnson.

"That's it! That's it!" cried Mrs. Smith with excitement. Then she quietened and dabbed a tear from her cheek. "I begged him not to come down here. But this Mrs. Rogers, the lady who owns the house, she's deaf and on her own, he knew her. She believes in him. She calls him Daniel. He's treating her for deafness, she can't hear a word, so we brought our things down after we closed up in Ealing, that's why it's so crowded, two of everything, I have to laugh."

"So you don't own the house?"

"Oh, no, dear—oh, no," Mrs. Smith said, frightened of the idea. "He wants something bigger. He wants space for his work."

Mrs. Smith hesitated and looked at the wall through which the sound of Mr. Smith's voice was coming. And then, fearing she had been disloyal, she said, "She's much better. She's very funny. She came down yesterday calling him. 'Daniel. Daniel. I hear the cuckoo.' Of course I didn't say anything: it was the man calling out "Coal." But she is better. She wouldn't have heard him at all when we came here."

They were both silent.

"You can't live your life from A to Z," Mrs. Smith said, waking up. "We all make mistakes. We've been married for forty-two years. I expect you have your troubles too, even in that lovely place."

After the hour Mr. Smith came into the kitchen to get Mrs. Johnson.

"What a chatter!" he said to her. "I never heard such a tittle tattle in my life."

"Yes, we had a fine chat, didn't we?"

"Oh yes," said Mrs. Smith boldly.

"How is it going on?" said Mrs. Johnson.

"Now, now," Mr. Smith corrected her. "These cases seemingly take time. You have to get to the bottom of it. We don't intend to, but we keep people back by the thoughts we hold over them."

And then, in direct attack on her—"I don't want you to hold no wrong thoughts over me. You have no power over Divine Love." And he turned to his wife to silence her.

"And how would I do that?" said Mrs. Johnson.

"Cast the mote out of thine own eye," said Smith. "Heal yourself. We all have to." He smiled broadly at her.

"I don't know what all this talk about Divine Love is," said Mrs. Johnson. "But I love Mr. Armitage as he is."

Smith did not answer.

Armitage had found his way to the door of the kitchen. He listened and said, "Goodbye, Mrs. Smith." And to Mr. Smith: "Send me your bill. I'm having the footpath closed."

* * *

They drove away.

"I love Mr. Armitage as he is." The words had been forced out of her by the detestable man. She hated that she had said to him what she could not say to Armitage. They surprised her. She hoped Armitage had not heard them.

He was silent in the car. He did not answer any of her questions.

"I'm having that path closed," he repeated.

I know! she thought. Smith has said something about me. Surely not about "it"!

When they got out of the car at the house he said to the chauffeur, "Did you see Mr. Smith when he came up here three weeks ago? It was a Thursday. Were you down at the pool?"

"It's my afternoon off, sir."

"I know that. I asked whether you were anywhere near the pool. Or in the garden?"

"No, sir."

Oh God, Mrs. Johnson groaned. Now he's turned on Jim.

"Jim went off on his motor bike. I saw him," said Mrs. Johnson.

They went into the house.

"You don't know who you can trust," Armitage said and went across to the stairs and started up. But instead of putting his hand to the rail which was on the right, he put it out to the left, and not finding it, stood bewildered. Mrs. Johnson quietly went to that side of him and nudged him in the right direction.

When he came down to lunch he sat in silence before the cutlets on his plate.

"After all these years! I know the rail is on the right and I put out my left hand."

"You just forgot," she said. "Why don't you try forgetting a few more things?"

She was cross about the questioning of the chauffeur.

"Say, one thing a day," she said.

He listened and this was one of those days when he cruelly paused a long time before replying. A minute went by and she started to eat.

"Like this?" he said, and he deliberately knocked his glass of water over. The water spread over the cloth towards her plate.

"What's this silly temper?" she said, and lifting her plate away, she lifted the cloth and started mopping with her table napkin and picked up the glass.

"I'm fed up with you blind people," she said angrily. "All jealousy and malice, just childish. You're so clever, aren't you? What happened? Didn't that good Mr. Smith do the magic trick? I don't wonder your wife walked out on you. Pity the poor blind! What about other people? I've had enough. You have an easy life; you sail down in your Rolls and think you can buy God from Mr. Smith just because—I don't know why—but if he's a fraud you're a fraud." Suddenly the wronged inhabitant inside her started to shout: "I'll tell you something about that Peeping Jesus: he saw the lot. Oh, yes, I hadn't a stitch on. The lot!" she was shouting. And then she started to unzip her dress and pull it down over her shoulder and drag her arm out of it. "You can't see it, you silly fool. The whole bloody Hebrides, the whole plate of liver."

And she went to his place, got him by the shoulder and rubbed her stained shoulder and breast against his face.

"Do you want to see more?" she shouted. "It made my husband sick. That's what you've been sleeping with. And" —she got away as he tried to grip her and laughed—"you didn't know! *He* did."

She sat down and cried hysterically with her head and arms on the table.

Armitage stumbled in the direction of her crying and put his hand on her bare shoulder.

"Don't touch me! I hate your hands." And she got up, dodged round him to the door and ran out sobbing; slower than she was, he was too late to hear her steps. He found his way back to the serving hatch and called to the cook.

"Go up to Mrs. Johnson. She's in her room. She's ill," he said.

He stood in the hall waiting; the cook came downstairs and went into the sitting room.

"She's not there. She must have gone into the garden." And then she said at the window, "She's down by the pool."

"Go and talk to her," he said.

The cook went out of the garden door and on to the terrace. She was a thin round-shouldered woman. She saw Mrs. Johnson move back to the near side of the pool; she seemed to be staring at something in the water. Then the cook stopped and came shouting back to the house.

"She's fallen in. With all her clothes on. She can't swim. I know she can't swim." And then the cook called out, "Jim! Jim!" and ran down the lawns.

Armitage stood helpless.

"Where's the door?" he called. There was no one there.

Armitage made an effort to recover his system, but it was lost. He found himself blocked by a chair, but he had forgotten which chair. He waited to sense the movement of air in order to detect where the door was, but a window was half open and he found himself against glass. He made his way feeling along the wall, but he was traveling away from the door. He stood still again, and smelling a kitchen smell he made his way back across the center of the long room and at last found the first door and then the door to the garden. He stepped out, but he was exhausted and his will had gone. He could only stand in the breeze, the disorderly scent of the flowers and the grass mocking him. A jeering bird flew up. He heard the gardener's dog barking below and a voice, the gardener's voice, shouting "Quiet!" Then he heard voices coming slowly nearer up the lawn.

"Helen," called Armitage, but they pushed past him. He felt her wet dress brush his hand and her foot struck his leg; the gardener was carrying her.

"Marge," Armitage heard her voice as she choked and was sick.

"Upstairs. I'll get her clothes off," said the cook.

"No," said Armitage.

"Be quiet," said the cook.

"In my room," said Armitage.

"What an idea!" said the cook. "Stay where you are. Mind you don't slip on all this wet."

He stood, left behind in the hall, listening, helpless. Only when the doctor came did he go up.

She was sitting up in bed and Armitage held her hand.

"I'm sorry," she said. "You'd better fill that pool up. It hasn't brought you any luck."

* * *

Armitage and Mrs. Johnson are in Italy now; for how long it is hard to say. They themselves don't know. Some people call her Mrs. Armitage, some call her Mrs. Johnson; this uncertainty pleases her. She has always had a secret and she is too old, she says, to give up the habit now. It still pleases Armitage to baffle people. It is impossible for her to deny that she loves Armitage, because he heard what she said to Smith; she has had to give in about that. And she does love him because his system has broken down completely in Italy. "You are my eyes," he says. "Everything sounds different here." "I like a bit of noise," she says.

Pictures in churches and galleries he is mad about and he likes listening to her descriptions of them and often laughs at some of her remarks, and she is beginning, she says, to get "a kick out of the classical stuff" herself.

There was an awkward moment before they set off for

Italy when he made her write out a check for Smith and she tried to stop him.

"No," he said, "He got it out of you. I owe you to him."

She was fighting the humiliating suspicion that in his nasty prying way Smith had told Armitage about her before *she* had told him. But Armitage said, "I knew all the time. From the beginning. I knew everything about you."

She still does not know whether to believe him or not. When she does believe, she is more awed than shamed; when she does not believe she feels carelessly happy. He depends on her entirely here. One afternoon, standing at the window of their room and looking at the people walking in the lemonish light across the square, she suddenly said, "I love you. I feel gaudy!" She notices that the only thing he doesn't like is to hear a man talk to her.

The Nest Builder

I have lost Ernest. We had been partners for a long time, but after a difficult year and the fiasco at Albine Rise, he went. Interior decoration is a hard, even a savage, trade; customers come to us not quite knowing what they want, but they know (and we know) that they want Perfection. That is very expensive. And there is a sad side to Perfection; there are losses, as you see around you in this shop now. They are Ernest's losses. The two cabinets in yellow lacquer, for example—Mrs. Cross, I call them. They were sent back by Mr. Cross, just when Ernest had finished the Chinese drawing room for her. Mr. Cross divorced her. There is Mrs. Raddock—the Empire sofa and the three chairs. She divorced Mr. Raddock, actually before we got the marble pillars into Mr. Raddock's study. The Hepplewhite four-poster, waiting to go into Cheyne Row while Ernest was still getting the Italian bathroom right—Mr. Fortescue died. A tragic business—but we get that, too, in the trade. The mirrors and consoles are Mrs. Hunstable, Mrs. Smith, and Lady Hatch, mirrors being a fate with Ernest. The moment he puts gilded mirrors with branches, cherubs, angels, scrolls, shells, or lions into a house, someone falls down the stairs, or there is a sarcastic scene between husband and wife or mother and daughter, and high talk of vanity, adultery, loss of looks or figure, even of camp or chichi; the next thing one hears is that the lease is for sale, then the accounts are disputed and the goods come back. The doctor or the lawyer, they say, sees deepest into the secrets of people's lives. I do not agree.

Yet it wasn't because of these losses that Ernest left us. They in fact stimulated his creative gift. When lacquer cabinets, Hepplewhite beds, mirrors, and so on, come back, he stands there stroking his small, soft beard, gazing at them at first as if personally affronted. Then one eyebrow goes up and he recognizes with admiration their extraordinary power to wreck human lives, and turns on me a gentle, conspiring, worldly young eye. "George, dear boy!" he says. "Mrs. Grant, I think—don't you? Or who was that woman who rang up yesterday?" And he would pay me a compliment, too. "George," he often said to me, "what a nose you have for booty!" He would be thinking of times when I came back from some place in the country with an Adam fireplace, a triptych, a gout stool, or a big chunk of Spanish choir stall, or had added to our collection of rare cattle pictures. My task was to go round to the auctions, to get into early Industrial Revolution houses in the North, to smell round rectories, look into the stabling of country houses, squint into the family detritus. That is, when I had the time, for I also had to deal with the trouble Ernest created for builders and painters, and his sneers at surly architects. It was Ernest—and this I gladly say—who brought the ideas to our business.

"My dear," I once said to him, "there are only two men in London who could turn a revolting Baptist chapel with Venetian excrescences into a Chinese pagoda. And you are both of them."

"You mean a Turkish bath, dear boy," he said. "Why two men."

"One to think up the ghastly idea, the other to persuade the people to have it."

"D'you know, you've got very bald since Easter," he said. "Shall we have a little Mozart?"

Ernest at work was a frightening sight. Generally, he did not like me to come with him, but I've seen him at it more than once. He is a slender, shortish man, with carefully styled hair—neither fair nor gray, but in some subtle pastel shade, as soft as moleskin. It fits his head like an old-fashioned ink pad. His beard is itself one of those small objets d'art that women itch to touch. He has a voice as soft as cigarette smoke, an utterly insincere listening manner—the head a little inclined—and when, to take an example, Mrs. Raddock talked pell-mell about enlarging her dining-room bookcases, he nodded with the air of a dignified mourner who is not a close friend of the family. This habit of grieving distantly and respectfully (after a wild, wheeling look at the ceiling, walls, and windows of the room, and with one rather cruel roll of the eye at the door he had just come through) had the effect of inducing dismay in many women. They would give a touch to their hair and a glance at their clothes, in order to recover fortitude; they had not realized, until that moment, that their dining room, their drawing room, their whole house, were dead, the interment long overdue.

"Yes, I see exactly what you mean, Mrs. Raddock. The thing that worries me is the height of the folding doors." Mrs. Raddock, a confusing talker, foolish and flirtatious but a woman of will who until then had known what she wanted, was torpedoed at once by this shot. Ernest's words showed her her personal disaster: it was not that she had been three times married but that she had never noticed the height of her folding doors. And Ernest struck again. "It is a pity the original chimney piece has gone," he accused.

"My husband found this one down in Wiltshire," said Mrs. Raddock, desperately pushing whatever blame that might arise on to him. Already Ernest was dividing husband and wife.

"Houses like this, so purely Regency, are getting rarer and rarer," said Ernest sadly. "So many are let go. I have been doing a library in Gloucestershire, a rather nice Georgian house—a room with a cupola, a small domed ceiling, you know?"

Mrs. Raddock blushed at her lack of cupola.

"I'd better measure the height of the door," Ernest said. "The top molding of your bookcase cannot possibly be below it. These houses put formality and balance first."

Ernest's steel ruler whizzed up the jamb of the door and lashed there for a second or two, then slipped back with a hiss into its holder. Mrs. Raddock stepped back. Formality and balance—how did you guess (her eager look seemed to say) that that is what I need in my life? She covered her defeat with a look of experienced irony at Ernest, but also of appeal. As I followed them around, I could hardly conceal my desire to protect the lady and Ernest from each other, and Ernest knew this. As we left the room to go upstairs to the drawing room, he gave me a glare. "Keep out of this," the look said, for I had the weakness of comforting suggestion to our customers. (At the shop, he once said to me crossly, "You are so tall, dear boy. It makes you look dispassionate.")

Now we were at the top of red-carpeted stairs outside Mrs. Raddock's drawing room. The door was open. We could just see in. Ernest paused and turned his back as if he had seen something dreadful, and nodded downstairs to the room we had just left. "Was it your idea or your husband's to have a black dining room?" said Ernest. He spoke of everything with the suggestion that it belonged to a past the customer was anxious to forget.

"Oh, mine," said Mrs. Raddock, making a guilty effort to take the blame herself this time. "Ten years ago," she said, breaking helplessly into autobiography, "when we moved up from the country."

"Ten." Ernest nodded. "That would be about the date." And Mrs. Raddock sank once more.

In two more visits, she was holding his arm, as he gazed up at the moldings of the ceiling and she gazed at his little beard, trying to formalize herself. The case of Mrs. Raddock differs little from that of Mrs. Cross, Mrs. Hunstable, or, indeed, all the others. Ernest seized their flats and their houses with the ruthless hands of the artist, shook the interiors out of their own windows, and re-created them. He was really shaking his clients out of the windows, too. Dark rooms appeared as monkey-haunted jungles; light was dispensed from chaste or unchaste vases, dripped like expensive tears, or shot out at piercing, agony-creating angles. Ceilings went up or down, alcoves appeared on blank walls. He had once a line in Piranesi dining rooms and in hairy pagan bedrooms where furs and lewd hints of the goat's foot were tossed around. He did sickening things with shot birds, which made the ladies scream first; put down tigerish carpets, which gave them voluptuous shudders. He created impudent or intimate congeries of small furniture, and could make a large piece look like an Italian church. A pushing career woman like Mrs. Greatorex was given a satiny nest of such kittenishness that it suggested to the visitor that here lived some delicate hypochondriac with little bones and sad pink rims to her sensitive eyes, instead of—as she was—a brassy, hard-bloused lady bawling down the telephone. Ernest penetrated to the hidden self of his client, discerned her so-far frustrated dream of perfection. And then a sudden practicality sprang up in his apparently passive personality and he took rough charge. It was they who then watched him—startled at first, then attentively, then gravely, then longingly. Here was the nest builder, and without realizing it they grew irritable with their husbands, who came home—or what used to be home—to find the place half closed or in chaos. These moneyed brutes trod on paint. The wives screamed out, "Don't go in there! Be careful! Ernest has moved the banisters." "Ernest"—

husbands wearied of the name. One or two coarse ones—Raddock and Cross were like this—threw out doubts about his sex. The ladies made a face, wriggled their shoulders, and sighed that men like Ernest understood what most men forget—that women are not merely female; they are feminine. The time came when a flat or a house was finished. There was Mrs. Cross's Chinese boutique. She stood entranced, hardly able to take a step, hardly able to see because of the sparkle that came to her excited eyes, which themselves looked jewel-like in this moment. She saw not only her house but herself, perfected. But, as always in the face of perfection, a mysterious sadness misted those eyes. There was the sense of loss that angels are said to have when they look back from Heaven upon the earth. A hunger made Mrs. Cross go limp, opened Mrs. Hunstable's uneasy mouth, brought a shiver to Mrs. Raddock's nervous bosom. Their houses were now perfect, but one thing was missing. What was it?

It was Ernest. They wanted him. For weeks he had been in and out, caressing yet masterful. The creation was empty without the creator. Mrs. Raddock rubbed herself against him; Mrs. Cross muttered in a low voice, leading him to the bedroom, where she had a final question to ask. Mrs. Greatorex frankly galloped at him. Our bad year began. Mrs. Raddock left her third husband; a load of chandeliers came back. Mr. and Mrs. Cross broke up, after years of bickering, in which the Chinese drawing room had been a last emotional bid; the lacquer cabinets were returned. Mrs. Greatorex went to Greece. Letters came in from bank managers and lawyers. There were last longing looks of farewell at Ernest. Some had wanted him socially, as a sparkler; others had wished to be sisters to him; others had wanted him as confidant, as an annoyance to their husbands. But why particularize? They wanted him. The final blow in that year came from Mrs. Hunstable. This florid and open-hearted lady, whose upper part suggested a box at the opera in which she was somehow living and sitting, and who spoke in a jolly mixture of aria and ravening recitative—this lady was caught, actually caught, lying rather sideways on a Recamier couch, having her tears wiped by Ernest while she stroked his neat pad of hair.

Mr. Hunstable caught them. She said she was comforting him.

"I was telling him," cried Mrs. Hunstable, jumping up and taking her husband in her arms and wiping her tears at the same time, "I was telling him he must not worry because he is different from other men. Ernest's on the point of breakdown."

Mr. Hunstable looked operatically doubtful.

"They feel it, Harry, you know," she appealed. "Ernest feels it. They all do."

Mrs. Hunstable was as near to telling the truth as a woman feels it necessary to be. The only correction needed here is that Ernest was comforting her. Ernest rarely spoke to me of his end-of-contract crises, but rumors are soon out. The telephone never stops in our trade, and more than half the calls are gossip. I often had to sweep up after Ernest emotionally. But Mrs. Hunstable was not easily put off. She came to the office when Ernest was out, her mouth wide open, her breasts in disorder, demanding to know more. She tried to ransack me. She was all out for confession. Naturally, I said nothing. "I see," she said to me with a cold smirk. "You hang together." She became the mortally insulted mother whose sons will not confide in her. She turned on us and sold the house, her husband landed the stuff back on us, and they went off violently to the Bahamas, leaving us to their lawyers.

The Hunstable episode was a shock to Ernest, and it worried me. As I say, it was the last one in a bad year. Until then I would have said that Ernest's successes with our clients depended on his skill in turning their desires into a ballet-like partnership from which he escaped by some beautifully timed leap, so to say, into the wings. But Mrs. Hunstable was no dancer. The world was no stage to her; it was property. It was to be owned. I confess that working with an artist like Ernest is apt to make a man at the business end, like myself, fall back on a vulgar tone in a crisis.

"It's a pity, dear boy . . . I mean—well, look, Ernest, let's not beat about the bush. Have another drink," I said. I stopped and gave a loud laugh.

"I mean," I said, "It's a pity you couldn't, just for once . . ."

"Be as other men?" Ernest said.

"I was only joking, dear boy."

"Not with Mrs. Hunstable," Ernest said. "Perhaps you, my dear—"

"Ernest," I said. "I'm sorry. I suppose we have to look at this in perspective. I've often wondered whether we realize what we are doing. I don't think you do—or perhaps you do?"

"Our mistake is that we deal with people," Ernest said.

"What a horrible thing to say," I said.

"People with inner lives," he said.

"You mean who send things back?" I said.

"Oh, all right!"he said angrily. "What d'you want me to do—the Flashback Bar, Nasty's Steak House? Or some self-service counter? Or the Svengali Room at the Metropole?"

"You cannot send a bar back. You can't return a restaurant," I said. "What happened at the Sea Urchin?" It was six o-clock in the evening, December, a wet day. I had persuaded him to see what the manager of the Sea Urchin wanted, and he had just come back.

"They want fisherman's nets on the ceiling. That was *out* ten years ago. They're going to sit on capstans."

"Not sit, surely, Ernest," I said.

"I don't know—perhaps it was anchors," Ernest said, covering his face with his hands.

I went to the cupboard in our office and reached for the bottle of gin, and as I did so the telephone rang. Ernest picked it up. "My name is Richards. I wrote you a letter . . ." I could hear a jubilant voice, fermenting like a small vat.

"Men! I'm sick of them," Ernest said, handing the telephone to me.

"Richards, Gowing, and Cloud," the happy voice went on.

"Lawyers," I whispered to Ernest.

"You wrote us a letter? Oh, dear," I said.

I found the letter on my desk. It was one I had not had the heart to answer, and I passed it to Ernest—or, rather, I dangled it before him. I have, as Ernest says, a suicidal voice, and now I used it. "Mr. Richards," I said to Ernest, "is engaged to be married shortly to a divine girl called Miss Staples and has taken one of those little musical boxes on Albine Rise. It's all here in the letter."

Then I turned back to the telephone. "Why, of course, Mr. Richards," I said. "When would you like us to come?" And when he rang off I looked strictly at Ernest. "Eleven tomorrow morning," I said. "Ernest, it's this or the Sea Urchin."

You find little enclaves like Albine Rise all over London if you know where to look. It was a group of nine small early-Victorian houses, enclosed in a terrace of weeping elms on an expensive hill. "Musical box" is the term for any one of them. Only three hundred yards from a thundering and whining main road but set above it, the houses seem—to a London ear—to tinkle together in rural quiet. One glance must have told Ernest when we arrived that there was little for us here: the couple had bought Perfection already. I turned away from it to study them.

Mr. Richards, of the Queen's Bench voice, was a set piece: bowler hat, black coat, striped trousers, old Etonian tie. Miss Staples was the shock. She was a fat little thing with a ruddy face, dressed in hairy brown tweed—a girl with a decided look and a hard hand-grip. She said little except that she was in a hurry and must get to something she called the Dairy Show. We went into the house. "I just want it done in white!" she shouted.

"White?" said Ernest.

"All this chichi off. I want plain white," said Miss Staples.

Mr. Richards looked at Ernest with appeal. "Save me from plain white," the look said.

"White?" said Ernest. "Do you mean chalk or ivory or—"

"Just white. Any white. White!" shouted Miss Staples cheerfully.

"Like sheep—clean ones," said Mr. Richards with fruity sarcasm, but also with a glance at Ernest screaming in a gentlemanly way for help. Ernest took in the pretty sitting room and the pretty staircase outside, but he was looking with astonishment at the vigorous, golden, untidy hair of Miss Staples, at her cheeks as fresh as ham, her eyes as blue as blackbirds' eggs. He was astounded. Most women, however bold their faces, were put in the wrong by him, but he failed—no, he did not even try—to put Miss Staples in the wrong. She was, he must have seen at once, his opposite—not a decorator but a de-decorator. "White? Very chaste," Ernest said in a louder voice than usual.

"Isn't that rather personal?" she said archly. Ernest was taken aback. Miss Staples showed small white teeth. "Let me show you what the frightful people did—the people who had the place before," she said, leading him up the stairs and showing him the bathroom. "It may be O.K. for Cleopatra and her asp, but I keep dogs."

"In the bathroom?" said Ernest.

"They scratch at the door," said Miss Staples heartily. "All this," she said, pointing round the room, "will have to go."

"We have dogs," apologized Mr. Richards. Ernest looked at him. Mr. Richards was a stout, pale young man choking with legal deprecation. The sentence sounded like "M'lud, my information is that my client keeps dogs."

"That bloody traffic," said Miss Staples from the window. One could scarcely hear the traffic.

"Better than calving cows," said Mr. Richards.

"Jerseys have such pretty eyes," said Ernest. I was dumfounded.

"Yes," said Miss Staples. "We've got fifty—two more coming this week. It's not the eyes, it's the yield! Isn't it, Robert? I want this place for Robert during the week. I hate London."

"This is where I shall be stabled," said Robert.

"We're keeping the oats in the country," Miss Staples snapped back offhand to her fiancé but gazing at Ernest. Ernest was entranced.

And so was Miss Staples.

Robert hated Ernest; Ernest despised Robert. Miss Staples looked Ernest over with open admiration, but with an occasional critical glance, her head on one side. "What a frightful tie you're wearing," she said. It struck me she was seeing what might, here and there, be altered. And Ernest was going over her in the same way, and was clearly finding, for the first time in his life, nothing that should be changed.

"The trees are very . . ." began Ernest, waving his hand at the weeping elms outside, but he was clearly indicating the waves of her hair.

"Give me twenty-five acres of kale any day," said Miss Staples.

"Me, too," said Ernest. I had never before heard Ernest lie.

"I'm afraid my wife—er, my future wife, it would be more correct to say—has rather drastic ideas. I hope Ernest will be able to exert an influence. In fact, that's why I asked . . ." Mr. Richards whispered to me.

"I've got to go. You'd better come down for the weekend," Miss Staples ordered. "There are the fox masks, the antlers, one or two prize cups—I don't see anywhere here to put a saddle."

"You're damn right there isn't," said Ernest, marveling at her.

This interview took place on a Tuesday. The following weekend, Ernest went to stay with Miss Staples and Mr. Richards at her parents' house in the country. On Monday, he came back. He came into the shop about twelve. His usual quiet gravity had gone. He walked up and down and said, "Stuffy in here. No air. I'll open the door." It was a cold day.

"We shall die," I said as the wind blew four yards of brocade off a screen and took the screen with it to the floor. "What were they like, the older Stapleses?"

"Wonderful," said Ernest. "Like moulting owls. Perfect . . . Blast this stuff," said Ernest, and he did something terrible. He kicked the brocade out of the way as it lay crouching on the floor—kicked it with boots that had obviously been in some country lane. I could have screamed, brocade at the price it is. There were probably not another four yards of that quality and color in London, and it takes months to get it from France.

"The order's off," Ernest said at last. "Albine Rise. We had a flaming row. Robert and Joanna—"

"Joanna?"

"Miss Staples. She's broken it off. He said he'd allow the hunting prints, if she insisted, but he bloody well wasn't going to have the heads of stinking dead animals and photographs of the Chester Cattle Show. And filthy white paint."

"Thank heaven, dear boy, it happened now, not later," I said.

"What d'you mean?" said Ernest curtly.

We moved into the inner office to get out of the wind while Ernest told me more. "Dear boy," I said, "what have you done to your eye?"

"Nothing," said Ernest. One eye was ringed in green and purple. "I was sawing a branch off a tree for her. She let go of the branch. It was too heavy for her. It sprang back and hit me in the eye. Wonderful girl. She didn't make a fuss."

"And I suppose she kissed it better and Robert saw you?" I said.

And then we heard a shout and dogs barking in the shop. We went to see what had happened. In at the open door came two dogs, fighting. One ran under the Chinese lacquer cabinet, and after them came Miss Staples with a leash and collars in her hand.

"Shut that bloody door! They've slipped their collars!" Miss Staples shouted at us. I shut the door, Ernest caught one dog by the neck. Miss Staples seized the other.

Reddened by the struggle, Ernest and Miss Staples stood excitedly looking at each other, with dogs' dribble on their clothes.

"Joanna and I are going out to lunch," Ernest said to me. "Do you mind if we shut Sydney and Morris in the office? Good fellow."

So our partnership ended. Ernest is farming now. Their house is terrible. It is the sort of house where dogs have their puppies on the sofa, where you can't see across the room for wood smoke, where the fake Jacobean furniture and brass trays are covered with old copies of the *Farmers Weekly*, where dogs' bones are found under rugs, where fox masks look down on you, where you can't see to read because the lamps are in the wrong place, and where Ernest sits in his gum boots reading the local paper and Joanna sits with a transistor mewing out the news in Welsh while she sews some awful cotton dresses.

"She's dead right here, isn't she? Exactly what a place like this needed," Ernest said to me, a flicker of the forgotten artist in him coming out—I flatter myself—at the sight of me. She had redecorated him.

A Debt of Honor

MRS. THWAITE got off the bus and turned the street corner, holding her key ready to get into her new flat. Every evening, for months now, she was eager to be home, to sniff the new paint and to stand looking at the place, wanting to put her arms round it. She ran up the stairs, let herself in and threw her old fur coat on the divan in the sitting room, put the gas poker in the fire and drew the curtains which did not quite meet, as if—by her intention—they had been carelessly made so as to let a little of the shabby Square and a stare of the London night into the flat. Then she went into the bedroom to see to the bed she had left unmade all day; almost at once she was sitting on the edge of it laughing, and telephoning to dear Argo—as she called him—to ask him to guess what she had found: his wristwatch under the pillow! And in a lower voice: "Oh, wasn't it lovely?"

She was swinging the wristwatch in her hand, Argo was saying he would be round, as usual, at half past seven and just then the doorbell gave its ugly little buzz.

"Hold on a minute, darling. Someone at the door."

When she got there, still dangling the watch, she saw a man with his hat in his hand standing there, a short figure with silver hair brushed straight back and wearing a silvery-gray overcoat. His face looked like a white blown-out paper bag. Long afterwards, she used to say he had the gleam of a simulacrum or a ghost. Then the paper bag burst and he showed his teeth in a smile. She instantly hid the watch in her hand. The teeth were unmistakable. They were not false teeth, but they looked false because they were not closely set; they were a squad of slight gaps, but the gaps were a little wider now than they had been nine years ago in her short married life. Her husband was standing there.

"Hullo, Phoebe," he said and with that he marched in past her across the little hall into the middle of the sitting room. He was much shorter than she was. She was a very tall woman and instinctively she stooped (as she had always done with him) when she followed the gleam of his overcoat into the room.

He turned round and said at once, "Nice place. Newly decorated. Frankly I didn't expect it in a neighborhood like this." He marked at once his disappointment with her. After nine years, he conveyed, she had gone downhill.

Mrs. Thwaite could not speak. A long scream seemed to be frozen in her. The shock was that, but for his teeth, Charles Thwaite was unrecognizable. She might have been telling lies about him for years.

He had been a bland little dark-haired pastry-fed fellow from the North when they had first gone off together, her fur-coat collar sticking to the frost inside the window of the night train. What a winter that was! He was a printer but had given that up, a man full of spit when he talked and his black eyebrows going up like a pair of swallows. The kind of man who said, "When I believe in a thing I put everything on it. Every penny in the bank, house, wife, children, shirt—everything." Even in those days his face had been blown out. Under the eyebrows there were a pair of earnest eyes fixed in an upward look, the eyes of a chapel-going boy caught with a finger in the jam pot; under them were curious, almost burned scoops of brown shadow—trademarks of a fate, the stamp of something salable they had seemed to her. She could never stop wondering what it was.

But now, as she stood there with her hands clenched upon Argo's watch, and looking down at her husband she saw that age had efficiently smoothed him. The stains were like hard coins; his effect was metallic. He looked collected, brisk and dangerous. And she had forgotten how short he was, for her Argo was a tall man.

What came back to her in the instant of this meeting was the forgotten, indignant girlish feeling—which living with Argo had cured her of—that she was lanky and exposed. If she had been able to move from where she was standing she would have made a grab at her coat in order to cover herself and especially to cover her legs. She had the sensation that she had become a joke once more.

For, to start with, her height had always been ridiculous. Men passing in the street turned to look up at her, startled and in dismay, and she was not a beauty; her features were too large. And jokes attract jokes; only stumpy little fellows—her husband was one of them—ever looked twice at her, and with a very trying ambition or impudence puffing themselves out. She had had the timid impression that men were playing a game of hide-and-seek round her, as boys playing in the street sometimes did still. This made her either stare crushingly over their heads or droop like a schoolgirl. In her early meetings with Charles she had got into the habit of finding a long low seat and at a distance from him where she could sit down, draw up her long legs, and listen on the same level as his. Being tall had turned her into a believer and listener, listening being a kind of apology; and she would look covertly down at her legs with a reproach that would change to a pout; for—when she had been with Charles—she was proud of the dashing way in which her legs had rushed her into this love affair and marriage and had disorganized her life. Nowadays, even with Argo, she would look at her legs with fear, thinking they belonged to someone else or were a pair of fine but disobedient daughters. What they had done to her, carrying her into that story of disaster! But the story itself, of course, had attracted Argo and she had come to feel that she had the grand distinction of being a woman to whom happiness and good luck were pettily irrelevant.

One Sunday Argo looked at his feet sticking out boastfully from the bottom of the bed and said, "Don't talk nonsense. Nine years is a long time. Your husband may be dead."

"Oh, no!" She still wanted her husband to be alive—and not for the sake of vengeance only.

"If he were, we could get married. Anyway, the law could presume death . . ." Argo went on.

She was happy with Argo after years of misery. But she wouldn't have *that.* She did not quite want to lose the gamble, the incompleteness—so breathlessly necessary to her—of her history.

* * *

History was standing there at ease, looking at the flat.

"I've given you a surprise," her husband said.

"What do you want?" She could speak at last. "I can't have you here. I have people coming."

"May I take my coat off?" he said and taking it off put it down beside hers on the divan.

"New?" he said, looking at hers.

At that her courage returned to her. "That's the only thing you left me with," she almost shouted and was ready to fly at him if he touched it. For in this frightened moment the coat, poor as it was, seemed to be her whole life—more than the office she worked in, more than Argo, more than her marriage. It was older than any of them. It was herself; it had known her longer than anything in the room.

Her husband turned away contemptuously, and while she unclenched her hands and put Argo's watch on the mantelpiece he sat down in an armchair. As his eyes stripped the room, he said, "Very nice, very nice. Kitchen there, I suppose. Bedroom through the door. Is that rug Chinese? I'm glad you're comfortable. You haven't changed. I must say you're very beautiful. By the way, I think you've left the telephone off in the bedroom—I can hear it crackling. Put it back, will you? Naturally I want to say a few words, to explain . . ."

"Say a few words"—how the phrase came back! There would be a lot of phrases.

She was determined not to sit down. The crackling of the telephone made her feel Argo was near.

An explanation! She wanted to demand it, rage for it, but she could not get the word out. She wanted to say, "Why? I just want to know why you left me. Don't imagine that I care, but I have a right to know. Then go."

"I found the address in the telephone book," he said, noting how well the world was organized. Then he made his announcement. It was more; it was a pronouncement, made with the modesty of an enormous benefactor.

"I have come back to you," he said.

"Argo, he's going to kill us," she wanted to cry out, and moved behind her chair for protection. The chair, the whole room seemed to be sickening, sliding her into the past, out of the window, into the flat she and her husband had had—the flat at the top of the small hotel she had bought for them with her own money—to those terrible scenes, to the sight of him opening the drawers of her desk in the little office, to that morning when she had unlocked the safe and found all the money gone—eight hundred pounds. Two of her father's pictures as well—but he left the frames behind!—and with them the foreign girl in Number 7. She held the chair tightly to hold the drifting room still. There he sat and, by merely sitting, occupied more and more of the room until only the few inches where she stood belonged to her. Nothing in the room, the pictures, the tables, the curtains, chairs, not even the little blue pot on the mantelpiece with pencils in it, came to her help. She would have to pass him to shout from the window.

"You are a very beautiful woman," he said in his praying, looking-skyward manner, but now the look was obsequious. "You are the most beautiful woman I have ever known. You are the only woman I have been in love with."

"You cannot break into my life like this," she said. "I have never been taken in by flattery."

"You are my wife," he said.

"I am certainly not," she said. "What is it you want?" And then she felt tears on her cheeks; ruinous tears, for this was the moment when he would get up and put his arms round her and she would be helpless. She tried to glare through her tears and did not know that this made her look brilliant, savage and frightening, indeed not helpless at all.

"I want *you,*" he said, without moving.

It was so wonderfully meaningless to hear him say this. Her tears stopped and she laughed loudly and did not know she was laughing. The laughter chased the fright out of her body. The joke restored her. That was the rock she stood on: a joke had been played on her when she was a child. She must put up with being a collection of jokes, but this joke was so preposterous that it drove all the others out. She could feel her laughter swallowing the little man up. It was wonderful also to see how her laughter took him aback and actually confused him so that he raised his chin and held up his hand to silence her. He had a small white hand. She remembered that this meant he was going to make a moral statement.

"I am a man who has sacrificed himself to women," he said, pointing to this as one of his unanswerable historic benefactions.

Another of his sayings! How she longed for Argo to come

in and hear it. Charles was a man who had always gone blandly back to first principles. Argo never quite believed the things she said about her marriage.

" 'I am a man who has sacrificed myself to women'—it was one of the first things he said to me when I met him. It was that cold winter, the worst winter for seventeen years —I told you my coat stuck to the frosty window in the train —shall I tell you about it? You don't mind? There was an election. He was—you won't believe, but it is true, it was one of his 'ideas'—standing for Parliament. Can you see him? He was standing as an Independent Republican—can you imagine it—in England, in the twentieth century! A gang of youths went round his meetings and sang 'Yankee Doodle' when he was speaking. Of course he didn't get in. He got two hundred and thirty-five votes. He lost his deposit. There was a row in the town. They were afraid he was splitting the vote. Splitting—he didn't even touch it! I was staying at the only hotel, a freezing-cold place. I had gone north to see my brother who was in hospital. Charles was always rushing in and out of the hotel, telephoning to his wife in London who was behaving very well—they were being divorced but she was holding the divorce up to stop the scandal—and to his mistress who was very tiresome. You could hear what he was saying all over the hotel because the telephone box was in the hall and he came out of it one evening and knew that I had heard. I was sitting wrapped up because I couldn't get near the fire.

" 'You look warm,' he said and then he looked back at the telephone box and said—well, that sentence. His set piece: 'I've sacrificed myself to women.' "

(What she did not tell Argo was that the remark was true. The scoundrel had "sacrificed" himself to women and that this was what had attracted her. She really had wanted in her naïve way to be the chief altar.)

"I told my brother when I went to the hospital. He said,

'He certainly doesn't sacrifice himself to anything else.' "

Now as he sat there in her flat and her laughter was warming her, Charles went one better.

"Everything I have done," he said. "I have done for you. Oh, yes, I have. You have been the cause and inspiration of it. You are the only woman who has influenced my mind. You changed my life. You were the making of me. When I went to South America . . ."

"Not South America!" she said. "Really! Think of something better than that. Monte Carlo. Cape Town."

"Buenos Aires first of all, then Chile—the women have beautiful voices there: it is the German and English influence," he went on, taking no notice of her. "Columbia—there's a culture that has collapsed. Bolivia, an extreme revolutionary situation, Ecuador, Indians in trilby hats looking like wood. I met the President. I've just come from Baranquilla. I flew."

"With that girl?" she said. A bad slip. He'd be the first to note her jealousy and mock it.

"Of course not," he said. He had a flat Yorkshire accent. "I have always been interested, as you know, in the Republican experience. You remember the book you made me write?"

"You didn't write it!" she said.

It was fabulous, after nine years, to see again his blank, baby-like effrontery, to hear his humorless, energetic innocence. He wasn't joking: the scoundrel *was* seriously, very seriously interested in republics! In a moment, he would tell her that he had stolen eight hundred pounds from her and deserted her out of a pure, disinterested passion for a harem of republics in South America!

The dangerous thing was that he was maneuvering her back to the time of their marriage. She could feel him recreating their marriage, against all her resistance, so that the room was filling with it. She feared he would wait for some sign of weakness, and then leap at her; the little man was very strong. She saw that he was already undressing the years from her and taking her back to her naked folly and credulity; until, if she was not careful, he would bring her to the point of the old passion. The Republic—it was incredible to remember—he had caught her with it.

It was a shock to her to remember what she had been like in those days—for example, how for years she had nursed her mother and had no friends. Every day she pushed the old lady down the sea front in her chair. Men looked at her or rather stepped back in half-grinning astonishment at a young woman so lanky, so gauche and shy and craving. The sight of her scared them. When her mother died, she got away to London. She had a little money which she knew she must be careful with and tried to find a job. Living alone, she simply read. Her tallness made her crave, and since no man came near her she craved for an idea.

So she was divided now between impatience and the memory he was rousing in her. She saw a half-empty room in that Town Hall in the North and him on the platform, uttering the fatal word, at the end of his speech. Republic—all men equal—equal height, perhaps that was the lure?—and so on: Republic. Quoted Plato even: "Love the beloved Republic." In a small industrial town, the war just over, snow frozen to black rock for six weeks on the pavements outside; and the small audience of men just back from the war, breaking up, drifting out, the gang of louts singing their "Yankee Doodle." She saw herself, exalted, turning in anger on the bored people around who were so rudely getting out and clattering their chairs; and gazing back at him, she signaled to him, "Yes, yes, yes, the Republic!" And when he lost, she really felt *she* would be the Republic! She had told Argo about this. "How I hate that word now. I can't even bear to read it in the newspapers. I was mad," she said. Argo could be very nasty sometimes.

He said, "I thought it was only men who went to bed with an idea."

She had to admit, as she listened, that dear Argo knew little about women. She had had two triumphs in her marriage: she had won a short period of power over her husband by persuading him that if he thought so much about republics he ought to write a book about them. She put her money into a small London hotel and drove him off to the British Museum to write it. If she had thought, she would have seen it was the ideal place for picking up foreign girls; but never mind about that. The other triumph was more important. She had beaten those two women, his wife in London and his mistress who was there in the North working for him. She—and the winter—had frozen them out.

* * *

Her husband was now in San Tomas—was it?—and in the midst of the mulatto problem.

"Where did you get the money?" she said coldly.

"Money?" he said. "I went back to the printing trade."

It was the first hint of reproach. She had persuaded him to give up that trade. Once she had got him she had been going to turn him into a political thinker. She had always said grandly to her friends: "He's in politics." Now she noticed a little color come to his face and that he was patting his small hand up and down on the arm of the chair in a dismissing way, as he had always done when money was mentioned. She had asked, she knew, the right question: indifference had made her intelligent.

"The heat was awful," he was saying. "When you go out into the street it is like a wall standing against you—I was glad you weren't there"—he had the nerve to say—"it shuts you in. I used to change my clothes four or five times a day . . ."

"Expensive," she said. "I couldn't have afforded it." He ignored this: no irony ever touched him.

"The only air-conditioned place was the casino and the cinema. The printing press was always breaking down. I was doing repairs half the time. I've not much use for casinos but I used to go there to cool off."

He raised his eyes seriously in the manner of the schoolboy now licking the spoon—who was he raising them to? Some feared schoolmaster, preacher or father?—and she remembered with pleasure that this presaged the utterance of some solemn, earnestly believed untruth.

"I have never been a gambling man," he said, "as you know—but there, the casino is packed every night. You have to get a permit, of course. Thousands change hands. I used to watch the tables and then go home along the shore road. I used to listen to the sea; you couldn't see the waves, except sometimes a flash of white, like Robin Hood's Bay on a rough night—remember, lass?"—dropping into broad Yorkshire—"Listen to this. One night when I went to the casino I had a shock: I saw *you*. I could have sworn it was you. You were standing there by one of the tables with a man, some politician: I knew him, the cousin of a man who owned one of the local papers. It was you, tall, beautiful, even the way you do your hair. I shan't forget the look in your eyes when you saw me. I thought: 'My God. I didn't do the right thing by her. I took her money. I have been a swine. I'll get the money and go back to her. I'll go down on my knees and beg her to take me back.' You don't know what remorse is."

"Oh, so you've come to pay me back?" she said.

"I knew it wasn't you, but it showed how you've haunted my mind every night for the last nine years," he said. "I couldn't take my eyes off that woman. She was playing. I went close to her and I played. I followed her play and won. I kept winning. Her husband came and joined us and we were all winning and I thought all the time 'This is for her. For her.' "

"For whom?" asked Mrs. Thwaite.

"For you."

"Did you sleep with her?"

"You can't sleep with those women. I was sleeping with an Indian girl," he said impatiently. "Don't interrupt me. It was for you. And then we started losing." I borrowed from her husband—he was excited like me. We all were. I'm not hiding anything. I lost everything I had. More than I had. A very large sum. I was ruined. Well, people are rich there. There was a thunderstorm that night. I couldn't pay for a taxi. The rain came down in sheets and the lightning was dancing about over the water in the streets. The whole place looked violet and yellow. I never saw anything like it. I wish you could have seen it. I stood there watching. You could see the sea, waves shooting up high, like hands. I thought, What have I done? What have I done to her?"

"Who?" she said.

"You. I thought, My God, suppose she is dead! I've never spent such a night in my life. At the door of the casino I heard that woman's voice. I thought it was yours. I went out. I went searching among the cars."

"And she wasn't there?"

"I was drenched. I was out in it for half an hour. I didn't know what I was doing."

"How did you pay back the money?" she said. *"Did* you pay it back?"

"Naturally," he said with stupendous coldness. "I had borrowed it from her husband. It was a debt of honor."

"Oh, honor," she said. "And what about the lady?" It shocked her that she felt that not quite conquerable disloyalty of the body when he mentioned the woman.

She had long ago admitted to herself that jealousy had been the foundation of her love for him. At the first sight of him in that hotel in the North, she had seen him sitting with three or four people near the fire. There was a cheerful vulgar fellow with drink-pimpled skin—his agent, no doubt. There was an elderly man who looked at him with a noble pathos and two gray-haired women who watched him with mistrust. They were talking about the meeting in the Town Hall and one said, "In this weather there'll be a poor turnout." A very thin young woman in a cheap black coat came in from the street kicking snow off her shoes and carrying a roll of posters which were packed in wet newspaper. Her stockings were wet. He went up to her quickly, scowling (but smiling too), and after taking the posters, he led the wretched girl by the arm not to the fire, but to the street door, speaking in a loud official voice about canvassing in the morning; at the door, he lowered his voice and said, shadily and sharply and intimately, looking into her defiant eyes: "I told you not to come here."

An intrigue! She heard it. A flare of desire to be part of it, and of jealousy, went through her, a sudden hungry jealousy. She had never felt like this until then, not at any rate since she was a child. She felt she had been set alight.

Now, nine years later, she said, "I don't know what you want. Why you're telling me this tale. It's all a lot of lies I know. I never wanted to see you again, but now I'm glad you've come. Where are you staying? Give me your address. I want a divorce. I shall divorce you. It's not a question of what you want. It is what I want now."

She was fighting for Argo and herself.

"Just a moment," he said. "I haven't come to talk about divorces."

"You can't stay here," she said. "I won't have you here."

"Let me speak," he said. "I haven't come here to quarrel." And shyly—how extraordinary to see him shy, for once—"I want your help. I know I must have made you suffer. You have something rare in a woman: integrity. You tell the truth."

"I'm certainly not going to help you about anything," she said.

"Divorce," he said. "Of course, I hadn't thought of that. It's natural, of course: I'm a Catholic, but still . . ."

"Yes?" she said.

He tapped one of his teeth with his finger thoughtfully.

"Let's get to the point. I'm in a little difficulty. Let me go on with what I was telling you. I've saved the printers a great deal of money—the firm in San Tomas. They were going to be forced to buy a new machine in New York, but I told them to wait, to let me work on it. That's what I've been doing. I've saved them thousands. These South Americans are no good at machinery. They just say, 'Buy a new one'—like that. They've got piles of money."

Perhaps he *has* come to pay me back? Is that the idea—buying me back? she wondered. The white hand went slowly up and down on the arm of the chair.

"What is it you really came here for?" she said reasonably. A full smile of pure, admiring pleasure made his white skin shine, a smile of polite tenderness and discreet thanks.

"I want twelve hundred pounds," he said. "I had to borrow it from the firm to pay that man—as I told you just now. I want it rather quickly. The accountants come in at the end of the month. I want you to lend it to me."

He said this in a voice of stupefying kindness and seriousness as if he were at last atoning for what he had done, unasked, in real friendship and generosity. It would, he gravely conveyed, be the most binding of ties. It would remind her of those happy days—ah, he too wished them to return!—when he had had money from her before. He conveyed that she would instinctively see the beauty of it—that he had come to her, the perfect woman, a second time;

that she was, in truth, the only woman in his life, that of no one else would he ask such a thing.

And the strange part of it was that as she gasped at the preposterous suggestion and was about to turn on him a small thrill went through her. She was a prudent woman, if anything a shade mean about the little money left to her, but he brought back to her the sense of unreason and danger that had turned her head when she had first met him. He brought back to her the excitement of the fact that he was—as she knew—unbelievable. It enhanced some quality in her own character: she was the kind of woman to whom mad things happened. And she saw herself running to Argo with her astounded mouth open and telling him, telling everyone. And, for a few seconds, she admired her husband. Twelve hundred pounds! In nine years his price had gone up!

"You stole twelve hundred pounds?" she said. "Fiddled the books?"

"Stole?" he said. "I don't like to hear you use a word like that. I borrowed it. I told you. It was a debt of honor."

"You must be mad to think I would be such a fool. I haven't got twelve hundred pence. I've never had such a sum in my life."

Stole! Arrest! Prison! Perhaps he had already been in prison? Was that why he was so pale? She was not frightened, but his case seemed to taint herself.

"But you can raise it," he said briskly, dismissing what she said.

"I work for my living. I go to my office every day. I've had to. Where do you think I could get the money?"

There was a silence filled by the enormity of that sum. He was proposing to come here, settle here, and tie that huge debt to her neck, like a boulder. Argo must turn him out. He must come and turn him out.

"I was very sorry to see—when was it? I saw an English

paper over there—that your aunt had died," he said in a changed and sorrowful voice. "I think you *can* raise it," he said suddenly, coolly threatening.

"Ah!" she woke up to it. *"Now* I see why you have come back to me. You thought I had just come into her money. You saw it in the paper and you came rushing back."

"It was coming to you. I remember you telling me. And I am your husband."

"Well, if you want to know, it did *not* come to me. When you left me, she blamed me, not you. But do you think even if I had, I would give it to you? She left it to her brother."

"Your brother?" he said sharply.

"No, *her* brother," she said triumphantly.

"Is that true?"

"Ask him."

He took out a pocket notebook and turned over a page or two. "The one in Newcastle?" he said. He had obviously been checking her family.

"You got nothing at all?" he said.

"No." And this time she really did shout at him.

"I can't believe it," he said curtly. "I just can't believe you can have been such a damn fool."

She could see he was affronted and injured. "I offer you everything," he seemed to say. "And you give me nothing."

There was a sneer on his papery face. The sneer, she knew, concealed desperation and she felt the beginnings of pity, but she knew now—what she had not known nine years ago—that this pity was dangerous to her; he would see it at once, and he would come towards her, grip her arm, press upon her, ignoring her mind but moving her body. He had a secret knowledge of her, for he had been the first to know that her body was wild.

She was frightened of herself. She had to get out of the room but each room was a trap. The only hope was the most dangerous room: the bedroom. It had a telephone in it.

"Argo, Argo, please come. Hurry," she was crying to herself. But her husband did not step towards her, he went over to the mantelpiece and he was looking at something on it. He picked up Argo's watch. She moved to snatch it from him, but he closed his hand. She actually touched his sleeve: touching him made her feel sick.

"Beginning all over again, I see," he said. "Does he live here?"

"That's my business."

"Snug under the coat?" He laughed and let the watch dangle by its strap. She was blushing, and almost gasping, fearing he would now attack her.

But he did not.

"You realize, I hope, that you are committing adultery?" he said stiffly. "I don't understand what has happened to you. You seem to have gone to pieces since I left you. I was surprised to see you living in a low-class district like this—what is he? Some clerk? You can't even manage your own money. Left it to her brother! How often I've told you—you never had any sense of reality. And by the way," he went on angrily, "if you had not left all your money in the safe, none of this would have happened. You should have paid it into the bank."

"He is not a clerk," she said. "He's a professor in the university."

He laughed. "That's what you wanted me to be. You are just romantic. The printing trade was not good enough for the lady."

"I didn't want you to be a professor."

"Write about the Republic. What republic?" he jeered.

"It was your idea," she said.

"Sitting in the British Museum, coming round to you for my money. I sacrificed myself to you. Why? I have always sacrificed myself to women. I loved you and you ruined me."

"I don't believe you ever went to the Museum," she said, "except to pick up girls."

"To think of my wife committing adultery!" he exclaimed. And—she could not believe her luck—he put the watch back on the mantelpiece with disgust. He ran his fingers on the mantelpiece and saw dust on his fingers.

"You don't look after your things. There are cigarette burns on this mantelpiece. I don't like your pictures—one, two, three nudes. Indecent. I don't like that. I suppose that is how you see yourself."

He mooched about the flat and pointed at the frayed lining of her coat on the divan.

"That ought to have gone to the furrier's," he said. He stared at the coat and his temper quietened.

"It was a very cold winter, wasn't it?" he said. "The worst winter for years. It cut down the canvassing, I couldn't get people to the polls. It wasn't that, though. Do you know what lost me that election? Your coat. That was a true thing Jenny said after you saw me tell her to keep out of the hotel. 'We're up against those hard-faced Tory women in their mink.' "

"It's not mink," she said.

"Whatever it is. Of course she was suspicious. But that wasn't the trouble. She was just freezing cold. Her room was an icebox. She couldn't stand it. She was coughing even when we started. She went off."

He suddenly laughed. "She was frozen out. You had a fur coat, she hadn't. Your coat won. Fourteen Purser Street, do you remember?—it kept us warm, after she had gone?"

"She didn't go for a week," she said. After all, she had sat her rival out. But Mrs. Thwaite was watching for her opportunity. How to get past him and snatch back the watch?

She saw her chance and grabbed it. He was taken by surprise and did not, as she feared he would, catch her arm.

"I feel sick," she said and rushed with her handkerchief to her mouth to the bedroom.

She sat on the bed and heard the crackling of the telephone receiver, which she had not replaced. She put it back and then took it off to dial Argo's number, looking in fear at the door she had left open.

"Darling, darling. Charles has come back. My husband, yes. Yes, he's here. I am frightened. He won't go. I can't get him out. Please come, he's horrible. What are we to do? No, if he sees you he will go. Call the police? How can I do that? He's my husband. He's in the sitting room, he's moving about. I can hear him. Get a taxi. I'm afraid. I'm afraid of what he'll do. I can't tell you. Get him out? How can I? Oh, please, thank you, darling, thank you, I love you . . . He's horrible."

She put down the telephone and moved away, standing with her back to the window. If he came into the bedroom she would open the window and jump out. But he did not. He seemed to be picking up things in the sitting room. She went back boldly now. He had picked up her coat and was holding it by the shoulders.

"Get out. Put that down. Get out. I have my own life now. I never want to set eyes on you again. I'm going to divorce you. I have rung for help." She was astonished by her own power and the firmness of her voice.

"Yes, I heard you," he said. He had put his overcoat on again.

"And put my coat down!" she shouted again.

They stood outstaring each other. He was half smiling with passing admiration.

"No," he said, "I'll take it with me. A souvenir. Goodbye."

She was flabbergasted to see him walk past her out of the room, open the door of the flat and go downstairs with her coat on his arm.

"Charles." She ran to the door. "Charles." He went on.

"Charles, come back here."

She was down at the street door, but already he was twenty yards away, crossing the street. He looked not so much ridiculous as luxurious carrying the coat. She felt he was carrying her off too. She shouted again but not loudly, for she did not want people to stare at them in the street. She was about to run after him when she saw the blind man who lived further down come tapping towards her with his white stick. He slowed down, sensing disturbance. He paused like a judgment. And in her pause of indecision, she saw her husband get to the bus stop and instantly, as if he were in league with buses and had bribed one or got it by some magic, a bus floated up beside him and he was off on it.

He had taken the last thing she had, he had taken twenty years of her life with him. She watched the bus until it was out of sight.

She went back to her door and she climbed the stairs and got inside and looked at the room where he had stood; it seemed to her that it was stripped of everything, even of herself. It seemed to her that she was not there. "Why are women so mad about furs?" he had once said to her. "To keep warm? No, so that they can feel naked." One of his "sayings." But that was what she felt as she sat waiting for Argo to come; her husband had taken her nakedness.

* * *

Argo found her sitting there. When she stopped crying in his arms he said, "He won't come back. I'll get on to the police."

"Oh, no."

"He'll sell it. He was just after anything he could get. He might get fifty pounds for it."

"He was very jealous. He used to try to make me say some man had given it to me." She was proud of that. "He's a funny man. He may not sell it."

"You mean," said Argo who, though placating, had his nasty side, "he'll give it to one of his girl friends?"

"No," she said angrily. She was not going to have that! An old feeling, one she used to have, that there was something stupid about very tall men like Argo, came back to her.

In the night she lay awake, wondering where her husband was. Perhaps everything he said had been true: that he did love her more than any of the women he had known, that he did want to be forgiven, that she had been hard and was to blame from the beginning. He had remembered Purser Street. Perhaps he *had* been in South America. She wished she had had twelve hundred pounds to give him. She would never forgive herself if he was arrested. Then her thoughts changed and she fell into thinking in his melodramatic way: he had taken her youth, her naked youth, with him and left her an old woman. She got up in the night and went to her mirror to see how much gray there was in her hair. She was not very much younger than Charles. She went back cold to bed and put her arms round Argo.

"Love me. Love me," she said.

She hated Argo for saying that her husband had given the coat to another woman.

In the morning she went to her office.

"Someone walked into my flat yesterday and stole my fur coat," she said.

What a life, they said, that poor woman has had; something is always happening to her. It never ends. But they saw her eyes shining brilliantly within their gloom.

The Cage Birds

JUST AS HE was getting ready to go to his office, the post came.

"A card from Elsie," Mrs. Phillips said. " 'Come on Wednesday. All news when we meet. I've got Some Things. Augusta.' " She turned the card over. There was a Mediterranean bay like a loud blue wide-open mouth, a small white town stretching to a furry headland of red rocks. A few villas were dabbed in and a large hotel. The branch of a pine tree stretched across the foreground of the picture, splitting the sea in two. Her husband had been brushing his jacket and stopped to look at the card: he started brushing again. In ten years, it seemed to her, he had brushed half the suit away: it was no longer dark gray but a parsimonious gleam.

They looked at each other, disapproving of the foreign scene; also of the name Elsie had given herself: Augusta. They had never got used to it.

"Ah ha! The annual visit! You'd better go," he said. And then he laughed in his unnatural way, for he laughed only when there was no joke, a laugh that turned the pupils of his eyes into a pair of pinheads. "Before her maid gets hold of the things."

"I'll have to take the boy. It's a school holiday."

"Half fare on the bus," he said. "She always gives you something for the fare."

And he laughed at this too.

"She forgot last year," she said.

He stopped laughing. He frowned and reflected.

"You shouldn't let her forget. Fares have gone up. All across London! When I was a boy you could do it for six-pence. Get off at Baker Street—that'll save four pence."

He put the brush down. He was a youngish man whose sleeves were too short, and he was restlessly rubbing his red hands together now, glistering at the thought of the economy; but she stood still, satisfied. When they were first married his miserliness had shocked her, but now she had fallen into abetting it. It was almost their romance; it was certainly their Cause. When she thought of the mess the rest of her family was in, she was glad to have years of girlhood anxiety allayed by a skinflint. She knew the sharp looks the shopkeepers and neighbors gave him when his eyes filled with tears as he haggled over a penny or two, and counted the change in his open martyred hand. But she stood by him, obstinately, raising her chin proudly when, giving his frugal laugh, he cringed at a counter or a ticket office. He had the habit of stroking his hands over the legs of his trousers and smiling slyly at her when he had saved a penny, and she, in ten years of marriage, had come to feel the same small excited tingle in her own skin as he felt in his.

"Get out of my way. We're going to Auntie's tomorrow," she said to the boy when he came back from school in the afternoon. "Here" and she gave him the postcard—"look at this."

She was in the kitchen, a room darkened by the dark blobs of the leaves of a fig tree hanging their tongues against the window. It was an old tree, and every year it was covered with fruit that looked fresh and hopeful for a few weeks, and then turned yellow and fell onto the grass, because of the failure of the London sun. The dirty-minded woman next door said those leaves put ideas into your head, but Mrs. Phillips couldn't see what she meant. Now she was ironing a petticoat to put on for the visit tomorrow and the boy was looking at the mole on her arm as it moved back and forth, her large gray eyes watching the iron like a cat. First the black petticoat, then her brassiere, then her knickers; the boy watched restlessly.

"Mum. Where is Auntie's house?" the boy said, looking at the card.

"There," she said, straightening up and dashing a finger at random on the card.

"Can I swim?"

"No, I told you. We're not going there. We haven't got the money for holidays. That's where Auntie Elsie lives in the summer."

"Where's Uncle Reg?"

135208

That was the trouble: the kid asking questions.

"I told you. He's gone to China, Africa—somewhere. Stop kicking your shoes. They're your school shoes. I can't afford any more."

Then she put down the iron with a clump and said, "Don't say anything about Uncle Reg tomorrow, d'you hear? It upsets Auntie."

"When are we going to see her?"

"Tomorrow. I keep telling you."

"On a bus?"

"On a bus. Here," she said, "give me those shirts of yours."

The boy gave her the pile of shirts and she went on working. She was a woman who scarcely ever sat down. She was wearing a black petticoat like the one she had ironed, her arms were bare and when she lifted up a garment he could see the hair in her armpits; hair that was darker than the tawny hair that was loose over her sweating forehead. What disturbed the boy was the way she changed from untidy to tidy and especially when she put on her best blouse and skirt and got ready to go out. The hours he had to wait for her when, going to the cupboard and looking at the dresses hanging there, she changed herself into another woman!

She was this other woman the next day when they went off to the bus stop. She was carrying a worn, empty suitcase and walked fast, so he had almost to run to keep up with her. She was wearing a navy-blue dress. She had tied a gray-and-white scarf round her head, so that the pale face looked harder, older and emptier than it was. The lips were long and thin. It was a face set in the past; for the moment it was urging her to where she was going but into the past it would eventually fall back. At the bus stop she simply did not see the other people standing there. The boy looked at her raised chin with anxiety and when the bus came, she came down out of the sky and pushed the boy on and put the case under the stairs.

"You sit there," she said. "And see no one takes it."

The annual visit! Her sister had come over from that island in June this year, early for her. It used to be Christmas in Reg's time and, for that matter, in the time of that other man she had never met. This new one had lasted three years; he was called Williams and he was buying the headland on the postcard, and he was a June man. He couldn't stand the mosquitoes. Her sister said, "They suck his blood. He's like beef to them." But who was the bloodsucker? You ask *him!* Those women have to get it while they can. At the Ritz one minute—and the next where are they? She called herself Augusta now. But Grace stuck to calling her Elsie: it was virtuous.

London was cabbaged with greenery. It sprouted in bunches along the widening and narrowing of the streets, bulging at corners, at the awkward turnings that made the streets look rheumatic. There were wide pavements at empty corners, narrow ones where the streets were packed. Brilliant traffic was squeezing and bunching, shaking, spurting, suddenly whirling round bends and then dawdling in short disorderly processions like an assortment of funerals. On some windows the blinds of a night worker were drawn and the milk bottle stood untouched at the door; at the Tube, papers and cigarette litter blowing, in the churchyards women pushing prams. The place was a fate, a blunder of small hopes and admired defeats. By the river one or two tall new buildings stuck up, prison towers watching in the midst of it. The bus crossed the river and then gradually made north to the park and the richer quarters.

"There's your dad's shop," she said to the boy. They passed a large store.

"There's his window, first floor," she pointed up. That was where he worked in the week.

Now the streets were quieter, the paint was fresher, the people better dressed. By a church with a golden statue of St. George and the Dragon outside it, she got the boy off the bus and walked to a new building where there was a man in blue uniform at the door.

In this instant the boy saw his mother change. She stopped, and her gray eyes glanced to right and then to left fearfully. Usually so bold, she cringed before the white building and its balconies that stuck out like sun decks. She lowered her head when the porter with the meaty despising nose opened the door into the wide hall. She was furtive, and in the lift she tried to push the suitcase out of sight behind the boy; she felt ashamed. She also nervously trembled, fearing to be suspected of a crime.

"Take your cap off in the lift when you're with a lady," she said to the boy, asserting to the porter that she was respectable. With both hands the startled boy clawed the cap off his head.

The porter was not going to let them out of his sight. On the eleventh floor the doors slid open. Across another hall of carpet and mirrors which made her feel she was a crowd of women at many doors and not one, he led her to the door. The boy noticed it had no knocker. No bang, bang, bang, iron on iron, as on their door at home; a button was pressed and a buzz like hair spray at the barber's could be heard. There were, he noticed, white bars behind the figured glass on the door where ferns were frosted.

Presently a maid wearing a pretty apron opened the door and let them in, looking down at their shoes. A green carpet, mirrors framed in mirror again, hotel flowers, lilies chiefly, on a glass-topped table of white metal: the flat was like the hall outside. It smelled of scent and the air stood warm and still. Then they were shown into a large room of creamy furniture, green and white satin chairs. There were four wide windows, also with white metal strips on them, beyond which the fat trees of the park lolled. Did Auntie own them? At one end of the room was a small bar of polished bamboo. Then out of another room came Auntie herself, taking funny short steps which made her bottom shake, calling in a little girl's voice, "Grace!" She bent down low to kiss him with a powdery face, so that he could see the beginning of her breasts. Her brooch pricked his jersey, catching it. "Oh, we're caught." She disentangled it.

"It's torn my jersey," the boy whined.

"There you are. Look. I'll take it off and put it here." She put the brooch on the table.

"Umph. Umph," she said, going back to him and kissing him again. Auntie had the tidiness of a yellow-haired doll. She was as pink as a sugared almond and her kiss tasted of scent and gin.

"You've lost a lot, Grace," she said to her sister. "Look at me. It's that French food. I've put on seven pounds. It shows when you're small. Mr. Williams is coming today. I flew in yesterday from Paris. I've got some lovely things.

It's no good anyone thinking they can leave me in Paris on my own."

"Is Uncle Reg in Paris?" said the boy.

His mother blushed.

"Keep quiet. I told you," she said with a stamp.

Elsie's round blue eyes looked at the boy and her lips pouted with seductive amusement. She wriggled a shoulder and moved her hips. The boy grew up as she looked at him.

"What do you like for tea? I've got something for you. Come with me and see Mary. Sit down, Grace."

When the boy had gone the two sisters took up what they felt to be their positions in the room. Grace refused to take off her scarf and refused also out of dread of contamination from the expense of the satin to sit back on the sofa; she kept to the edge from where she could get a good view of everything. Elsie sat with her beautiful silk legs drawn up on the seat of a chair and lit a cigarette and touched the hair that had been made into a golden crust of curls that morning.

Grace said, "The carpet's new."

"They never last more than a year," Elsie said with a cross look. She was pretty, therefore she could be cross. "People drop cigarettes. I had the whole place done." And with that she restlessly got up and shut a window.

"The curtains as well. Mr. Williams paid five hundred pounds for the curtains alone! I mean—you've got to be kind to yourself. No one else will be. We only live once. He spent nearly as much in the bedroom. I saw the bills. Come and look at it."

She got up and then sat down again. "We'll see it in a minute."

"You're all barred in," Grace said.

"We had burglars again. I just got in—Mr. Williams took me to Ascot. He likes a bit of racing—and I rushed back, well, to tell you the truth I must have eaten something that didn't agree with me, duck pâté I think that's what it was, and I had to rush. He must have followed me in, this man, I mean, and when I came out my handbag was open and he had cleared a hundred and fifty pounds. Just like that." She lowered her voice. "I don't like the man on the lift. Then at Christmas when we were on the island they came in again. The staff here were off duty, but you'd have thought people would see. Or hear . . . That's what staff is like these days."

"What happened?"

"They took my mink coat and the stole, and a diamond clasp, a diamond necklace and Mr. Williams's coat, a beautiful fur-lined coat—he carried on, I can tell you—and all my rings. Well, not all. We got insurance but I don't keep anything here now except what I'm wearing. The brooch—did you see it? Mr. Williams gave it to me as a consolation, I was so upset. Pictures, that's where he puts his money usually. Everything's going up. You want to put your money into things. That's why we put those bars on the door and the windows. And—come here, I'll show you."

They walked into the bedroom and on the door that gave on to the balcony there was a steel grille that closed like a concertina.

"You're caged in," said Grace.

Elsie laughed.

"It's what Mr. Williams said. Funny you should say it. He likes a joke—Reg could never see one, d'you remember? 'Birdie—we'll keep you in a cage.' Ah now," she pointed to the white bed where dresses were laid out. "Here it all is. I've picked them all out."

But Grace was looking at a white cupboard with a carved and gilded top to it. The doors were open and thrown inside was a pile of summery hats, some had fallen out onto the violet carpet of the bedroom. Half of them were pink —"My color."

"Oh," said Elsie in a bored voice, already tired of them. "That's what I got in Paris. I told you. On the way back."

Elsie led her sister out of the bedroom again.

The cringing had gone; Grace sat stiffly, obstinately, hardened, without curiosity, looking at the luxury of the room.

"I heard from Birmingham the day before yesterday," she said in a dead voice.

Elsie's pretty face hardened also.

"Mother's ill," said Grace.

"What is it?" said Elsie.

"Her legs."

"I hope you didn't tell her this address," Elsie accused.

"I haven't written yet."

"Grace," said Elsie in a temper, "Mother has her life. I have mine. And she never writes."

She went to the bar, saying in the middle of her temper, "This is new. I know its no good asking you," and she poured herself a glass of gin and vermouth and then resumed her temper, raising her small plump doll's chin so that Grace should know why her chin and throat and shoulders could, when her lips pouted and her eyes moistened, draw men's eyes to the hidden grave gaze of her breast. Men would lower their heads as if they were going to jump and she kept her small feet nimble and ready to dodge. It was a dogma in the minds of both sisters that they were (in different but absolute ways) who they were, what they were, on their own and immovable in unwisdom. This was their gift, the reward for a childhood that had punished them.

"Listen," said Elsie in her temper, "you haven't seen me.

'How is Elsie?' 'I don't know. I don't know where she is.' I've got my life. You've got yours. If Dad had been alive things would be different."

"I never say anything," said Grace grimly. "I mind my own business. I wouldn't want to say anything."

Suddenly Elsie became secretive.

"Mary," she nodded to the room where the maid and the boy were, "always has her eye on the clothes. I don't trust anybody. You know these girls. You have to watch them. 'Where's my red dress?' 'At the cleaner's, ma'am.' I wasn't born yesterday. But you can *use* them, Grace, I *know*. Let's go and look."

Gay and confiding she took Grace back to the bedroom and looked at the dresses spread out on the bed. She held up a blue one.

"It's funny, I used to be jealous of your clothes. When we went to church," Elsie said. "Do you remember your blue dress, the dark-blue one with the collar? I could have killed you for it and the bank manager saying, 'Here comes the bluebird of happiness.' Aren't kids funny? When you grew out of it and it came down to me, I hated it. I wouldn't put it on. It was too long. You were taller than me then, we're the same now. Do you remember?"

"And here is a black," she said, holding up another. "Well, every picture tells a story. Mr. Williams threw it out of the window when we were in Nice. He has a temper. I was a bit naughty. This one's Italian. It would suit you. You never wear anything with flowers though, do you?"

She was pulling the dresses off the bed and throwing them back again.

"Reg was generous. He knew how to spend. But when his father died and he came into all that money, he got mean—that's where men are funny. He was married—well, I knew that. Family counted for Reg. Grace, how long have you been married?"

"Ten years," said Grace.

Elsie picked up a golden dress that had a paler metallic sheen to it, low in the neck and with sleeves that came an inch or two below the elbow. She held it up.

"This would suit you, Grace. You could wear this color with your hair. It's just the thing for cocktails. With your eyes it would be lovely. Mr. Williams won't let me wear it, he hates it, it looks hard, sort of brassy on me—but you, look!"

She held it against her sister.

"Look in the mirror. Hold it against yourself."

Against her will Grace held it to her shoulders over her navy woolen dress. She saw her body transformed into a sunburst of light.

"Grace," said Elsie in a low voice. "Look what it does to you. It isn't too big."

She stepped behind and held the dress in at the waist. Grace stood behind the dress and her jaw set and her bones stiffened in contempt at first and then softened.

"There's nothing to be done to it. It's wonderful," said Elsie.

"I never go to cocktail parties," said Grace.

"Look. Slip it on. You'll see."

"No," said Grace and let go of a shoulder. Elsie pulled it back into place.

"With the right shoes," Elsie said, "that will lift it. Slip it on. Come on. I've never seen anything like it. You remember how things always looked better on you. Look."

She pulled the dress from Grace and held it against herself. "You see what I look like.

"No," she went on, handing it back. She went to the bedroom door and shut it and whispered, "I paid two hundred and forty pounds for it in Paris—if you're not going to wear it yourself you can't have it. I'll give it to Mary. She's had her eye on it."

Grace looked shrewdly at Elsie. She was shocked by her sister's life. From her girlhood Elsie had wheedled. She had got money out of their aunt; she drew the boys after her but was soon the talk of the town for going after the older men, especially the married. She suddenly called herself Augusta. It baffled Grace that men did not see through her. She was not beautiful. The blue eyes were as hard as enamel and she talked of nothing but prices and clothes and jewelry. From this time her life was a procession through objects to places which were no more than objects, from cars to yachts, from suites to villas. The Mediterranean was something worn in the evening, a town was the setting for a ring, a café was a looking-glass, a night club was a price. To be in the sun on a beach was to have found a new man who had bought her more of the sun.

Once she giggled to Grace: "When they're doing it—you know what I mean—that's when I do my planning. It gives you time to yourself."

Now, as Grace held the golden dress and Elsie said in her cold baby voice, "If you don't keep it to wear I'll give it to Mary," Grace felt their kinship. They had been brought up poor. They feared to lose. She felt the curious pleasure of being a girl again, walking with Elsie in the street and of being in the firm humoring position of the elder sister of a child who, at that time, simply amused them all by her calculations. Except for their father, they were a calculating family. Calculation was their form of romance. If I put it on, Grace thought, that doesn't mean I'll keep it for myself. I'll sell it with the rest.

"All right. I'll just try it," she said.

"I'll unzip you," said Elsie, but she let Grace pull her dress over her head, for the navy wool disgusted her. And Grace in her black slip pouted shyly, thinking, Thank heavens I ironed it yesterday. To be untidy underneath in an expensive flat like this—she would have been shamed.

She stepped into the golden dress and pulled it up and turned to the long mirror as she did this, and at once to her amazement she felt the gold flowing up her legs and her waist, as if it were a fire, a fire which she could not escape and which, as Elsie fastened it, locked her in. The mirror she looked in seemed to blaze.

"It's too long."

"We're the same height. Stand on your toes. Do you see?"

Grace felt the silk with her fingers.

"Take off your scarf."

Grace pulled it off. Her dead hair became darker and yet it, too, took on the yellow glint of the flame.

"It's too full," said Grace, for her breasts were smaller than Elsie's.

"It was too tight on me. Look!" Elsie said. She touched the material here and there and said, "I told you. It's perfect."

Grace half smiled. Her face lost its empty look and she knew that she was more beautiful than her sister. She gazed, she fussed, she pretended, she complained, she turned this way and that. She stretched out an arm to look at the length of the sleeve. She glowed inside it. She saw herself in Elsie's villa. She saw herself at one of those parties she had never been to. She saw her whole life changed. The bus routes of London were abolished. Her own house vanished and inside herself she cried angrily, looking at the closed door of the bedroom, so that her breasts pushed forward and her eyes fired up with temper: "Harry, where are you? Come here! Look at this."

At that very moment, the bedroom door was opened. The boy walked in and a yard behind him, keeping not quite out of sight, was a man.

"Mum," the child called, with his hands in his pockets, "there's a man."

The boy looked with the terror of the abandoned at the new woman he saw and said, "Where's Mum?" looking at her in unbelief.

She came laughing to him and kissed him. He scowled mistrustfully and stepped back.

"Don't you like it?"

As she bent up from the kiss she had a furtive look at the man in the room: was it Mr. Williams? He was gazing with admiration at her.

But Elsie was quick. She left Grace and went into the sitting room and Grace saw her sister stop suddenly and heard her say, in a voice she had never heard before—a grand stagy voice spoken slowly and arrogantly as if she had a plum in her mouth, her society voice: "Oh, you! I didn't invite you to call this afternoon." The man was dark and young and tall, dandified and sunburned. He was wearing a white polo-neck jersey and he was smiling over Elsie's golden head at Grace, who turned away at once.

Elsie shut the bedroom door. As she did so, Grace heard her sister say, "I have got my dressmaker here. It's very inconvenient."

To hear herself being called "my dressmaker" and not "my sister," and in that artificial voice, just at the moment of her stupefying glory, to have the door shut in her face! She stared at the door that separated them, and then in anger went over to the door and listened. The boy spoke.

"Ssh," said Grace.

"I am annoyed with you. I told you to telephone," Elsie was saying. "Who let you in?"

Grace heard him say, "Get rid of her. Send her away."

But Elsie was saying nervously, "How *did* you get in?"

And quite clearly the man said, "The way I went out last night, through the kitchen."

Grace heard a chair being pushed and Elsie say, "Don't, I tell you. Mr. Williams will be here. Stop."

"Here, help me," said Grace to the boy. "Pick them up." She had the suitcase on the bed and quickly started to push the dresses into her case. "Come on."

She tried to unzip the yellow dress but she could not reach.

"Damn this thing," she said.

"Mum, you said a word," said the boy.

"Shut up," she said. And, giving up, she pushed the navy dress she had taken off into the case, just as Elsie came back into the room and said to the boy, "Go and talk to the gentleman." The boy walked backwards out of the room, gaping at his mother and his aunt until Elsie shut the door on him.

"Grace," she said in an excited, low voice, wheedling. "Don't pack up. What are you doing? You're not going? You mustn't go."

"I've got to get my husband his supper," said Grace sharply. Elsie opened her handbag and pulled out a five-pound note and pushed it into Grace's hand. "There's time. That's for a taxi. Something awkward's happened. Mr. Williams will be here in a minute and I can't get rid of this man. I don't know what to do. It is a business thing about the villa and he's pestering me and Mr. Williams loathes him. I met him on the plane. I was very, very silly. If Mr. Williams comes, I'll say he's come with you from the dress shop. And you can leave with him."

"You *said* Mr. Williams knew him," said Grace with contempt.

"Did I? I was a bit silly," Elsie wheedled. "You know what a fool I am—I let this gentleman drive me from the airport—well, that's harmless, I mean . . . Grace, you look wonderful in that dress. I only mean go out of the flat *with* him." She looked slyly and firmly at Grace.

Into Grace's mind came that scene from their girlhood outside their school when Elsie made her stand with a young man and hold his arm to prevent him getting away while she fetched a new red coat. The young man had a marvelous new motor bike. It was the first time Grace had held a young man's arm. She would never forget the sensation and the youth saying: "She's a little bitch. Let's go."

And how, just as she was going to say wildly, "Oh, yes," and he squeezed her arm, Elsie came running back and pulled him to the motor bike and shouted to Grace, "So long!"

Grace hesitated now, but then she remembered Elsie's society voice: "My dressmaker." And with that she had a feeling that was half disgust and half fear of being mixed up in Elsie's affairs. For Grace the place was too grand. The lies themselves were too grand. And there was this revelation that for years, in every annual visit, Elsie had concealed and denied that they were sisters, just as she denied the rest of the family.

"No, Elsie," Grace said. "I've got to get back to Harry."

She was tempted to leave the suitcase, but she thought, She'd only think I'm a fool if I leave it.

"I'll take the case and I'd best go. Thanks, though, for the taxi."

"Goodbye, ma'am," she said to Elsie in a loud, proud voice as they went into the sitting room.

"Come on," she called to the child. "Where are you?"

He was sitting on a chair staring at the man, and particularly at his jacket, as if his eyes were microscopes. The man had walked over to the window.

Grace took the boy by the hand.

"Say goodbye to the lady," Grace said, pulling the boy who, scared still by the strangeness of his mother in her glory, said, "Goodbye, Auntie."

* * *

They sat in the taxi.

"Sit down," said Grace to the boy. He had never been in a taxi before. He took a timid look at her. She was overpowering.

"I haven't been in a taxi since your dad and I came back from our honeymoon," she said. London had changed. There were only doors to look at, doors at first of the rich houses in the park and herself arriving at them, being taken into drawing rooms. She wished her suitcase was not so shabby. She would go into the doorways of hotels; palaces seemed familiar; streets wider; she looked at the windows of shoeshops. She looked at the handbags women were carrying. The taxi came to the river and there she gleamed, as she passed over the sad, dirty, dividing water, but through the poorer streets, past the factories, the railway arches, the taxi went fast, passing the crowded buses. She was indignant with traffic lights that stopped them.

"Mum," said the boy.

She was daydreaming about the effect she would have on her husband when she opened the gate of her house.

"Do you like it?" she said.

"Yes. But Mum . . ."

"Look," she said, excited. "We're nearly there. There's Woolworth's. There's Marks's. Look, there's Mrs. Sanders. Wave to Mrs. Sanders. I wonder if she saw us."

Then the taxi stopped at the house. How mean it looked!

"Your dad is home," she said as she paid the driver and then opened the gate and looked at the patch of flower bed. "He's been watering the garden." But when she was paying the taxi driver the door of the house opened and her husband stood there with his eternal clothes brush held in horror in the air. He gaped at her. His eyes became small.

"You took a cab!" he said, and looked as if he were going

to run after it as it grunted off. "How much did you give him?"

"She paid," she said.

"Come in," he said. "Come in." And he went into the dark hall, put the brush down and rubbed his hands as she lifted the suitcase into the house. The boy crept past them.

"What did he charge?" her husband said.

Not until then did he see the dress.

"Couldn't you get it into the case?" he said when they were in the small room that was darkened by the drooping bodies of the leaves of the fig tree. "That color marks easily."

"That's why I took the cab."

She watched her husband's eyes as she posed, her own eyes getting larger and larger, searching him for praise.

"It wants the right shoes," she said. "I saw some as we came back just now, in Waltons."

She looked at him and the ghost of her sister's wheedling attitude came into her head as she let it droop just a little to one side.

"And my hair done properly. It blew about in the taxi. Jim was at the window all the time."

Her husband's eyeballs glistered with what looked like tears.

"You're not thinking of keeping it for yourself?" he said, his face buckling into smiles that she knew were not smiles at all.

"Why not?" she said, understanding him. "There's eighty pounds' worth in the case there."

"You're rich," he said.

She opened the case.

"Look," she said.

"You'd better get it off, you'll mark it cooking," he said, and went out of the room.

From her bedroom she saw him in the back garden

spraying his roses and brushing the green fly off with his finger. He was shaking the syringe to see if there was a drop more in it and she heard him ask the boy if he had been playing with the thing and wasting the liquid.

She gave a last look at herself in the mirror. She despised her husband. She remembered the look of admiration on the face of the man in her sister's flat. She took off the dress and pulled her woolen one out of the case and put it on. The golden woman had gone.

That evening as they sat at their meal, her husband was silent. He grunted at her account of the visit. She did not tell him she had been called "the dressmaker." Her husband was sulking. He was sulking about the dress. She tried to placate him by criticizing her sister.

"There was a man there, someone she picked up on the plane. She was trying to get rid of him because this man with all the property, Mr. Williams, was expected. I don't envy her. She lives in a cage. Two burglaries they've had."

"They're insured." His first words.

She could still feel some of the gold of the dress on her skin, but as she went on about her sister, the gray meanness which in some way was part of her life with her husband, which emanated from him and which, owing to the poverty of her life as a girl, seemed to her like a resource—this meanness crept over her and coated her once more.

"And you talk of wearing the dress of a woman like that," he said. And then the boy said, with his mouth full of potato: "The man took Auntie's brooch off the table. I saw him. The pin was sticking out of his pocket. I saw it. It tore my best jersey."

"Tore your jersey!" said her husband.

"What's this?" they both said together, united. And they questioned the child again and again.

Husband and wife studied each other.

"That wasn't a pin," the father said to the boy.

"No," said his wife, in her false voice. "She'd got the brooch on." And she signaled to her husband, but her husband said to the boy, "Did he come in the taxi with you?"

"No," said the boy and his mother together.

"I asked the boy."

"No," said the boy.

"Just as well," he said to his wife. "You see what they might say when they find out. I told you I don't like you going to that place. You lose your head."

The next day she packed the gold dress with the rest and sold them all, as usual, to the dealers.

The Skeleton

AWFUL THINGS happen to one every day: they come without warning and—this is the trouble, for who knows?—the next one may be the Great Awful Thing. Whatever that is.

At half past seven, just as the new day came aching into the London sky, the waiter-valet went up in the old-fashioned lift of the Service Flats with a tray of tea to Mr. Clark's flat on the top floor. He let himself in and walked down the long, tiled hallway, through part of Mr. Clark's picture collection, into the large sitting room and putting the tray down on the desk, drew back the curtains and looked down on the roofs. Arrows of fine snow had shot along the slate, a short sight of the Thames between the buildings was as black as iron, the trees stuck out their branches like sticks of charcoal and a cutting wind was rumbling and occasionally squealing against the large windows. The man wiped his nose and then went off to switch on one bar of the electric fire—he was forbidden to put on two—and moved the tray to a table by the fire. He had often been scolded for putting the tray upon Clark's valuable Chippendale desk, and he looked around to see if anything else was out of place in this gentlemanly room where every flash of polish or glass was as unnerving to him as the flash of old George Clark's glasses.

With its fine mahogany, its glazed bookcases which contained a crack regiment of books on art in dress uniform, its Persian rugs, its bronzes, figurines and silken-seated chairs and deep sofa that appeared never to have been sat on, and on the walls some twenty-five oil paintings, the room had the air of a private museum. The valet respected the glass. He had often sat for a while at Mr. Clark's desk, gossiping with one of the maids while he saw to it that she did not touch the bronze and the Chinese figures—"He won't allow anyone to touch them. They're worth hundreds—thousands"—and making guesses at what the lot would fetch when the old man died. He made these guesses about the property of all the rich old people who lived in the flats.

The girls, an ignorant lot, Irish mainly these days, gaped at the pictures.

"He's left them all to the Nation," the valet would say importantly. He could not disguise his feeling that the poor old Nation had a lot to put up with from the rich. He could always get in a sexy word to the maids when they looked at the cylindrical nude with a guitar lying across her canister-like knees. But the other pictures of vegetation—huge fruits, enormous flowers that looked tropical, with gross veins and pores on stalk and leaves—looked humanly physical and made him feel sick. The flowers had large evil sucking mouths; there were veined intestinal marrows; there was a cauliflower like a gigantic brain that seemed to swell as you looked at it. Nature, to this painter, was a collection of clinical bodies and looked, as Seymour said, "nood." The only living creature represented—apart from the cylindrical lady—was a fish, but it, too, was oversized and gorged. Its scales, minutely enumerated, gave Seymour "the pip." It was hung over the central bookcase.

"It doesn't go with the furniture," Seymour had often said. The comforting thing to him was that, at any rate, the collection could not move and get at him. Like the books, the pictures, too, were cased behind glass.

"All by the same man. Come into the bedroom. Come

on. And don't touch anything there because he'll notice. He sees everything," he'd say.

In the bedroom he would show the girls the small oil painting of the head of a young man with almost white hair standing on end and large blue eyes.

"That's the bloke," the valet would say. "He did it himself. Self-portrait. John Flitestone—see, the name's at the bottom—cut his throat. You watch—his eyes follow you," he would say, steering the girl. "He used to come here with the old man."

"Oh," the girls were apt to gasp.

"Stop it, Mr. Seymour," they added, taken off their guard.

"Years ago," Seymour said, looking pious after the pinch he'd given them.

The valet left the room and went down the passage to George Clark's bedroom. Carpet stopped at the door of the room. Inside the room the curtains were blowing, the two sparse rugs lifting in the draft on the polished floor and snow spitting on the table beside the bed. He caught the curtains and drew them back and tried to shut the heavy window. The room contained a cheap yellow wardrobe and chest of drawers which old George Clark had had since he was a boy. The sitting room was luxurious but his bedroom was as bleak as a Victorian servant's. On a very narrow iron bedstead he lay stiff as a frozen monk and still as a corpse, so paper-thin as to look bodiless, his wiry black hair, his wiry black moustache and his greenish face and cold red nose showing like a pug's over the sheet. It sneered in sleep.

"Seven-thirty, sir. Terrible morning," he said. There was no answer. "By God," the valet said after a pause, "the old man's dead." In death—if that was what it was—the face on the pillow looked as if it could bite. Then the old man gave a snuffle.

The old man opened a wicked eye.

"The old bastard," murmured the valet. Often the old boy had terrified and tricked him with his corpselike look. It was Clark's opening victory in a day, indeed a life, devoted to victory. Then he woke up fully, frightened, reaching for his glasses, to see Seymour's blood-colored face looking down at him.

"What?" George Clark said. And then the valet heard him groan. These groans were awful.

"Oh my God!" George Clark groaned, but spoke the words in a whisper.

"It's a terrible morning. Shall I put on the fire?"

"No." The old man sat up.

The valet sighed. He went and fetched a cup of tea.

"You'll need this." He put on his bullying voice. "Better drink it hot in here. You'd better have your lunch here today. Don't you go to the club. It's snowing, the wind's terrible."

George Clark got out of bed in his flannel pajamas. He stepped barefooted to the window, studying the driving gray sky, the slant of snow and the drift of chimney smoke.

"Who closed the window?" he said.

Oh, dear, said the valet to himself, now he's going to begin. "The snow was coming in, Mr. Clark. You'll get pneumonia. Please, sir."

Clark was upright and tall. His small head jerked when he talked on a long, wrinkled neck. His voice was naturally drawling but shortness of breath was in conflict with the drawl and the sounds that came out were jerky, military and cockerel-like. At eighty-two he looked about sixty, there was hardly any gray in his moustache, the bridge of his gold-framed glasses cut into his red nose. Seymour, who was fifty, was humped and lame and looked seventy. In a fight old George would win and he gave a sniff that showed he knew it. In fact, he got up every day to win; Seymour knew that and accepted it.

What reduced him to misery was that the old man would *explain* his victories. He was off on that now.

"No, I won't get pneumonia," old George snapped. "You see, Seymour, it's a north wind. The north wind doesn't touch me. There's no fat on me, I'm all bones. I'm a skeleton, there's nothing for it to bite on."

"No, sir," said Seymour wretchedly. Ten to one George Clark would now mention his family. He did.

"My father was thin, so was my grandfather, we're a thin family. My youngest sister—she's seventy-eight—she's all bones like me."

Oh God (Seymour used to moan to himself), I forgot—he's got a sister! Two of them! He moved to get out of the room, but the old man followed him closely, talking fast.

"One day last week I thought we were going to catch it, oh yes. Now we're going to get it, I said! Awful thing! That clean white light in the sky, stars every night, everything clear, everything sparkling. I saw it and said, Oh no! No, no. I don't like this, oh no."

He had now got Seymour in the doorway. "You see—I know what *that* means."

"Yes, sir."

"East wind," said George victoriously.

"That's it, sir."

"Ah, then you've got to look out, Seymour. Oh yes. Awful business. That's what finishes old people. Awful thing." He drove Seymour forward into the sitting room and went to this window, studying the sky and sniffed two or three times at it.

"We're all right, Seymour. You see, I was right. It's in the north. I shall have lunch at the club. Bring my cup in here. Why did you take it to the bedroom?"

It was a cold flat. George Clark took a cold bath, as he had done ever since his schooldays. Then he ate a piece of toast and drank a second cup of tea and looked eagerly to see what was annoying in the papers—some new annoyance to add to a lifetime's accumulation of annoyances. It was one of the calamities of old age that one's memory went and one forgot a quite considerable number of exasperations and awful things in which, contrary to general expectation, one had been startlingly right. This forgetting was bad—as if one were the Duke of Wellington and sometimes forgot one had won the Battle of Waterloo.

In fact, George sat in comfort in a flat packed with past rows, annoyances and awful things, half forgotten. It was an enormous satisfaction that many of his pictures annoyed the few people who came to see him nowadays. The Flitestones annoyed violently. They had indeed annoyed the Nation to such an extent that, in the person of a "nasty little man" called Gaiterswell, the Nation had refused them. (Seymour was wrong there.) George was very proud of this: his denunciation of Gaiterswell was one of the major victories of his life. George had been the first to buy Flitestones and even Flitestone himself, and had warned the vain and swollen-headed young man against Gaiterswell, years and years ago. "Modish, Jack, he's merely modish. He'll drop you when it suits him."

* * *

At twelve o'clock George walked across the park to one of his clubs. He belonged to three. The park was empty. He blew across it like a solitary, late leaf. The light snow was turning Whitehall black, and spat on his gold glasses, but he arrived, a little breathless, but ready to deal with that bugbear of old men: protective sympathy.

"George! You ought not to be out on a day like this!" several said. One put his arm round his shoulder. They were a sneezing and coughing lot with slack affectionate faces and friendly overburdened bellies, talking of snowed-up roads, late trains and scrambles for taxis.

"You *walked* through this! Why didn't you make your chauffeur bring you?"

"No car."

"Or a cab?"

"Fares have gone up. I'm too mean."

"Or a bus?"

"Oh no, no, you see," said George, glittering at them. "I don't know if I told you"—he had told them innumerable times—"when you're brought up by a rich brute of a father, as I was—oh yes, he was very rich—you get stingy. I'm very stingy. I must have told you about my father. Oh, well, now, there's a story," he began eagerly. But the bar was crowded; slow to move, George Clark found his listener had been pushed away and had vanished. He stood suddenly isolated in his autobiography.

"Oh God," he groaned loudly, but in a manner so sepulchral and private that people moved respectfully away. It was a groan that seemed to come up from the earth, up from his feet, a groan of loneliness that was raging and frightening to the men around him. He had one of those moments which, he had to admit, were much commoner than they used to be, when he felt dizzy; when he felt he was lost among unrecognizable faces, without names, alone, in the wrong club, at the wrong address even, with the tottering story of his life, a story which he was offering or, rather, throwing out as a lifeline for help. His hand shook as he finished his glass of sherry. The moment passed and, recovering and trembling, he aged as he left the bar and crossed the hall to the dining room, saying aloud to himself, in his fighting drawl: "Now, now, now, we must be careful."

The side tables were already taken but there were gaps

at the two long tables. George stood blinking at the battlefield. He had in the last years resigned from several clubs. Sometimes it was because of bridge, central heating, ventilation, smoking, about house committees, food and servants, usually over someone who, unknowingly, had become for a period uncommonly like the Arch Enemy, but who turned out to be no more than an understudy for the part. After a year or so George would rejoin the club. For him the dining room was one more aspect of the general battlefield. Where should he place his guns? Next to Doyle? No, he was "a Roman." George hated "Romans." He hated "Protestants" too. He was an atheist who never found anyone sufficiently atheistical. George was tired of telling Doyle how he had happened to be in Rome in '05 staying with one of the great families ("she was a cousin of the Queen's") and had, for a year, an unparalleled inside view of what was going on in the Vatican. "Oh yes, you see, a Jesuit, one of their relations, became a great friend and exposed the whole hocus-pocus to me. You see, I have often been in a position to know more of what is going on than most people. I was close to Haig in the war." There was Gregg, the painter—but it was intolerable to listen to Academicians; there was Foster who had been opposed to Munich and George could not stand that. There was Macdonald—but Scots climb. Look at Lang! There was Jefferies, such a bore about divorce reform: the bishops want it but daren't say so. "I told the Archbishop in this club that the moment you drag in God you lose your reason. My mother ought to have got a divorce. You should have seen his face. Oh no, oh no, he didn't like it. Not a bit."

George looked at the tops of heads and the tableloads of discarded enemies, casualties of his battles, with a grin. At last, glancing around him, he chose a seat beside a successful, smirking pink man of fifty whose name he had forgotten. "Pretty harmless," muttered George. "He thinks Goya a great painter when we all know he is just a good painter of the second rank. Ah, he's eating oysters." This stirred a memory. The man was talking to a deaf editor but on the other side there were empty chairs. It was against George's military sense to leave an exposed flank but the chance of attacking the club oysters was too good to miss.

"I see you've risked the oysters. I never eat oysters in this club," said George, sitting down. "Poisonous. Oh yes, yes—didn't I tell you? Oh, you see, it was an awful thing, last year . . ."

"Now, George," said the man. "You told me that story before."

"Did I? Nothing in that," sniffed George. "I always repeat myself, you see I make a point of telling my stories several times. I woke up in the night . . ."

"Please, George," said the man more sternly. "I want to enjoy my lunch."

"Oh ah, ah, ah," said George, sniffing away. "I'll watch your plate. I'll warn you if I see a bad one."

"Oh, really, George!" said the young man.

"You're interrupting our conversation, George," the editor called across. "I was telling Trevor something very interesting about my trip to Russia."

"I doubt if it is interesting," said George in a loudish whisper to the other man. "Interesting! I never found a Whig interesting."

"Dear George is old. He talks too much," said the deaf editor, speaking louder than he knew.

"Not a lot of rot," said George in a loud mutter.

"What's he say?" said the deaf editor.

"You see," George continued to interrupt. "I talk a lot because I live alone. I probably talk more than anyone in this club and I am more interesting than most people. You see, I've often been in a position to know more than most people here. I was in Rome in '05 . . ."

But George looked restlessly at the vacant chair beside him. "I hope," he said, suddenly nervous, "some awful bore is not going to sit here. You never know who, who—oh no, oh no, no . . ."

* * *

It happened as simply as that, when one was clean off one's guard. Not a single awful thing: but the Great Awful Thing. He saw a pair of small, polished, sunburned hands with soft black hair on them pull back the chair and then a monkeyish man of seventy, with wretched eyes and an academic heaving up of the right shoulder, sit beside him. And heard the voice: "Good morning, George," uttering the name George as if it contained a lifetime's innuendo.

"Oh God," George said.

The man was the Arch Enemy and in a form he had never expected. Out of the future he should have come, a shape at a slowly opening door, pausing there, blocking it, so that one could not get out. Who he would be, what he would be, was unknown: he was hidden in next week, next year, as yet unborn.

But this man was known. He had sneaked in not from the future, but from the past. It was Gaiterswell.

"Just the man I want to speak to," said Gaiterswell, picking up the menu in hands that George could only think of as thieving.

"I didn't know you were a member," George choked out in words like lead shot.

"Just elected."

George gave a loud sniff.

"Monstrous," said George, but holding on to manners said it under his breath. He grasped his table napkin, ready to fly off and at once resign. It was unbelievable that the Committee, knowing his feelings as they must do, had allowed this man in. Gaiterswell who had stolen Flitestone from him; who had turned down Flitestone; who had said in the *Times*—in a letter, above all—that George's eccentric tastes had necessarily taught him nothing about the chemical composition of oil paint; Gaiterswell of the scandalous official appointment!

George had forgotten these Waterloos; but now the roar of them woke up in his brain. The fusillades he had let off in committees were heard again. The letters to the *Times* were shot off once more. Gaiterswell had said there were to many "gentlemen" in the art world. It was a pity (he was known to have said), it was a pity that the Empire had gone and there were no more natives for them to pester. George had replied, around the clubs, that "the nasty little man" suffered glaringly from merit and the path of the meritorious was strewn with the bodies they had kicked down the ladder as they climbed.

After he had said things like this, George considered that Gaiterswell was dead. The body could no doubt be found still lying, after twenty-five years, in that awful office of his with the fake Manet—of course it was a fake—on the wall.

"Just the man I want to speak to," Gaiterswell said to the menu. (You noticed he never looked you in the face.)

"Wants to speak to me. For no good reason," George murmured loudly to the man sitting on the other side of him.

"I bet you won't guess who came to see me the other day," Gaiterswell said. "Gloria Archer, Stokes that was. She's married to a Frenchman called Duprey. You remember her? What are you eating? The pie? Is it any good? She's got a lot of poor Jack Flitestone's letters. She's short of money. You wrote the Memoir, didn't you, George? Charming little book, charming. I told her to drop in on you. I said you'd be delighted to see her."

George was about to put a piece of pie into his mouth. He put his fork down. He was shaking. He was choking.

"Drop in!" he said, astounded. "Drop in?"

"Look here," he called out, pushing his chair from the table. "Oh, this is monstrous." And he called to one of the waiters, who rushed past and ignored him. "Look here, I say, why do we have to have meat like this in this club . . . It's uneatable . . . I shall find the secretary . . ."

And getting up, with his table napkin waving from his hand, he hurried to the end of the room, the light tossing in his glasses, and then after wild indecision, left the room.

"Where has George Clark gone?" said an old gentleman who had been sitting opposite. "He never finishes a meal."

"It's his teeth," the deaf editor said.

* * *

George had made for the Morning Room of the club where he circled like a dog.

"What manners!" he said to the portraits of dead members on the wall. Happier than he, they were together; he was alone. He was older than most of them had been, and with a flick of ironic pride which never quite left him in any distress, he could not but notice that he was rather better connected and had more inside knowledge than most of them had had. He addressed them again: "Drop in! What manners! I shall resign."

The Arch Enemy had appeared in a fashion unpredictable: from the Past—and now he saw—not as a male but as a female. Gloria Archer—as he had always said: "What a name!" It recalled (as he firmly pronounced it), the "Kinema," striking a blow for classical scholarship. Her portrait, if one could call it that, was in his sitting room, cylindrical and naked. It had been there for over twenty-five years, with the other Flitestones, and he had long ago stopped remembering her or even Flitestone himself as human beings he had known. They were not life; they were art—not even art now, but furniture of his self-esteem. He had long ago closed his mind to them as persons. They had become fossilizations of mere anecdote. Now that damn little shot-up official, Gaiterswell, who had been polished off long ago, had brought first Gloria back to life, and the name of Gloria had brought Flitestone back. The seals of anecdote were broken; one of the deepest wounds of George's existence was open and raw again. A woman's work: it was Gloria who had shown how dangerous Flitestone was to him; it was Gloria who had shown him the chaos of his heart.

He left the Morning Room, got his hat and coat, buttoned himself up to the neck, and walked out into the street, where the snow was coming in thicker shots. At once he felt something like a film of ice form between his shirt and his bony chest and he stepped back, afraid.

"No, no," he said very loudly and passersby raised their ducked heads thinking he was talking to them. But he was speaking to the wind: it had gone round to the east.

Seymour met him in the lift at the flat. He smelled of beer.

"You shouldn't have gone out, sir," said Seymour. Seymour looked murderous with self-righteousness.

George sat down on his sofa, frightened and exhausted. He was assaulted by real memories and was too weak to fend them off: he had felt frightened to death—he now admitted—in that so enjoyable 1914 war. Flitestone's pictures took on life. Flitestone, too. The cliché vanished—"Not a bad minor painter, like a good many others ruined by the school of Paris": the dangerous Flitestone appeared. He saw again the poor boy from a Scottish mill town, with gaunt cheeks, light-blue eyes and almost white hair that stood up like a dandelion clock ("took hours brushing it, always going to expensive hairdressers"). A pedant, too, with morbid and fanatical patience: it took him longer to paint a picture than anyone George Clark had ever known;

the young man was rather deaf, which made him seem to be an unworldly, deeply innocent listener, but there was—as George Clark saw—nothing innocent about him, there was a mean calculating streak ("After all he realized I was a rich man"—George swaggered) and he was soon taken up by wealthy people. He was clever and made them laugh. He was in trouble all the time with women, chasing them like a maniac and painting them with little heads and large bottoms, like pairs of enormous pink poppies. ("Now, there's a bloody fine bottom, George.")

Very annoying he was, too, especially when he got into Society. That was one thing George Clark knew all about and to be told about Lord This or That or a lot of duchesses, by a crude young genius from the slums, was infuriating.

"He's got five bloody great castles . . ."

"Only one. Forstairs and Aldbaron belong to his half brother who married Glasnevin's sister. Jack, I wish you wouldn't pick your teeth at meals. I can't bear it. It's such frightful manners."

"Lord Falconer does. He's got a gold toothpick."

But these squabbles were merely annoying. Flitestone was the only human being George ever loved. Jealously loved. He was his prize and his possession. And the boy liked him. Here was the danger. George had dreaded to be liked. You lose something when people like you. You are in danger of being stripped naked and of losing a skin. With Flitestone he felt—ah, there was the danger: he did not know what he felt except that it was passion. He could listen to him for hours. For eleven years, George had the sensation that he had married late in life someone who, fortunately, did not exist, and that Flitestone was their fantastic, blindly invented son. Like a son he clawed at George's bowels.

His love affairs? Well, one had to avert the eye. They

were, nevertheless, an insurance against George's instant jealous fear: that Flitestone would marry. The thought of that made George shrink. "Marriage will ruin you"—he nagged at it. And that was where Gloria came in.

When Gaiterswell spoke of Gloria, a shot of jealous terror and satisfaction had gone through George. She bored him, of course. Yet in the last years of their friendship, Flitestone's insane love for this girl who would have nothing to do with him was the real guarantee. George even admired the young girl for the cruelty of her behavior, for being so complete an example of everything that made women impossible. He was so absorbed in this insurance that he forgot the obvious: that Gloria might marry. She did. In a month on the rebound, Flitestone had married some milky student girl whose first act was to push her husband into the influence of Gaiterswell. For Gaiterswell was the Nation. A breach with George was inevitable.

He went to his desk and started writing to Gaiterswell.

"I shall be obliged if you will inform Miss Stokes, Mrs. Archer, or whatever her name is, that I have no desire to meet her or enter into correspondence . . ." His hand shook. He could not continue.

"Awful business" was all he could say. The Arch Enemy had deprived him even of the power to talk to himself.

The east wind. Impossible to go out to any of his clubs that night. After dinner, he poured himself a very large whiskey and left the bottle, uncorked, on his desk—a sinister breach of habit, for he always locked up his drink.

"I always reckon to be rather drunk every evening," George used to say. It was a gesture to the dignity of gentlemanly befuddlement. But now, he felt his legs go; he was rapidly very drunk. He tottered to his bedroom, dropped his clothes on the floor and got into bed with his shirt, collar and tie on and was asleep at once. Often at night he had enjoyable dreams of social life at Staff H.Q. in the 1914 war. Haig, Ronnie Blackwater and others would turn up. A bit of gunfire added an interest; but this night he had a frightful dream. He dreamed that at the club, before all the members, he had kissed the teeth of George V.

This woke him up and he saw that it was daylight. His heart was racing. He could not find his glasses. He got out of bed. The room was getting light; he wondered if he were dead and he pulled back the curtain and what he saw convinced him that he was. The snow had stopped, the sky was hard and clear, and the sun was coming up in a gap between two high buildings. It was still low and this made it an enormous raw yellow football that someone had kicked there, without heat or radiance yet. It looked like a joke or some aimless idea; one more day (George realized as he became more conscious) had begun its unsolicited course over the blind slates of the city. "Old men are lonely," he often said, but now he saw a greater loneliness than his own.

"I want those letters." The desire came out before he could stop it. "I must see Gloria. I must get Gaiterswell's dirty little hands off them." He was longing for the past. Then he saw he was wearing his day shirt, his collar and tie.

"Oh God," he said. And he got into his pajamas and back into bed before Seymour should catch him.

* * *

At half past seven Seymour let himself into the flat. His demeanor was of one whose expectations were at last being fulfilled. He had warned several of the old people in the flats about the weather; he had seen Mr. Clark come back yesterday exhausted when, against all advice, he had gone to the club. Reaching the sitting room, Seymour saw a decanter of whiskey standing on the table. This was a sight that he had thirsted for for years and he gazed at it entranced, unbelieving and with suspicion. He listened. There was no sound. Seymour made a grab at the decanter and took a long swig, letting a drop rest on his chin while he replaced what he had drunk with water from the hot-water pot on the tea tray. He stood still, trying to lick the drip off his chin but, failing, he wiped it off with his sleeve, and after looking at the letters on Mr. Clark's desk, walked confidently to Mr. Clark's bedroom.

"Good morning, Seymour. Half past seven," said George. He was sitting up in bed. Seymour heard this reversal of their usual greeting with alarm. He stood well away and slopped the tea in its saucer. He was even more alarmed to see Mr. Clark had switched on his own fire and that his clothes were dropped in a muddle on the floor. George caught his glance and got out of bed to show that he was properly dressed and stood with one foot on his rumpled jacket. Panic and the whiskey brought guilt into Seymour's face: he suddenly remembered he had made a disastrous mistake. He had forgotten to give Mr. Clark a message.

"A lady rang last night, sir, when you were at dinner."

"A lady—why didn't you tell me?"

"The headwaiter took the call. He said you were out. She didn't leave a name."

To distract an angry question, Seymour looked at the clothes on the floor.

"Dear, dear, dear, what a way to leave a suit." He pulled the trouser leg from under George's foot and held the trousers up. "Look at it."

"What lady?" said George.

"She didn't leave a name. She said she'd drop in."

"Drop in!" The horrible phrase.

"That's what she said, she'd drop in."

"Who was it?"

"I don't know, sir. I never took the message. I told you—it was the new headwaiter."

"Don't stand there waving my trousers about like a fool, Seymour. It's your business to know."

"They're all foreigners downstairs."

George had his glasses on now and Seymour stepped away. In his panic he took a gamble.

"Might have been Miss Stokes," he said. He had read the name on George's unfinished letter. The gamble was a mistake.

"Archer!" cried George. "Where is the headwaiter?" And hurrying to the sitting room, he started banging the telephone. There was no answer.

"What time do the servants come on?" he called to Seymour. Seymour came in and listened to George banging away. He was very scared now. He dreaded that the headwaiter would answer.

"They come when it suits them, now. They suit themselves," said Seymour, putting on a miserable manner. And then he got in his blow, the sentence he often used to the old people in the flats when they got difficult. It always silenced them.

"Might just as well sell the place," he said.

"Sell!" George was silenced, too. He stared at Seymour, who straightened himself and said, accusingly, "Where's the jacket of this! Dear, dear, I suppose that's on the floor too," and walked out, leaving George shivering where he stood.

"Sell?" said George.

On a long ledge of the stained building opposite, thirty or forty dirty pigeons were huddled, motionless, with puffed-out feathers, too cold to fly.

"Out on the street! Homeless." Like Stebbing-Walker, crippled and deaf, who had married Kempton's half sister

—she was a Doplestone—and now lay in his nursing home, or Ronnie Blackwater who sat paralyzed in the army infirmary. Sell—it was the awful word anxiously whispered in the lift by the old ladies as they went up and down to their meals. Was the place being sold? Were the rents going up? Were they going to pull the whole place down? For months there would be silence; everyone breathed again; then once more, mostly from Seymour, the rumors began. Fear made them sly and they believed Seymour rather than the management. He moved among them like a torment.

George Clark went down early to luncheon, to get in before the restaurant vanished; rushed upstairs afterwards to barricade himself, so to speak, in his flat. There were few pigeons on the ledge now. What? Had tenancy gone out of Nature too? At seven o'clock he went to dinner. Instead of the two or three tables of old doll-like couples in the middle of the room, there was a large table at which ten large young men, loud and commercial, were laughing together. One or two had briefcases with them. Obviously this was the group who were going to pull down the flats. George raced through the meal, feeling that, possibly, even before the apples and custard, he might be sitting out alone on a vacant site. George's fighting spirit revived over his wine. "Ha," he sneered at them as he left the table and went to the lift, "I'll be dead before you can turn me out."

The lift wheezed and wobbled upwards, making the sound of all the elderly throats in the building. He was startled to see the door of his flat open and, for a moment, thought the men had broke in already; but Seymour was standing in the cold hall. His heavy face looked criminal. In insinuating, lugubrious voice he said, "The lady's waiting to see you, sir."

"Seymour, I've told you, never . . ." George hurried to his sitting room. Gloria was standing by his desk reading the letter he had begun so often.

"Dear Gaiterswell, I would have thought that common decency . . ."

"Oh, oh, no, no, I say," said George greeting her, but was stopped.

A fur coat and a close-fitting black hat like a faded turban with brass-colored hair sticking out of it rushed at him; a hot powdery face kissed him with a force that made him crack in his joints like a stick.

"Oh, George, darling, I dropped in." Gloria shouted at him through large stained teeth and laughed.

All he could see was these teeth and lipstick and blue eyes and she was laughing and laughing as she wiped the lipstick off his face.

"Oh, well," he said, "they're selling the place . . ."

Then she stood back in a pair of cracking shoes. "George," she said in a Cockney voice. "It's marvelous. You haven't changed at all. You're not a day older."

And she let her fur coat fall open and slip back on her shoulders and he saw the cigarette ash and one or two marks on the bosom of her black dress. She was a big woman.

"Oh," George recovered and gave a victorious sniff. "I'm eighty-two."

"You're a boy," she cried.

"Oh no, don't think I'm deceived by that sort of talk—er, well, you see, I mean . . ." George nearly smiled. By his reckoning she was in her fifties and he could see what she wanted, what all women wanted, compliments. He was not, at his age, going to fall for that old game. She sat down on the sofa so as to show off her fine legs.

"Did you recognize me?" she asked.

"Oh, well, you know . . ."

"Oh, come on, George."

"I daresay I—er—might have done. You see, I forget

names and faces, its an awful business . . . old people . . . they're selling this place . . ."

"Oh, you crusty old thing. What do you mean—selling?" she said. "You always were crusty. I knew you'd be at dinner, so I got that man to bring me up. What is his name? Is he all right? I didn't feel very comfortable with him in the lift."

She moved her body and pouted.

"When your lady friends call, you ought to tell them to keep an eye—well, George, how are you? How many years is it? It must be twenty-five. You weren't living here then."

"It was the beginning of the war," said George, but he could not remember. He had discarded memory as useless a long time back. He had seen her a lot, yet one of his few clear recollections was of sitting with Flitestone in the old Café Royal waiting for her to come in and arguing with him that she was not a woman who would stick to any man: he remembered her really as an absence.

"You've put on weight," he said. But she hadn't changed much.

"Yes," she said. "I like it, don't you?"

The Cockney voice came warm and harsh out of the wide mouth. Her skin was rougher and was now looser on her bones but still had a wide-pored texture and the colorlessness which Flitestone used to say was like linen. One spot of color in her cheeks and Flitestone would probably never have fallen for her. "She's like a canvas. I'd like to paint on her," Flitestone used to say to George. He did remember. The bare maleness of face on a girlish body was still there on the body of the full woman.

George stood, shaking at the sight of her.

"You're still an old bachelor, George?" she said. "You didn't marry?"

"No," said George with a grin of victory. "You see, in my

day, one never met any girls, everyone was chaperoned, you couldn't speak and we had no one to the house, oh no, my father wouldn't allow anyone and then the war, and all that. I told you about my father, oh, now, there's a story—"

"Oh, I've been. Three times," she cut in, parading herself.

"Oh, three! Well, that's interesting. Or I suppose it is. It doesn't surprise me. Please sit down. Let me get you a drink. Now, let me see, keys. I have to keep it locked —well, with the servants it isn't fair to leave drink about. Ah, in this pocket. I keep them here."

He fussed at the cupboard and brought out a bottle of whiskey and a bottle of sherry.

"Oh, gin, please," she said. "Can I help?"

"No, no, it's here. I keep it at the back. I'll put this bottle down here, yes, that's the way . . ." he chattered to himself.

Gloria walked across the room to look at the pictures, but stopped instead to look at her reflection in the glass of the bookcases and to rearrange the frilled neck of her dress. Then she looked up at the large picture of the fish.

"George! You've got my fish."

"Ah, yes, the fish. He painted four fish pictures. One is in the Tate, one is . . . now, where is it?"

"*My* fish, I mean," she said. "Don't you remember, it's the one I made you carry to Jack's place and the paper came off . . ."

"No, no," said George.

"Yes, you must remember. You're not still cross, are you? You looked so funny."

She took a deep breath in front of the picture, inhaling it.

"I don't know why we didn't eat it."

"Ah yes. Awful business. Café Royal," said George, a memory coming back.

She turned to the cylindrical woman in a shift, with enormous column-like legs, who was playing a guitar, and looked with flirtatious annoyance at it, paying off an old score.

"That's me," she said.

"Oh no," said George sarcastically. He was beginning to enjoy himself. "It was done in Paris."

"It's me," said Gloria. "But they're Violet's legs." Gloria turned abruptly away, insulted, and taking her drink from George went back to the sofa. Once more she gave a large sigh and gazed with admiring calculation at the room. She leaned her head to one side and smiled at George.

"You are a dear, George. How cozy you are. It's wonderful to see old friends," said Gloria sweetly. "It brings it all back."

She got up and put more gin in her drink and then leaned over his chair as she passed him and kissed the top of his head.

"Dear George," she said and sat down. "And you live here, all alone! Well, George, I've brought the letters, all Jack's letters to me. I didn't know I had them. It's a funny thing: François found them, my husband, he's French. We live in France and he has an antique business. He said 'They ought to fetch a bit,' you know what the French are about money, so I remembered Monkey—"

"Monkey?"

"Monkey Gaiterswell, I always used to call him Monkey. We used," said Gloria very archly, "to be friends and he said, 'Sell them to America.' Do you think he's right—I mean Monkey said you'd written a book about Jack and you'd know? He said I'd get five hundred pounds for them. I mean they're all about painting, famous people, the whole circle . . ."

Ah, it was a plot!

"Five hundred," said George. "You won't get five

pounds. No one has ever heard of Flitestone in America. None of his pictures went there."

"But the letters are very *personal,* George. Naturally you're in them."

"I doubt it."

"Oh, you are. I remember. I know you are. You were his best friend. And you wrote so beautifully about him. Monkey says so."

Obviously there was a plot between Monkey and Gloria.

"I've no doubt they are full of slanders. I should tear them up," said George shortly.

"George," she appealed. "I need the money. François has gone off with some woman and I'm broke. Look."

She opened her black shopping bag and took out a parcel of crumpled brown paper and put it on George's desk.

"Open it. I'll leave them with you to look at. You'll see."

"Oh, no. I can't do that," said George. "I don't care to be responsible. It leads to all sorts of awful business."

"Read them. Open it. Here."

She put down her empty glass and untied the string. A pile of letters of all sizes in Flitestone's large hand, each word formed carefully like the words of a medieval manuscript, slid onto George's desk.

George was sitting there and he withdrew his hand so as not to touch the letters. They brought Jack Flitestone into the room. George wanted them. He knew now what was meant when she said *he* was in them. It was not what *she* meant. The letters contained the to-him-affronting fact that he had not after all succeeded in owning his own life and closing it to others; that he existed in other people's minds and that all people dissolved in this way, becoming fragments of one another, and nothing in themselves. He had known that once, when Jack Flitestone had brought him to life. He knew, too, that he had once lived or nearly lived.

Flitestone, in his dangerous way, had lived for him. One letter had fallen to the floor and Gloria read aloud:

> ". . . Archie's car broke down outside Medley and we didn't get to Gorse until the middle of dinner. La Tarantula was furious and I offered to eat in the kitchen and the Prime Minister who was already squiffy . . .

"There you are, George. The Prime Minister," cried Gloria.

George took the letter in the tips of his fingers and Gloria helped herself to another drink.

"Jack was an awful snob," said George, but admiringly, putting the letter back. "No manners, writing about people when he was a guest."

"Oh, come off it, George," said Gloria, picking out one or two more. "You know, I haven't read them for years. Actually Jack frightened me. So morbid. Here's one. Oh, this is good. It's about the time you and Jack went to Chartres. The tie drawer, George!"

The new blow from the past struck him. He remembered it: the extraordinary thing about small French hotels—they never gave you a drawer for your ties. He took the letter and read:

". . . George surpassed himself this morning . . ."

He had walked down the corridor to Flitestone's room and knocked.

"Here. I say, Jack. I want to speak to you."

"What is it?" Flitestone had called. Ordinary manners, one would have thought, would at least have led Flitestone to open the door. Jack was so *thoughtless.*

"Jack, Jack, I've no tie drawer in my room."

Flitestone came to the door naked and pushed a drawer from his wardrobe into George's hand. "Take mine."

"Jack, here, I say, dear fellow. Chambermaid."

"Umph," said George to Gloria. "Inaccurate."

He reached out for the next letter she offered to him. He looked at it distantly, read a few lines and stopped.

"Here, I say, I can't read this. It is to you." He sneered a little.

"They're all to me."

"Yes, but this is—er—private, personal."

George looked quizzically and sternly at her; it was "not done" to look into another's moral privacy. It was also shameless and woman-like to show letters like these to him. But the phrases he had run into head-on had frightened him, they brought back to him the danger he had once lived in: his heart had been invaded, he had been exposed once to a situation in which the question of a victory or a defeat vanished.

"You see," he said, turning his head away nervously from her as he handed back the letter to her.

Gloria took it. She put on her glasses and read. Immediately she smiled. The smile became wider and she gave pleased giggles. She was blushing.

"Jack ought to have been a writer," she said. "I hated his paintings. It's quite true what he says, George. I was very attractive. I had marvelous legs."

She turned to look at her reflection in the glass of the bookcase and took her fur coat off and posed. Gradually she lifted her skirt above her knees and pleased by what she saw, she lifted her skirt higher, putting one leg forward, then the other.

"Look, George," she said. "Look. They're still good. There aren't many women of my age with legs like these. They're damn fine, George. You've never seen a pair like that." She turned sideways and pranced with pleasure.

"Gloria, please," said George sharply.

But she marched over to the picture of the woman with

cylindrical legs and said, "I could have killed him for that. What's the matter with painters? Didn't he have enough to eat when he was a boy? He was always carrying on about his hard times."

She lowered her dress and sat down to go on reading the letter.

"The pink peony, did you get to that?" she said. "Really, Jack's ideas! Not very nice, is it? I mean, not in a letter. He wasn't very . . ." She stopped and was sad. "No," she checked herself. "I'll tell you something, George: we only went to bed together once . . ."

"Gloria," said George in agitation. "Give me the letter. I'll put it with the others . . ."

She was making Flitestone far too alive.

"It was your fault, George. It was the dinner you gave us that night, the night I bought the fish. You say you don't remember? At the Café Royal. I made you go off to the Café Royal kitchen and get the largest fish they had. I don't know why. I wanted to get rid of you and I thought it would annoy you. I was getting plastered. Don't you remember? I said, 'Tell them we want it for our cat. Our cat is enormous. It eats a salmon a day.' And Jack kept on saying—we were both drunk—'I want to paint a large salmon. You're bloody stingy, George, you won't buy me a salmon.' "

"Awful business," snapped George. "Jack never understood money."

"You remember! Isn't that wonderful?" cried Gloria, pulling off her hat and looking into her empty glass.

"You followed us out of the restaurant, all up Shaftesbury Avenue and he was going to show me his new pictures. You had no tact, George. He was carrying the fish and he suddenly gave it to you and made you carry it and the paper blew off. George," she said, "do you mind if I have just a teeny-weeny one? There's a letter about it."

And she pushed him aside and got at the parcel on his desk.

"I think you've had enough, Gloria."

"For old times' sake," said Gloria, filling her glass. She unfolded the parcel again and scattered the letters. George looked at the clock.

"I can't find it," she said. "It's here somewhere."

"Gloria, I don't want drink spilled on my desk. I've forbidden Seymour . . ."

Gloria stopped and, now red in the face, smiled amorously.

"That man?" she said. "Is he here?"

"Gloria," said George. "I'll have to—er—I'll have to— It's eleven o'clock, I . . ."

Gloria replied with dignity. "Jack had no sense of behavior. I could see it was spoiling your suit. I begged him, begged him," she said grandly, "to carry it himself. I was furious with him. He could see you had an umbrella as well, you always carried one and wore a bowler hat. He said, 'Stick it on the umbrella.' I was terribly upset when he slammed the door in your face when we got to the studio. We had a terrible row and I made him swear to go round to your flat and apologize. It was awful, George. What did you do?"

"I took a cab, of course," said George.

"Well, I mean, you couldn't leave a salmon in the street," said Gloria. "It was a suit like the one you are wearing now, dark gray. That isn't the one, is it? It can't be."

"Gloria, I am sorry, but . . ."

Gloria frowned.

"I am sure it's there," she said and went to the letters on the desk again. "No, not that. Not that," she began throwing the letters on the floor. "Ah, here."

She waved the letter and looked through it in silence until she read aloud:

". . . I apologized to George and he said he had left the fish with the hall porter, so I went down there. We had a bit of a row about my low-class manners. I said I thought half the salmon in England had been to Eton. He told me to ask Seymour, the hall porter, for it—"

"Inaccurate," interrupted George. "Seymour was never hall porter."

". . . I said I have called for the specimen I loaned to Sir George Clark, the marine biologist, who is doing research on spawn . . .

"You see, George," she said. She went back to the sofa. "Come and sit here, George, don't be so stuffy. We can talk, can't we, after all these years? We are friends. That is what we all need, George, friends. I'm serious, George." She had tears in her eyes.

"It was wicked of Jack to call you stingy. You gave him money. You bought his pictures."

"But I *am* stingy," said George. "You see, rich people never give their children a penny. We never had anyone to the house at Maddings . . ."

"It was his jealousy," said Gloria darkly. "He was jealous of you."

"Oh, well, class envy—" George began.

"No, of you and me," she said. "Oh, yes, George, he really was. That's why he tried to shake you off, that night, that's why we had such terrible scenes . . . You were rich . . ."

"Don't be ludicrous, Gloria."

"Letters by every post, pursuing, bombarding me, I couldn't stand it."

"Nonsense."

"It isn't nonsense. You were very blind, George. And so

you live in this place, alone. Jealous men are so *boring,* George. I've had four. I said 'Oh, to hell' and I went off to France. Vive de Gaulle! You know?" she said, raising her glass.

"To *les feuilles mortes d'automne,*" she said. "That's what my husband says."

He bent to take her glass to prevent her drinking more and she stroked his spiky hair. He put the glass away out of reach.

"That is why Jack married that stupid student girl," she said in a suddenly sharp calculating voice. "That broke up you and Jack, didn't it?"

"I don't wish to talk about it," said George. "It ruined him. Marriage is the ruin of painters."

"George, come clean. After all, we all know it. You were in love with him, weren't you?"

There was a silence.

"Weren't you?" she persisted.

He recovered and achieved his worldly drawl. "Oh, I know there's a lot of that sort of thing about, was in my time, too. I paid no attention to it . . . Women don't understand talent. I understood Jack's talent. Women ruined it."

"Jack said you'd never been to bed with a woman in your life," she said.

"It wasn't possible, it wasn't possible," said George angrily, "Not in my day. Not for a gentleman." And he turned on her. "I won't be questioned. I should burn those letters. You treated him badly. You killed his imagination. It's obvious in his work."

He looked at the clock.

"George," she said. "You don't mean that. You don't know what you are saying. You were always so sweet to me."

"I do mean what I said. Read your letters," said George.

And briskly he collected them off the floor and packed them up and tied the parcel. He was going to turn her out now.

She was staring stupidly.

"You don't want them?" she said. "Monkey said you'd jump at them."

"You've got one in your hands," he said. "No," he added, "I won't give a penny for them. I won't be blackmailed."

Gloria got up to give the letter to him. She could not walk and put her hand on the table beside the sofa. It fell over, carrying her glass with it.

"What's that man Seymour doing in here? Tell him to get out. Out with Seymour," she suddenly shouted. "Out. Out. What d'you mean? Stop playing the innocent. You've never lived. That's you, George, that fish." And she tried to point at the picture.

"Gloria, I won't have this," shouted George. "You're drunk."

"You won't have it? You've never had it. My coat, who's taken that?"

But when she turned she fell heavily onto the sofa, twisted her body and fell asleep instantly with her skirt above her knees and one majestic leg trailing on the floor.

"Gloria. How dare you! In my house!"

"Darling," she smiled.

* * *

"Women," George always said, glittering dryly, "they contribute nothing." She was contributing a stentorian snore.

He had couples up after dinner sometimes, elderly friends, and you could see how it was: they either couldn't let their husband speak—poor Caldicott, for instance—or they sat as stupid as puddings. The men aged as they sat: rather them than me. Eighty-two and not a day's illness.

Gloria was contributing more than a snore. She was contributing an enormous haunch, an indecent white thigh—"Really." He would have to cover it. Couldn't she pull her skirt down? Couldn't she be drunk like a—like a lady? She contributed brutality, an awful animality, to the room.

He went over and tried to pull her skirt down.

"Gloria," he shouted.

He couldn't move the skirt. He gave her a shake. It stirred an enormous snore and a voluptuous groan and it seemed that she was going to roll off the sofa onto the floor. He couldn't have women lying on the floor in his flat. He could never get her up. He moved a chair against the sofa.

He sat down and waited. Gaiterswell was responsible for this. In the promiscuous Bohemian set he had lived in, the dirty little man would be used to it.

George could not ring for Seymour. Think of the scandal. She had trapped him. He hated her for what she had done to Jack, driving him out of his mind with jealousy of other men, encouraging him, evading him, never letting go. She, more than his expensive wife, was responsible for Jack's suicide. Gloria had paralyzed him. You could see it in his paintings, after they had broken up: the paintings had become automatic, academic, dead, without air, without life. There were ten drawings of that fish. He had become obsessed with it.

It was a death of the heart: of George's heart as well. This body lying in the room was like the brutal body of his father. The old brute with his rages and his passions, his disgraceful affairs with governesses and maids in the very next room to where he slept as a boy—awful business—he would never forget that—the manners!—the shouts, his terrible behavior to his wife: it had paralyzed the whole family. They all hated him so violently, with a violence that so magnetized them all, that none of them had heart for others. He had killed their hearts; not one of them had been able to love. For a moment, George left these memories and went off into anecdotes about how he fought back against his father, sniffing triumphantly, as he did at the club. But the sight of Gloria there smashed the anecdotal in him. He recognized that he had *not* fought back and had *not* been victorious. He had risked nothing. He had been whipped into the life of a timid, self-absorbed scholar.

He poured himself a large whiskey. It was gone midnight. Perhaps by the time he checked up on the windows in the flat and saw all the doors were closed she would wake up. He carried his glass to his bedroom and put it by the bedside; and there exhaustion drove him to his habits. He took off his watch and put it on the table. He forgot why he had come into the room. It was not what he intended to do, but he was tired, and murmuring to himself, "Coat, hanger, shirt, trousers, shoes, socks," he undressed, and shivering he got into bed. He finished his whiskey, turned out the light and—Gloria forgotten—he was at once asleep. And at once dreaming he was back in the sitting room, parceling the letters, watching her. He dreamed that he called Seymour, who got a taxi, and they hauled her into it. But as fast as they got her into the cab she was back upstairs on the sofa, and his father and Jack were there too, but ignoring him, standing a yard or two away, though he shouted at them to help. And then the awful thing happened. He picked her up himself. He was at a railway station; he could go no further; he dropped her. With an appalling noise, the enormous body fell just as a train came, steaming, blasting, wheels grinding, a massive black engine, advancing upon him. He gave a shout. It had hit him and crushed him. He was dying. He had had a heart attack. He screamed and he woke up shouting, sitting up in bed.

In the bedroom Gloria was standing in her stocking feet and her petticoat, holding her skirt in her hand, her hair in disorder.

"What's the matter, George?" she said thickly.

George could not speak.

"What is it? I woke up. I heard you shout." Her breathing was heavy, it was the sound of the engine he had heard. George gaped at her.

"Are you ill?" she said. "I passed out."

"I . . . I . . . I . . ." He could say nothing more. He got out of bed. George was shuddering. "What's the time?"

"Get into bed. You're freezing. You're ill." She came over and took him by the arm and he allowed himself to be put back to bed.

"What an icebox," she said. She shut the window, switched on the fire.

"I'd better get a doctor," she said.

"No," said George. "I'm all right." He was panting. She felt his head.

"Where is my watch."

"It's half past three nearly. George, for God's sake, don't do that again. Have you got any aspirins? What happens when you're alone and there is no one here?"

"Ah, you see, I have an arrangement with the . . ."

"What? The doctor?"

"The telephone," said George.

"The telephone? What the hell's the good of that? You might die, George. Where are those aspirins, be a dear and tell me. I'm sorry, George. You screamed. God, I hadn't time to put a skirt on," she said archly.

"Oh, well, so I see," said George sarcastically.

"Ah, thank God," said Gloria sighing. "Now you sound more like yourself. You gave me a turn. I would have fallen on the floor if you hadn't put the chair there. I'll make you a cup of tea. Can you make tea in this awful museum?"

"No," said George victoriously. "You can't. I never keep tea here. Tea, I never drink it. Seymour brings it."

"Well, my God, how you live, George, in this expensive barn," she said, sitting on the bed.

"Awful business. Awful dream," said George, coming round. "I had an awful dream the other night, oh yes . . ."

"You look green, George. I'll get you a drink."

She brought it to him and watched him drink it.

"I've been round your flat. There are no beds. If you don't mind I'll go back to the sofa. Now, stop talking."

For George was off on some tale of a night in the war.

"This is the only bed," he said. "I used to keep a spare bed but I stopped that. People exploit you. Want to stay the night. It upsets the servants here."

"There's not room for two in it, George," she said. George stopped his drink.

"Gloria," he stammered in terror of her large eyes. She came closer and sat on the bed. She took his free hand.

"You're cold," she said.

"No," he said. "I'm not. All bone, you see, skeleton. My sister . . ."

She stood up and then bent over him and kissed him.

"I'll find a blanket," she said. "I'll go back to the sofa. I'm terribly sorry, George. George, I really am."

"Well," said George.

"George, forgive me," she said and suddenly kneeled at the bed and put her arms round him. "Let me warm you."

"Oh no, no. No. Awful business," said George.

She went away. George heard her opening cupboards. looking for blankets. He listened to every movement. He thought, Seymour will find her in the morning. Where could he hide her? Could he make her go to the bathroom and stay there till Seymour left? No, Seymour always ran his bath. He was trapped. He heard her go to the sitting room. It was six before he fell asleep again.

At half past seven she came to his room with Seymour.

"My brother was taken very ill in the night," she was saying to Seymour. "I cannot find out who his doctor is. He oughtn't to be alone like this. At his age."

"No, ma'am," said Seymour, looking guilty.

"Bring me his tea. Where does he keep his thermometer? Get me one."

"I told him not to go out, ma'am," said Seymour.

"Thank heaven I came in."

When Seymour left she said to George, "Don't talk. It's tiring. A little scandal would have done you good, George, but not at your age."

"Umph," said George. "That man knows my sister. She's as thin as a pole. She's meaner than me," he cackled. "She never tips anyone."

"I told him I was the fat one," she said. "You stay there. I'm calling a doctor."

* * *

Waiting for him to come was a nuisance. "Awful business" having a woman in the house. They spend half their lives in the bathroom. You can't get into it. When George did get to it he was so weak he had to call for her. She was sitting in a chair reading Flitestone's letters and smiling. She had—George had to admit—made herself presentable.

"You're right, George," she said. "I'm going to keep them. He was so full of news. They're too . . ." she said demurely, "personal."

And then the doctor came.

* * *

At the club George was sitting at luncheon.

"You're looking well, George," said the academician, who had just passed him the decanter.

"I never drink until the evening. I always reckon to

drink a bottle of wine at dinner, a couple of glasses of port. I usually have a whiskey here and one more back at the flat when I get home. I walk home, taxis are expensive and oh, oh, oh, I don't like the underground. Oh no, I don't like that."

"You're looking fine."

"I have been very ill. I had pneumonia. I was taken very ill a month ago, in the night. Luckily my sister has been looking after me. That is the trouble with old people who live alone, no one knows. They can't reach the bell. I told you about that awful night when I ate the oysters . . ."

"George, not now, please. I didn't know you had a sister?"

"Oh yes, oh yes. Two," said George sharply. "One is very thin, all bones like me, the other very fat."

"But you're better? You look fine. I hear, by the way, that Sanders is getting married."

"Oh, I knew about that. I advised him to, at his age. I warned him about the loneliness of bachelors in old age. I'm used to it. Keep occupied. See people. That's the secret. Oh yes, I worked it out. My father lived till he was ninety. You see, when I was young one never met any women. Just girls at deb parties, but speak to them, oh dear no. Not done. That's a big change. The bishops don't like sex, though Canterbury is beginning to come round. The Pope will have to make a move, he's been the stumbling block. A scandal. Oh yes, I happened to be in Rome in '05, staying with a papal count and, well, I was able to tell him the whole inside story at the Vatican, you see I knew a very able Jesuit who was very frank about it privately . . ."

"What happened about Gloria?" said a voice. It was the Arch Enemy, sitting opposite.

"Hah," said George. "I recommended her not to sell. She offered to give me the letters, but I didn't care to take them. They were very intimate, personal."

"I thought her husband had left her and she was short of money?"

"That's not the worst thing to be short of," sniffed George.

"The trouble with Gloria was that she was also so sentimental," said the Arch Enemy. "The moment she sees a man her mind simply goes. Still does, and she must be sixty if she's a day," he said, looking at George.

By God, George thought, the Arch Enemy is a fool.

The Speech

"It's a funny turnout. You don't know what front to take up for the best," the chatty doorman replied to the big-bellied woman as he opened the door and let her and the other speakers into the hall.

"You'd better bloody well make your mind up or you'll be dead," she said to him with a grin over her shoulder as she passed and followed the others up the steps onto the cold, dusty platform. And she said to the young man with heavy fair hair who was next to her when they sat down: "That's this place for you. Did you hear him? It's dead. They've had the bomb already."

A man's voice shouted from the audience, just before Lord Birt got up to introduce the speakers: "Good old Sally."

No smile of pleasure moved her double chin, nor did she nod. She was counting. That one shout echoed. It revealed the emptiness of the hall. It would hold eight hundred; she had seen in her time twice that number fighting their way in. Now (she reckoned it up) there were no more than fifty or sixty.

The weather, the sleet whipping across all day—the secretary had said—not having had longer notice, couldn't get through to headquarters on the phone. A lot of people on short time. Excuses. They had even spelled her name wrong on the notice outside: Sally Proser, leaving out the second "s" and the sleet spitting on it made the red ink run into the blue as if the poster were sobbing and ashamed of them all. They couldn't get her name right, even in her own town.

Lord Birt had sat down. The first speaker was up.

"Friends," he was saying, "I shall not take up your time . . ."

She looked at her watch. "We'll be here half the night," she said to the young man next to her. He was trying to keep a piercing look on his face. "Who is he?"

"Doctor," hissed the young man, crossing his legs. "Quaker. Liberal."

"God," she said very audibly.

It was a large hall, a yawning historic fake in a Gothic baronial style, built out of cotton profits a hundred years before, shabbied by hundreds, thousands, of meetings, the air staled and exhausted by generations of preachers, mayors and politicians. The damp had brought out a smell made of floorboards, the municipal disinfectants, the sweet, sooty cellulose effluence of the city. It was a smell provided by a dozen mills whose tall chimneys penciled the pink fume of the sky, and by something of the fouled, milky green industrial river and the oily canal. A mist hung across the middle of the hall like breath left behind for years and although all the chandeliers were lit, the light fell yellowish and weak on the audience sitting in their overcoats in the first five rows and on the long funereal stretch of empty chairs behind. One person after another turned around in discomfort, looking at the distant glass doors at the back and then at the side, to see where the Arctic draft came from; and then, reproaching themselves, lifted their chins stiffly and stared with resentment at the platform.

The doctor was still going on. He was a tall, very thin man, vain of his eagle face, his blossom of white hair, his gentle, high-pitched, doubting vocables. They were moving equably out of "the situation before all of us today"; then went on derisively to "the international plane" and "the lessons of history": (his past); to what he had said "in this very hall" (references to local elections thirty years ago), and emerged into the benignancy of the "moral issue" and circled impatiently to what he had "always said." Beside him sat young Lord Birt, ace flyer, Matisse owner, lecturer in America, with a dark, prompt electric black moustache, like a too-recent political decision, and next to him the very young man.

"It's a scandal, a meeting like this," Mrs. Prosser was saying to him audibly through the doctor's speech. "I'll take it up with headquarters. Where have they put you up—in an hotel? I was out last night, God knows where, in the treasurer's house, and there's been a death in the family. Imagine the atmosphere."

"Someone just died?" said the young man, astonished.

"Twenty-five years ago!" she said sarcastically. "I've made fourteen speeches on this tour, in the last six days, and they hadn't the decency to put me into a hotel. "It's all wrong."

And Mrs. Prosser's head, mouth and jaws, even her big arms, seemed to gather themselves together until she looked like a fist.

"What about Hungary?" shouted a man from the audience.

"Yes, what about Hungary?" shouted two or three others.

"They're waking up," said the young man.

"I'm glad you asked me that question," said the doctor, going on.

"No, it's nothing," she said, giving an experienced glance at the shouters. "They're dead. How did you get here? They didn't even have a car, borrowed it from the treasurer's son, it broke down. We sat on the road for half an hour, on a night like this. Ah, well, the old bastard is drying up. It's you."

The young man got up.

"Ladies and gentlemen," he began.

(Oh God, thought Mrs. Prosser, but forgave him.) He had learned his speech, he was sawing it off, it fell in lumps to the floor. The women looked sympathetically, the men looked ironical, one or two of the shouters leaned forward to egg him on at first, and then leaned back, with their hands on their knees, giving up. Handsome, his hair flopping, he seemed to have some invisible opponent in front of him whom he was angrily trying to push away so that he could see the audience. He struggled and at last he stopped struggling. He came to an end, looked back nervously to see if his chair was still there, and when the audience clapped he looked back at them with suspicion and anger.

"I made a mess of it," he murmured to Mrs. Prosser as he sat down.

"Here we go." Mrs. Prosser ignored him. "Watch me, if I don't wet my drawers before I've done with this bloody lot . . ."

She was up, adroitly slipping her old fur coat off her shoulders and into the hands of the young man, stepping in one stride to the edge of the platform. She stared at the audience, let them have a good look at her. She was a short woman of forty-seven. Robust. She was wearing a tan jumper that was low on her strong neck and pulled on anyhow, and a shabby green skirt. She had big breasts, which she had been ashamed of in her young days, wanting to hide them, but that was before she joined the Movement; a stout belly, hard as a drum, which made her laugh when she got up in the morning. Her face was round and she had a double chin and the look on her face said: Go on! Take a good look. It's your last chance.

Suddenly, she let out her voice.

"Fellow workers," she shouted. The words, slow, deep and swinging in delivery, rocked them. They stopped fidgeting and coughing. She heard with pleasure her full plain Northern voice sweep out over them and to the back of the hall, filling it to the baronial beams and spreading over the seats and into the empty galleries.

"Good old Sally," shouted a man.

"Come on, Sally," shouted another, wet-lipped with love at the sight of her and nudging his neighbor. She paused in the middle of her sentence and smiled fully at him—the first broad smile of the night.

She loved these opening minutes of her speeches. I'm an old potato, she thought, but my hair is brown and alive and I've got a voice. I can do anything with it. It was as powerful as a man's, yet changeable. Now it was soft, now violent; riotous in argument yet simple; always firm and disturbing. It could be blunt and brutal and yet it throbbed. It had sloshed its way through strikes and mass meetings; it had rebounded off factory walls, it had romped and somersaulted over thousands of heads. It had rung bitterly out through the Spanish War, when she was a young woman; through the rows of the Second Front, the peace campaigns, the Hungarian quarrel; it was all out now for Banning the Tests. It had never worn out, never coarsened, never aged; in these first few minutes it was her blood, the inner, spontaneous fountain of her girlhood, something virginal she would never lose. At every meeting it was reborn.

Even her shrewd brown eyes were bemused by her utter pleasure in hearing this voice, so that all of her early sentences surprised her by their clarity and the feeling that was in them; she was proud to feel her lungs heave, to watch the next thought form in her brain, the next argument assemble, the words, the very vowels and consonants fall into place. It was thrilling to pause and throw in a joke, a flash of hate or a line of wit that would sometimes recklessly jump into her head and make it itch with pleasure. This was the moment when she caught the crowd, played with them and made them hers. It was the time, for her, of consciousness, like a sudden falling in love, when the eyes of the audience answered her signals, when she could look carelessly from face to face, watching her words flick like an angler's line over them, looking for the defaulter. And, picking this man or this woman out, she would pause, as it were, to ask the audience to watch her make her catch, as if she had come down off the platform to be down among them with an intimacy that teased them and made their minds twist and flick and curl with fear and pleasure.

And then—it happened: the break, almost painful for her. The virginal voice that was so mysteriously herself would separate from her and perform alone as if it had nothing to do with her at all. It became, simply, the Voice. It left her—a plain, big-bellied, middle-aged woman—a body, to stand there exposed in all the woundedness of her years, while it went off like some trained dog barking round the audience, rounding them up, fetching in some stray from the back, flinging itself against the rows of empty chairs.

"And I say and I say again: we've got to stop these tests! We tell the Americans to stop these tests. We tell this Tory government that if it does not stop these tests . . ."

Now it was barking down derisively from the gallery at the end of the hall, barking at the City Arms, at fire extinguishers, at the Roll of Honor in gold, at the broom left by the cleaner, at the draft coming in at the doors, it was barking round walls below and the feet of the audience.

The light went out of Mrs. Prosser's face. She let the Voice carry on and she looked with boredom at the people. There was the elderly man, deaf and impatient; there was the big married woman with folded arms who kept glancing down her row to see everyone was listening, like a policewoman. There were the two girls, shoulder to shoulder, with pretty false faces, waiting for a chance to whisper. There was a woman with mouth open, ravenous, as if she were going to rush the platform and kiss her. There were the threes or fours of men frosted with self-respect. There was the man who seemed, nowadays, to come to all her meetings, a man neither young nor old, listening with one ear and sly, who sat at the end of the row with one bent leg sticking out of the neat block of the audience and who glanced often at the side door, as if he were waiting his chance or for a sign to make a bolt for it. For what? For the pubs before they closed, for the last tram, to meet someone, even just to stand in the street—why? Had he got—a life? It always troubled her. She wanted to follow him. And there was that swing door which kept gulping like a sob as someone pushed in and gave a glance at the meeting and then went out and the door gave another gulp like the noise of a washbasin as if all the words of that Voice of hers were going down a drain. She heard the Voice go on:

"For you can take it from me, if the Americans don't stop these tests, if the Russians don't stop these tests, if the Tory party just sits on its bum . . ."

Loud cheers. That was a word made for the North. Mrs. Prosser grinned at the Voice's joke. She had a good big bum herself.

The Voice went on. It carried nearly thirty years of her life. At a meeting like this—no, not like this, but much larger and in the open streets, in the Blackshirt days—she had met her husband. There was a shouting, arm-wrenching, tearing, kicking fight with the police. What solid lumps their bodies were! She (when she remembered it) had felt as light as air. A gale had lifted her suddenly so that she, like the rest of the scattering and re-forming crowd, was blown about and with a force in her big arms and body that was exalted. Bodies swung about like sacks of meal. The houses and all their windows seemed to buckle and bulge towards her, the cobbled street heaved up and down like a sea. You could pick up the street in your hands. A young man near her gave a shout and she shouted, too, and her shout was his and his was hers; for an extraordinary few moments they had the same body. A policeman struck at the young man, the blow fell on his neck and *she* felt the pain. She could not remember how—but she was clawing at the policeman and the young man's blood struck her cheek. They spent that night in prison.

The pupil teacher at the Adderdale Road School (Girls) to be in prison! That was when the hate started—her mother saying she would never hold her head up again; they had always been decent people. The father saying: "All stuck-up with those books and too good for her own family." And now she had disgraced them. If young Prosser, the little weed, came round the house again—the father said—he'd belt him. In this very city. They sacked her from the school. From that time on her life had been committees, lectures, meetings. Always traveling, always on platforms, her husband at one end of the country and she at the other. He with the shout on his face and she with the shout on hers, a drawing back of the lips over the teeth: that was their love, too. Love a shout, marriage a shout. They saw each other for an hour or two, or a day or two, eating anything, anywhere, usually a sandwich or a few bars of chocolate. It was the choclate that had made her put on weight. "I'm a fighting sweetshop." At first, he had been the nimble one, the leader, wearing himself out and often ill; he had the ideas; then, one week, when he was sick with an ulcer, she had taken a meeting—and the Voice, this strange being inside her, came out and now it was she who not only commanded him, but audiences by the hundreds, then the thousands. The Voice took over her own and her husband's life.

And they stick me at a place nine miles outside the city (her body, her bullying breasts and affronted belly were saying), in weather like this! I don't say I wasn't comfortable. That'd be a lie. I was glad to see a coal fire. Three-piece suite too and the telly on, very nice. You wouldn't have seen that in our home when I was a girl. We had a laugh too about Lord Birt's house, all those chimneys. Mrs. Jenkins was a maid there when she was a girl and they used to bless those chimneys! My husband and I did our courting up there in the woods above. Mrs. Jenkins and I had a good laugh about old times.

And then the old lady, Mr. Jenkins' mother, got restless. "Eh," says Mrs. Jenkins, "Mother wants her telly. We turned it off when you came. She sits there in front of it, tapping her toes on the floor when the cowboys go by, rocking up and down."

"You want to get on your horse and ride the range, Gran, don't you?" says Harry Jenkins, the lad. "Gran's in her saddle, reaching for her gun when the Westerns come on. She gets excited, don't you, Gran?"

Of course, the old lady was stone-deaf and couldn't hear a word he said. But she looks at me and says, suddenly, "That's Sally Gray." Just like that, her eyes like pistols. "That's Sally Gray."

"No, Gran, that's Mrs. Prosser. Excuse her, Mrs. Prosser, the mind . . . she's failing."

"It's Sally Gray," says the old lady.

"Now, Gran!" says Mrs. Jenkins. "You be a good girl."

"It's the girl that killed our Leslie. It's Sally Gray that sent our boy to Spain and killed him."

"Gran," says Mrs. Jenkins. "Stop that. I won't have you upset us. Excuse her, Mrs. Prosser. My husband's brother was killed in the Spanish War. She doesn't forget it."

"It's Sally Gray, the schoolteacher, who went to prison and got her name in the papers and broke poor Mrs. Gray's heart." The old lady stands flapping her little hands about and turning round and round like a dog.

The atmosphere—you can imagine it!

"Now, Gran, Mrs. Prosser didn't do anything to Les. It's a long time ago."

"Tuesday, we heard," the old lady said.

"Gran," says the lad, taking the old lady's arm to steady her, "don't carry on. It'd be a bad day for the workers if they didn't fight for themselves. Uncle Les was an idealist."

Nine miles outside the town in weather like this.

"I'm sorry, Mrs. Prosser," says Mrs. Jenkins. "Switch on the telly, Harry. She's a great problem. Definitely. I could kill her," says Mrs. Jenkins, standing up stiff. And she suddenly picks up the teapot and rushes out of the room, crying.

"Excuse us," says Mr. Jenkins, giving the old lady a shake.

What a committee to put me in a house like that with a mad old woman. Where's the consideration? And they bring me here in a borrowed car that breaks down and we stand there on the moor, with the sleet coming through my stockings. And they spell your name wrong and scrape up an audience of ten or twenty people.

There was a cheer from the audience. The Voice had got into them. Mrs. Prosser paused: she was startled herself. She paused for the cheer and the Voice cracked a thin joke about the Foreign Secretary: "They fly about from Bonn to Washington, from Washington to London; you don't see them flying down here. They're afraid of getting their feathers dirty," and got a laugh from them, a dirty, drafty laugh, which gave the man at the end of the row a chance to inch his leg out further and get ready to make a bolt for it; and at that very second she saw the dead white face of the clock at the end of the hall, its black hands like a jack-knife opening.

Twenty to nine! Her husband down at Plymouth, the other end of the country. And Jack? Where is Jack? But as her Voice picked up its freedom again and sailed on, she silently asked the audience: Where's my son? What have you done with my son? A year ago I could tell you what he was doing. He'd come home from school, get himself some supper, that boy could cook, oh yes, and clean up afterwards—and then settle to his homework. He could look after himself better than a grown man. From the age of nine he could manage on his own. My husband and I could leave him a week at a time and he didn't mind. And I'll tell you something else: a boy with a real political conscience!

You've done it—her body was shouting to the audience —*you've* done it! For twenty-five years my husband and I have been fighting for *you,* fighting the class enemy, getting justice for you and you sit there—what is left of you—pulling in the big money, drunk on hire purchase, mesmerized by your tellys and your pools—and what do you do for *us?* When I knew I was going to have that boy I said to my husband, "We won't let this stop the work." And we didn't. But you and your rotten society just did nothing. A year ago he was the best boy in this country and you couldn't stand it. No. You had to get him out and start him drinking with a lot of thieving hooligans, you put a knife in his hand. You know what he said to his father? "Well, you were in prison, you and Mother, you told me." "Son," his father said, "We were fighting for justice for the people." "Oh, that crap!" he says. That's what the great British people did while we were working for them. Those people out there lost a son twenty-five years ago in Spain. I want to tell you I lost mine last year—killed by his own side.

"Good old Sally," the audience shouted. "Hit 'em. Listen to her."

Mrs. Prosser paused with a smile of victory.

"But, my friends, you will say to me," the Voice suddenly became quiet and reasonable, "this government cannot act alone. It has got to consider the American government and the Russian government. You will say the British people cannot isolate itself from the human family . . ."

But Mrs. Prosser was saying to them: Before I came here this evening they took me to this Lord Birt's house, the one I told you about with all those chimneys; very friendly those chimneys looked when we were courting in the woods above. My husband and I used to look down at the house. And the time I liked the best was when the smoke was going up straight from them in the autumn. Some weekends when there was company at the house the smoke went up from many of them like it does from his Lordship's mills, but pleasanter, homey. You'd see rooks turning round and round over it and hear a dog drag its chain and bark, or hear pails clash where they were washing the car or swooshing out the yard at the back: I always wanted to see inside when I was a girl. Well today I saw it. Oh, yes! There I was inside sitting by the fire with a cat on my knees. Can you see me with a cat? There were some people there and after we'd had our meal this young man who just made that bad speech was there looking at the books in the white bookcases. And there was a young girl, plump with brown hair, talking to him about them. Lord Birt asked him where they'd been that morning and they said, "Up in the woods at the back." I'll tell you something. I was jealous. I was jealous of that young girl talking to that young man. I felt old and ugly and fat. Mind you, I don't like the way these girls wear trousers, so that they look as naked as the tadpoles we used to catch when we were kids. I'd split them myself, you'd have a laugh—but it wasn't that that made me jealous. I couldn't *talk* about anything. That lad can't make a speech, but he can talk and so could the girl. I sat there dumb and stupid. Every day, morning and evening, year after year, generation after generation, this was a home and they could talk about a subject in it. If you talked about a subject in my home when I was a girl they'd call you stuck-up. All I can do is to make bloody fine speeches in bloody empty halls like this.

There was coughing in the audience and now the Voice was quieter. The man sitting at the end of the row with his leg out made up his mind. He got both legs out, and bending slightly, thinking to make himself invisible, he slowly tiptoed out across the bare space to the door at the side. And half those forty or fifty heads, in the midst of their coughing, turned to watch, but not that widely smiling woman who was still looking ravenously up at the platform as if she were going to rush at Mrs. Prosser and swallow her.

Mrs. Prosser saw the man tiptoeing out to that life of his and she did what she always could do, at any meeting, startle it out of its wits with a sudden shout, and make any escaper stop in his absurd delinquent steps.

"Fellow Workers (the Voice rang out), Don't kid yourselves. You won't escape. It is you and your children who are being betrayed by this cowardly government. It is you . . ."

But her life was the forty-seven-year-old body with the big white mournful bottom saying to them: And if you want to know what I thought when I passed the long mirror in the hall of Lord Birt's house when we were getting in the car to come to this place where I was born and brought up and where you can't even spell my name, if you want to know what I thought, I can tell you. It's you have made me ugly! Working for you! You never gave me a minute to read a book, look at a picture or feed the spirit inside me. It was you who made me sit dumb as an old cow back there. You fight for justice and you lose half your life. You're ugly and you've made me as ugly as you are.

The applause went up sharp and short near the platform and echoed in the emptiness behind the audience. Chairs shifted. Mrs. Prosser sat down. Lord Birt and the young man congratulated her. She looked scornfully and boastfully at them.

"I've wet them," she said to the young man as they walked away down the steps off the platform. Out of the little crowd of people who had stayed behind to talk to the speakers, the young girl came forward and secretively, not to embarrass him, squeezed the young man's arm and said, "You were wonderful." He hardly listened but was looking eagerly into the crowd that surrounded Mrs. Prosser.

"We'll wait for her," he said fiercely. "She had them"—he held out his cupped hand—"like that." And he clenched his fist.

The Liars

"WE'RE ALL DRESSED up today," said the landlady, going downstairs to her husband in the kitchen from the old lady's room. "Diamond rings, emerald necklace—she's put the lot on. I said to her, 'You're all dressed up for company, I see.' 'Yes,' she said, 'Harry's coming.' I mean, it's childish. I don't trust that man. He'd stop at nothing and he tells lies. And do you know what she said?"

"What did she say?" said the landlady's husband.

" 'It's Thursday, Mrs. Lax,' she says. 'It's my day for telling lies.' "

It was a February afternoon. Under her black wig, the old lady upstairs was sitting up in bed reading her father's Baudelaire. She read greedily; her eyes, enlarged by her glasses, were rampaging over the lines; with her long nose and her long lips sliding back into her cheeks, she looked like a wolf grinning at the smell of the first snow and was on the hunt restlessly among the words.

Vous que dans votre enfer mon âme a poursuivies
Pauvres soeurs, je vous aime autant que je vous plains"

she was murmuring avidly as she read. All over the bed were books, French and English, papers, detective novels that she had picked up and pushed away. On and off, in the long day, she had looked to see what was going on in the street; rain had emptied it. The only thing that still caught her eye was an old blackbird gripping the branch of the plane tree outside her window; its wings hanging down, alone.

"You're late," said the old lady, pulling her shawl violently round her arms, taking off her glasses and showing her strong, expectant teeth, when Harry came up to her room at four o'clock. The bold nose was naked and accusing. Harry put the library books he had brought for her on the table under the window by her bedside. He was a tall, red-faced man with the fixed look of moist astonishment at having somehow got a heavy body into his navy-blue suit and of continually hearing news.

"I had my hair cut," he said, moving a small cane-seated chair out of the muddle of furniture into the middle of the room. The old lady waited impatiently for him to sit down.

"No," he said. The old lady took a deep breath and gave a small hungry smile.

"No," he said. "A terrible thing happened when I came out of the barber's." The old lady let out her breath peacefully and let her head slip aside on her pillow in admiration.

"I saw my double," Harry said.

Two years ago she had been in hospital, but before that, Harry had the job of pushing her along the sea front in a bath chair on fine mornings. When she had been taken ill, he had started working in the bar and dining room of the Queens Hotel. Now that she was bedridden he brought her books. First of all, in the days when he used to wheel her out, it was "Yes, Miss Randall" or "Is that a fact, Miss Randall?" while she chattered about the town as it was when she was a child there, about her family—all dead now—and about her father, the famous journalist, and what he had done at Versailles after the 1914 war and his time in the Irish troubles, and her London life with him. And Harry told her about himself. "I was born in Enniskillen, ma'am." "Now that's a border town, isn't it, Harry?" "It's like living on a tightrope, ma'am. My father fought against the British." "Very foolish of him," said the old lady. "Oh, it was," said Harry. "He had us blown up." "The British *bombed* you, Harry?" "Not at all, it was one of father's bombs, homemade thing, it went off in the house." "Were you hurt, Harry?" "I was at my auntie's. So I went to sea." "So you did, you told me, and the ship blew up too." "No, ma'am, it was the boiler. It was a Liverpool ship, the *Grantham*." "Two explosions, I don't believe you, Harry." "It's God's truth, ma'am. It was in New York harbor. But I'd left her in Buenos Aires—there was always trouble on her." "And then you went to that hacienda—no, you got a job in an hotel first of all—isn't that it?" "Yes, in two or three hotels, ma'am, until this American lady took me up to her hacienda." "To look after the horses?" "That is correct." "This was the lady who rode her horse up the steps into the dining room?" "No, ma'am," said Harry, "she rode it right inside and up the marble staircase into her bedroom." "She couldn't, Harry. A mule yes, but not a horse." "That part was easy for her, ma'am, it was getting the horse down that was the trouble. She called us, the Indian boy and myself, and we had to do that. Down twenty-five marble steps. She stood at the top shouting at us 'Mind the pictures.' " "I suppose there was an explosion there, too, Harry?" "No ma'am, but there were butterflies as large as plates flying through the air, enough to knock you down . . ."

"Harry," said the old lady one day, "You're as big a liar as my sister's husband used to be."

Harry looked at her warily, then around him to see if there was anyone he could call to for help if there was trouble.

"It's God's truth," said Harry rapidly and anxiously.

"There's truth and there's God's truth," said the old lady. It was after this that she had to be taken off to hospital.

* * *

"So you saw your double, Harry," the old lady said. "Stand up and let me look at you."

Harry stood up.

"They've cropped you at the back, you're nearly blue. I'll tell you whose double you are, Harry. My sister's husband. He was in the hotel business like you."

"Is that a fact?" said Harry. "Did your sister marry?"

"I've been thinking about it ever since you went to work at the Queens," said the old lady. "He was taller and broader than you and he had fair hair, not black like yours, and a very white face, a London night face—but the feet were the same, like yours, sticking out sideways. Sit down, Harry."

"I suppose," said Harry, who had heard versions of this story before. "I suppose he'd be the manager?"

"Manager!" shouted the old lady. "He wouldn't have considered it! Ambassador, archbishop, prime minister, more like it. That is what he sounded like and what he looked like—anyway what we *thought* he was. He was the headwaiter at a night club."

She stared herself into silence.

"No, it's God's truth," said Harry, taking his chance. "I was coming out of the barber's and I forgot your books and went back for them and when I came to cross the street, the lights changed. There was a crowd of us there on the curb and that was when I saw this fellow. He was standing on the other side of the street waiting to cross. I stared at him. He stared at me. We were the double of each other. I thought I was looking in a mirror."

The old lady let her head slip back peacefully on the pillow, a happy smile came on her face and she took a biscuit from the tin.

"Same clothes?" said the old lady slyly.

"Except for the hat," said Harry. "Same height. He was staring at me. Same nose, eyes, everything. And then the lights changed and he stepped off the curb and I stepped off and we were still staring at each other. But when we got to the middle I couldn't look at him any longer and I looked away. We passed each other and I felt cold as ice all down one side of my body."

"Did he turn round? Did *he* recognize *you?*"

"He did not. But after we passed I looked back and he wasn't there. No sign of him at all. I got to the curb and I had a second look. He'd gone."

"He was lost in the crowd."

"He was not. There wasn't a crowd. He was the only one crossing from that side of the street. Except for the hat, it was me."

The pupils of Harry's eyes were upright brown ovals. He had been wronged, so wronged that he looked puffed out, full of wind.

"It was like passing an iceberg in the Atlantic. Or a ghost," Harry said.

"You could say Deb's husband was a ghost," said the old lady. "He was living upstairs in the flat above us for three years before we met him. We used to hear his taxi at four in the morning. He was out all night and we were out all day. Deb at her art school and I worked on the paper my father used to work on."

"You mightn't have met at all," Harry said. "I never saw the night porter at the Queens for a year."

"I wish we hadn't," said the old lady.

"It would be accidental if you did. Would there have been an accident?" Harry said, putting on an innocent look. "When I was working on that hacienda with the American lady, the one with the horse in her bedroom . : ."

"There *was* an accident!" said the old lady. "You know there was. I told you, Harry."

"He left the stopper in his basin," Harry said.

"With the tap dripping," the old lady said. "Deb got home one evening and heard the water dripping through the ceiling on to Father's desk. She put a bowl underneath it and it splashed all over Father's books—we had a very pleasant flat, not like this. Father left us some very beautiful things. When I got home I was angry with Deb. She was a very dreamy girl. 'Why didn't you get the housekeeper up instead of letting it ruin everything?' I said. *I* had to ring for him—stone-deaf, like your cook. Didn't you say the explosion on that ship, the *Cairngorm,* made your cook stone-deaf?"

"On the *Grantham,*" Harry said.

"You told me the *Cairngorm* before," said the old lady. "But never mind. He got his keys and went upstairs to see what was going on. That flat, Harry. It was empty. When I say empty, just the lino on the floor . . ."

"I've got lino at the Queens," said Harry. "Brown with white flowers."

"Nothing—nothing but a table and a bed and a couple of chairs. It was like a cell. It was like a punishment hanging over us. Not a book. There was a parcel of shirts from the laundry on the bed—that would have told us something if we'd looked."

"It would," said Harry.

"Four o'clock in the morning," said the old lady, "he came home. The taxi ticking down below in the street! Like a ghost in the night. Of course he came down to apologize about the water. Harry, the moment he stood in the room, I knew I'd seen him before! I said to my sister, 'I've seen that man somewhere.' The way he stopped in the doorway, looking across the room at Deb and me and the chairs, nodding at them as if he were telling us where to sit, the way he held his hands together as he spoke, with his head bent. He had one of those kissing mouths—like a German. He looked at the books that had been splashed and said, 'Balzac and Baudelaire, very great men,' and looked fatter in the face after he said it. More important. We said they were Father's books and my sister said 'Father was a special correspondent. Perhaps you've heard of him.' He said he'd heard people mention him at his club and it sounded as if he'd eaten Father." The old lady laughed out loud at this idea of hers and left her mouth open for a while after she had laughed. "I'll tell you who he was like," she said excitedly, "that statue of George the Second. Or do I mean the Duke of Bedford?

"I wanted to get rid of him: he was so large and serious and he sounded as if he was making a speech to Parliament about what some painter he knew had said about art and the public. He knew a lot of people—cabinet ministers, actors, judges. Well, I said, when he'd gone, I don't know who he is but he's a man 'in the know'! Deb did not like my saying this. 'He's a journalist, I expect.' Before he went Deb asked him to have a drink with us one day. 'Let me look at my diary. Thursday I'm free and Sundays, unless I go away to stay,' he said. 'Come on Sunday,' Deb said. He came. We had people there. The first thing he did was to start handing round the drinks. It was *his* party. He owned us. He'd eaten us too. I couldn't take my eyes off him. One or two people were as curious as I was. 'Who is he? The editor of the *Times?* What does he do?' He wasn't like any of our friends, we were all younger. You know what I think drew us to him—girls are such fools—his conceit! He was as conceited as a gravestone. I watched him moving about. There was his round white face, rather puffy, and his head bowing like the whole of the House of Hanover—the House of Hanover were very stiff, I know, Harry, but you know what I mean—and talking about the Prime Minister and politics in a pooh-poohing way; but down below were his feet sticking out sideways and scampering about beneath him—like messenger boys. 'Which paper do you work for?' I asked him. 'I'm not a journalist,' he said. 'Oh,' I said, 'the housekeeper said you were a journalist on night work. We hear your taxi every night.' And do you know what he said? 'I asked the housekeeper about *you* when I took my flat here. I wanted to be sure it was a quiet house. He said you were two ladies out all day.' Snubs to us, I said to my sister after he had gone, but she said 'Fancy him asking about us!' and she danced round the room, singing up at the ceiling, 'I'm a lady out all day.' We could hear him upstairs walking about."

"Yes, but that's what I can't make out about this man," said Harry. "I was thinking about it yesterday. Why wouldn't he tell you what his job was?"

"He thought we were a pair of snobs," said the old lady. "I expect we were."

"Out all night, he could have been a printer," said Harry.

"Or the post office! Or the police! Night watchman. Actor. We thought of that," the old lady raced along. "It was clever of him: you see what he did. He didn't tell a single lie but he started us imagining things and telling lies to ourselves. Deb couldn't leave it alone. Every time he dodged our questions, she made something up."

The old lady pulled her arms out of the shawl and spread her arms wide.

"Burglar came into *my* head," she shouted. "I came home from the office one evening and there they were, both of them, sitting on the sofa and he was saying he had heard on the 'highest authority'—the highest authority, he actually used those words, I always called him the highest authority after that to annoy Deb—that the Cabinet had decided to legalize street betting. When he left I said to Deb, 'Deb, that man is not in politics: he is in crime.' 'I can tell you he is *not* in crime,' Deb said, 'I asked him straight out.' "

Harry leaned forward and began to rub his hands up and down his sleeves making a sound like breath.

" 'I asked him straight out what he did,' Deb said, 'and he said he was very sorry but it was secret work, something he couldn't talk about, but not crime.' He made her promise not to ask or try to find out, but he said he would tell her when he was free to say."

"If you'd looked at those shirts on his bed you'd have known the answer," Harry said. "Dress shirts."

"The headwaiter at a smart night club," the old lady said.

"And earning good money, I suppose," said Harry. "That is where he picked up his talk."

"I've told you all this before, Harry," said the old lady.

"Things come back," said Harry.

"The chief steward on the *Grantham,*" said Harry, "used to pass himself off as the captain when he went ashore. That was to girls too."

"Oh, he talked very well and took us in. You can call him a waiter if you like but you know what I call him? Bluebeard."

"Bluebeard?" said Harry, very startled. "Was he married?"

"No, but he had Bluebeard in him," said the old lady. "A girl will do anything to find out a secret."

"That's true," said Harry.

The old lady stared at Harry, weighing him up. Then she said, in a lower voice: "I can talk to you, Harry. You're a married man. I mean you've been a married man. Show me your wife's picture again."

Harry opened his wallet and took out an old snapshot of a young girl with smooth dark hair drawn in an old-fashioned style round an oval face.

"She was pretty, Harry. Deb was fair and a bit plump."

She looked at the photograph a long time and then gave it back to Harry, who put it in his wallet again.

"You miss her, Harry."

"I do that."

"You would have had a home," said the old lady. "I haven't got a home. You haven't got a home—and yet, years ago, before we moved to London, my family had a large house in this town."

The old lady suddenly changed her mood and her voice became sarcastically merry. "Bluebeard! Oh, we were all mystery! Secret service, Russian spies. When Deb went to bed at night, she started drawing back the curtains, turning out the lights and undressing by the light of the street lamp down below. And she would open the window wide—in the winter! The fog blowing in! She would stand in her nightdress and say, 'Can't you feel the mystery of London? I want to feel I am everywhere in London, seeing what everyone is doing this minute. Listen to it.' 'You'll get pneumonia,' I said. But it was love. He came down to see us very often now. One day he was saying something about the French ambassador and French foreign policy, it sounded boastful and I said (I remember this), 'Father was one of Clemenceau's very few English friends'—which wasn't true. I told you he made us tell lies. That impressed him because before he went he asked us both out to dinner—at the Ritz! The Ritz! And that was where something funny happened—only a small thing. A party at another table started staring at him and I was sure I heard someone mention his name. I'm sure I heard one of the men say, 'There's Charles,' and I said to him: 'Someone knows you over there.' 'No,' he said. 'They were talking about you.

They were saying it was unfair a man taking out two pretty sisters.' Deb was very pleased. 'He's very well known,' she said. 'In that case, he can't be secret, can he?' I said. He never took us out again."

The old lady scowled. "After that it was champagne, caviar, lobster. Up in his flat and Deb took her gramophone —I never went. 'He must be a cook,' I said and she said, 'No, he sends out for it,' and wouldn't speak to me for a week afterwards. She was clean gone. She gave up her classes because she couldn't see him during the day except on Thursdays and Sundays. She was mad about him. And she got very secretive, hiding things, not like her at all. I told her she'd have a bigger secret than she bargained for."

The old lady sniggered.

"I was jealous," said the old lady in a moping voice.

"Ah, you would be, I expect," Harry agreed.

"Yes," moped the old lady.

"And then," said Harry, giving a loud slap to his knee. "There was this ring at the bell . . ."

The old lady looked suspiciously at him.

"The same as the time I told you about, when we docked at Marseilles—with that Algerian. Short black socks he had on and . . ."

The old lady woke up out of her moping, offended.

"Algerian! He was not an Algerian. It was a Cypriot. I was very surprised to hear a ring at that time of the evening. I thought it must have been one of those Jehovah's Witnesses. I went to the door and there he was, this little dark Cypriot with a bottle sticking out of his pocket—I thought he was drunk. He asked for Mr. Charles. 'There is no Mr. Charles here,' I said. 'What number do you want?' 'Six,' he said."

"And you were four!" said Harry.

" 'This is four,' I said, pointing to the number on the door. Well, you'd think people could read. 'Number six is upstairs.' And I shut the door quickly, I was frightened."

"You can mark a man with a bottle," said Harry. "I've seen that too."

"I heard him ring the bell upstairs. I heard talking. And then it was all quiet. Then suddenly I heard a shout and I thought the ceiling was coming down, like furniture being thrown about."

"An argument," said Harry.

"An argument?" said the old lady. She tightened her shawl round her and leaned back as if she were warding off blows.

"Screams, Harry! Lobster, Harry. Glass! And Deb rushing out to the landing, making a horrible squeal like a dog being run over. I rushed out of our flat and up the stairs and there was Deb in her petticoat shrieking and just as I got to her the Cypriot rushed out with ketchup or blood, I don't know which, on his boots and ran downstairs. I pulled Deb out of the way. Her scream had stopped in her wide-open mouth and she was pointing into the lobby of the flat. There was Charles getting up from the floor, in his shirt-sleeves with blood all over his face. You couldn't walk for glass."

The old lady stared at Harry, and picking up Baudelaire's poems, contemptuously threw them to the end of the bed. Then slowly she smiled and Harry smiled. They smiled at each other with admiration.

"Yes," said Harry with a nod. "It's feasible."

The old lady nodded back.

"It's feasible, all right," Harry said. "The same as I was saying happened in Marseilles when I was in the *Grantham*—Egyptian onions from Alexandria—you could smell us all over the port. I went ashore with the second mate and we were having a drink in one of those cafés with tables on the street—only there five minutes and this Algerian comes in, a young fellow. He walks straight between the tables to the headwaiter who was flicking flies off the fruit and shoots him dead. Not a word spoken. Same idea. The headwaiter had been fiddling chicken and brandy, selling it on the side and when the boss tumbled to it, the waiter said this Algerian kitchen boy—that is what he was—had done it and the boss fired him. Same story. They're very hot-blooded down there. It was all in the papers."

"The Cypriot was kitchen boy at the club. Champagne, lobster, caviar, it all came from there! Week after week," said the old lady.

"Yes," said Harry.

"We kept it out of the papers, of course," said the old lady loftily.

"You don't want a thing like that in the papers," Harry agreed. "Just sweep up and say nothing, like that time at the Queens when Mr. Armitage . . ."

"We had a reason," said the old lady. "I'll tell you something I never told you before. When Deb came screaming to the door, I didn't tell you—she had a broken bottle in her hand."

"Is that so!" said Harry, very startled.

"It's true. That is what happened. It was Deb that did the fighting, not the Cypriot. It was Deb."

"God Almighty," said Harry. "And she married him after that!"

"She didn't marry him," said the old lady. "I know I said she did, but she didn't. 'I wouldn't marry a man who cheated like that,' she said. She wouldn't speak to him. Or look at him. She wouldn't get a doctor to look after him. He had a terrible cut on his forehead. I had to clean it and bandage it and get him to the hospital and nurse him. She wouldn't go near him. But it wasn't because he'd cheated. Now she knew about him, the secret, she didn't want him. She was a girl like that. It was a pity. He did well for himself. I showed you the postcard of his hotel—it must be one of the biggest in Cannes. When you sit like that with your feet turned out, you remind me of him. He could tell the tale too," she suddenly laughed. "You're the double."

And then the landlady came in with tea and put the tray across the old lady's lap.

"There," she said. "Tea for two, as the saying is. And don't you tire her out, Mr. O'Hara. Another quarter of an hour."

The old lady frowned at the closed door when the landlady went, and listened for her steps going down the stairs.

"I *could* have married him," the old lady said.

"Now, this woman, Harry," she said quickly. "With the horse. She was after you, wasn't she? Why did she make you come up and get that horse down? Why couldn't she ride it down, she rode it up. You're trying to throw dust in my eyes . . ."

"No, it was a fine horse and Irish bred," said Harry, "she bought it off a man who had lost his leg . . ."

The afternoon had darkened. The bird that had been sitting on the tree all day had gone. Harry said goodbye to the old lady. "See you next Thursday," he said.

"And don't be late. Don't let that woman at the Queens keep you. It's your day off," she called as he stood by the open door at the top of the stairs.

He went back along the front, listening to the laughter of the sea in the dark and then into the bar of the Queens Hotel. But because it was his half day off, on the other side of it, as a customer, drinking a small whiskey and listening to what people had to say.

Our Oldest Friend

"LOOK OUT!" someone said. "Here comes Saxon."

It was too late. Moving off the dance floor and pausing at the door with the blatant long sight of the stalker, Saxon saw us all in our quiet corner of the lounge and came over. He stopped and stood with his hands on his hips and his legs apart, like a goalkeeper. Then he came forward.

"Ah! This *is* nice!" he crowed, in the cockerel voice that took us back to the Oxford years. He pulled up a chair and placed it so that none of us could easily get out. It passed through our heads that we had seen that dinner jacket of his before. He must have had it since the last term at school. It was short, eager and juvenile in the sleeves, and now his chest had bolstered it, he seemed to be bursting with buns and toffee. A piece of stiff fair hair stuck up boyishly at the back. He crossed his short legs and squeezed them with satisfaction as his sharp blue eyes looked around our circle over his strong glasses.

"How awfully nice." For niceness was everything for him. "Everyone is here," he said and nodded back to the people on the dance floor. "Jane Fawcett, Sanderson-Brown, Tony Jameson and Eileen—I missed them in Brussels, they'd just left for Munich—very nice catching them here. With the Williamsons!"

He ran off a list of names, looking over one lens of the glasses that were not quite straight on his young enthusiastic nose as he spoke them, and marking each name with a sly look of private knowledge. We were the accused—accused not so much of leaving him out of things, as of thinking, by so doing, that he *was* out of them. His short, trotting legs were infallible in old acquaintance. Names from the past, names that we had forgotten from school and then Oxford, came out, and made our wives look across at us at first with bewilderment and then set them to whispering and giggling.

"What are you doing, Saxon?" someone said. "Are you still on the Commission?"

"In principle, yes; in practice," said Saxon, uttering his favorite words, "I'm the liaison between Ways and Means and the Working Party."

"The liaison!" one of the wives said.

"Yes. It's awfully nice. It works very well. We have to keep in touch with the subcommittees. I saw the Dustman the other day. He's a trustee now, he came in from Arbitration."

"The Dustman?" Mrs. Selby said to her husband.

"Oxford," said Selby. "Lattersmith. Economist. Very old. He was called the Dustman because he was very dirty."

"Tessa's father," Saxon said. And as he shot the name of Tessa at us, he grinned at each one of us in turn to see what could be found in our faces. There are things in the past that become geological. Selby's face became as red as Aberdeen marble; some of us turned to sandstone; one or two to millstone grit or granite; that was how alarm and disclaimer took us.

"Your oldest friend," said Mrs. Selby to her husband, grinding out the phrase.

"In principle, yes, in practice, no," said Selby, bitterly mocking Saxon's well-known phrase.

"My oldest friend, if you please," said Thomas, always a rescuer.

"And mine!" two of us said together, backing him up.

"Is she yours?" said kind Jenny Fox to me.

"She is the 'oldest friend' of all of us."

We laughed together loudly, but not in unity of tone. Hargreaves was too loud, Fox was too frivolous, Selby was frightened and two or three laughs were groans. There was something haphazard, hollow, insincere and unlasting about our laughter, but Day saved us by saying in his deep grave voice to Saxon: "We ought to settle this. Who *is* Tessa's oldest friend? When did *you* meet Tessa, Saxon?"

"Selby and I were at school with her, at Asaph's."

"You didn't tell me that," said Selby's wife to her husband.

"I tried to get her to come tonight," said Saxon. "She's gone out with the Dustman. He said they might drop in later."

Our wives put on stiff faces: one or two picked up their handbags and looked at the door on to the dance floor, as if they were going to search it, and even the building. The incident was one of Saxon's always unanswerable successes but once more Thomas saved us. He said to Saxon, "So *you're* her oldest friend."

And Selby said grimly, "Yes, you were at Asaph's a year before me."

"Saxon! You've been holding out on us," we said with false jollity.

One of the ladies nodded at us and said to her neighbor: "They seem to be a club."

The pious pretense on the part of our wives that they did not know Tessa Lattersmith was, in its way, brilliant in our embarrassed state. It brought out the hypocrisy in Harry James, who said in a light-headed way, "She's married now, I suppose?"

"Oh, no," said Saxon. "She's carrying on." And he meant carrying on, as it were, in the sense of working hard on the joint committee, himself informed because he was, after all, the liaison.

"You mean," said Mrs. Selby, "she hasn't found anyone's husband willing?"

"Shame!" said Saxon as at an annual general meeting. "Shame."

"Perhaps," said the kind young Jenny Fox, "she doesn't want to be married."

"She's very rich," said James.

"Very attractive," said Day.

"Big gobbling eyes."

"Lovely voice."

"I don't agree," said Fox. "It bodes. It comes creeping into you. It gets under your shirt. It seems to come up from the floor. Expensive clothes, though."

"Not like the Dustman's!" shouted Thomas, rescuing us again. "D'you remember? I used to see him at the station waiting for the Oxford train. He used to walk up to the very last bench on the platform, and flop down. I thought he was a tramp kipping down for the night, the first time. His clothes were creased as though he'd slept in them. He had that old suitcase, made of cardboard I should say, tied with string—and parcels of books tied up. Like Herbert Spencer. You know Herbert Spencer had to have everything tied to him? He sat there looking wretched and worn-out, with his mouth open and his thick hair looked full of dust—a real layabout from the British Museum. He hardly got his feet off the ground when he walked, but sort of trudged, as if he was wading through sand. He must be well past seventy."

"No, he's barely sixty. Tessa's only thirty-two."

"Thirty-seven," said Mrs. Selby.

"He's sixty-two," said Saxon. "Tessa is a year younger than me."

"The Lattersmiths were rich," said James again. "I mean compared with the rest of us."

"The Dustman's wife had the money," said Thomas.

"She belonged to one of those big shipping families. Did you ever see her? She's like Tessa—oh, she comes after you with those big solemn eyes."

"We went to see her, didn't we?" Day said to his wife. "She saw Diana's necklace, her eyes were fixed on it . . ."

"And my rings!"

"She just wanted them. Greedy. She couldn't bear it that Diana had something that she hadn't got."

"She wanted you as well," said Diana.

"Oh," said Tom, the rescuer. "There's nothing in that. Old Ma Dustman wanted me too, in fact she wanted all of us. 'I am so worried about Tessa, I wish she'd settle down. I wish she'd find a nice husband—now *you,* you're fond of Tessa, I'm sure.' "

"Shame!" called Saxon again.

We had forgotten about him; he was sweating as he watched us with delight.

"No, it's true," I said to Saxon.

"And she couldn't have them, poor things," one of the wives said and the others joined in laughing at us.

James once more pushed us into trouble.

"Did you ever go on a picnic with them? I mean when they came down to school? No? Saxon, didn't you and Selby? Didn't you? None of your camp fires with damp sticks, thermos bottles and tea slopping over the tomato sandwiches. Oh, no! And it never rained: old Ma Dustman had ordered sun down from Fortnum and Mason's. They brought the Daimler and the butler came—how did they fit him in, I wonder? I bet he went ahead in the Rolls. He set tables and chairs. Silver teapot, the best Rockingham . . ."

"Not Rockingham, it can't have been."

"Well, old Spode. Something posh. The butler handed round the stuff. I only just knew Tessa then. I had brought a girl called Sadie and Tessa brought a girl called Adelaide with her and Tessa said, 'I want you to meet Harry James. He's my oldest friend.' Sadie looked sick."

"It had started then?" some of our wives cried out.

"Long before that," I said. "In the cradle."

"Exactly what she said just before we were married when you introduced me," said Mrs. Day to her husband.

"She said it to me at our wedding," said Mrs. Selby, and glaring at her husband, "I don't know *why*."

"I don't get what her fascination for you all was!" said sly Mrs. James.

"Oh," we all said largely, in a variety of voices, "I don't know . . . She was about . . ."

"You know, I think it was sex," said Jenny Fox.

"Was it sex?" we looked at each other, putting as much impartiality as we could into the inquiry.

"Sex! Of course it was sex," said Mrs. Selby, putting her chin up and gripping her handbag on her knee.

"Not for me," said Harry James.

"Nor me." One wife squeezed her husband's hand.

"Why not?"

This dumbfounded us. We huddled together. Why had none of us made a pass? Were we frightened?

"You took her to picture galleries," said Mrs. Selby.

"Yes," said Selby. "She did nothing but talk about a man called Cézanne."

"That's it. A whole party of us went to Parma and she did nothing but talk of a man called Fabrice," said Tom.

"Fabrice?"

"Stendhal," said Saxon.

"I had Lawrence in Rome."

"There was always another man. Anyone have Picasso? Or Giacometti?" said James.

"Who did you have, Selby? Russell? Einstein?"

Selby had had enough. With the treachery of the desperate, he said, "She talked of nothing but you, James."

"No," said Tom the rescuer. "You can't have had. *I* had you, James."

"I had Tom."

"Day was my trouble."

"With me it was Bill."

"What a lovely daisy chain," one of the wives said. "The whole distinguished lot of you. Who's missing?"

"Saxon," Jenny Fox said.

We all stared accusingly at him. Saxon went on squeezing himself. He looked archly over his glasses.

"I had the Dustman," he said complacently.

We laughed but Mrs. Selby silenced us and said to Saxon, "Go on. You're the only one who's telling the truth."

"She was always very worried about the Dustman," he said. "They're a wretched family. He scarcely ever goes home."

And at this, the band started again and Saxon got up and asked my wife to dance. We were left with Saxon's picture of that rich girl alone in the world. Before the evening was out he had danced with each one of our wives. We all grinned and said, "Look at old Saxon at the end of term dance."

If there was one non-dancer on the floor it was he. His feet, rather like the Dustman's, trudged, in straight, fated lines, deep in sand, enthusiastically deep. He danced, as it were, in committee. Our wives found themselves in the grip of one who pushed them around, all the time looking askance from side to side as if they were sections or subsections for which he was trying to find a place in some majority report. They lost their power to dance. The matter had become desperately topographical to them; while he, as he toiled on, was running off the names of people.

"I saw him in Paris on the second day of the conference." Or:

"They were in New York when Foreign Relations met the working party."

Or:

"They ran into one another in Piccadilly when the delegation met the trustees. Thompson, Johnson, Hobson, Timson, Richardson, Wilkinson—" Our wives returned to us like new editions of *Who's Who.*

Except Mrs. Selby. She was much taller than he and on the floor she had the prosecuting look of one who was going to wring what she wanted out of Saxon. She did not look down at him but over his head at the piece of fair hair that stuck up at the back of his head. He soon had to give up his committee style. She got a grip of him, got him into corners, carried him off to the middle, turned savagely near the band, and in this spot she shouted to him, "What's all this stuff about Tessa and the Dustman?"

And as she said it, seeing him turn to the right, she swung him round to the left, and when the dancers were thinning on the floor she planted him in a quiet spot in the middle.

"Tessa's slept with all of you, hasn't she?" she said.

"Shame!" Saxon said, stopping dead. He took off his glasses and there was a sudden change in him. Often since, seeing that naked look on his face, I have thought: How he must have hated us. I remember at school how we stuffed sausage down his neck and how he just let us do it. Sausage after sausage went down. Then off came the glasses and he backed to an open window. Now, on the dance floor, with his glasses off, Saxon suddenly began to dance—if that is the word for it—as if he had been stung. Where had he learned these extraordinary steps?—that sudden flinging wide of his short legs and arms, that strange buckling and straightening of the body, the thrusting forward and back of his punchball head, those sudden wrenchings of Mrs. Selby back and forth, and spinning her round, that general air of looking for a knockout on the rebound off the ropes. Mrs. Selby's firm eyes were disordered as she tried to foresee his movements, and amid the disorder she was magnetized by the fiendish rhythm of his feet and by the austere look of his unforgiving face.

"Hasn't she?" called Mrs. Selby, in a last pitiable attempt.

The band stopped and she stood there getting her breath in the middle of the floor. Saxon, without music, dropped back into the goalkeeper stance we knew so well, with his hands on his hips and short legs apart. She was staring at Saxon, he was staring at her. It was a long stare. Selby and his partner passed them and he saw what Mrs. Selby saw: obstinate tears were forming in Saxon's naked eyes; water filled them; it dropped on his pink cheeks. He took out his glasses and pretended to wipe them with his handkerchief and put them on. He was sternly, silently, crying. Mrs. Selby put out her hand repentantly; no doubt he did not see her hand but walked with her off the floor. We were clapping in the silly way people do and someone called out: "Where did you learn that one, Saxon?"

He looked with bewilderment at us.

"I'll be back in a minute," he said and walked across the room to the outer hall of the hotel.

Mrs. Selby put herself with kind Jenny Fox and whispered to her for a long time and Mrs. Fox said, "It's not your fault. How could you know?"

"I only *said* it," Mrs. Selby said wretchedly, looking at the swing door that let cold air in from the outer hall when it flashed round and where Saxon had gone.

"What was the matter with Saxon?" Selby accused.

"He's upset—nothing," said Mrs. Fox, turning to Selby as she patted Mrs. Selby's hand. And then, arguing for herself, Mrs. Selby told us.

Presently the swing door flashed and Saxon came back and three of us got up to offer him a chair. We gave him the best one, beside a low table which had a brilliant lamp on it. Instantly it threw his shadow on the white wall—a shadow that caricatured his face—the long nose, the chin that receded, the glasses tilted as he looked askance at us, the sprig of schoolboy hair.

"They haven't turned up yet," he said.

We looked at our Saxon with awe. It was obvious he was in love with that rich, beautiful woman. He must always have been in love with her. We had pulled her to pieces in front of him. What he must have been feeling as he pretended and as he submitted to our joke! And, after all this, she had not come. Where was she? One or two of us wanted to get up and find her. Where would she be? We could not guess. We had to admit that Tessa merely slummed with us. She would never think of coming to a second-rate hotel like this or to an old Asaphians' reunion. She'd be at some smart dinner party, something very grand—she certainly had "oldest friends" in very grand circles. One could imagine her long neck creeping up close to the conscience of an archbishop. Or disturbing the shirt of an ambassador, or her boding voice creeping up the sleeve of a banker who would be saying: "Young lady, what are all your hippie friends up to nowadays?" at one of old Ma Dustman's dinner parties. *She* would be stripping the jewelry off the women and telling Sir Somebody Something that one would be a fool to sell one's Matisses yet. The Dustman would not be there. We tried not to look at the unmarriageable silhouette of Saxon's head on the wall.

"Where did you pick up that wonderful step, Saxon?" Mrs. Selby said gaily, to make amends.

Saxon gave a forgiving glance. He had recovered.

"At the Cool It," he said.

"What's the Cool It?" Thomas said.

"A club," said Saxon.

"Never heard of it."

"In the docks," said Saxon.

"The docks?"

Saxon in the docks! The liaison committees in the docks! Saxon in low life! Saxon a libertine!

"What on earth takes you to the docks? Research? Come clean. Having fun?"

In our repentance, we made a hero of him. The old sly Saxon, pleased and pink, was with us again.

"In principle, yes," said Saxon. "I sometimes go with the Dustman."

We could not speak. Saxon and the Dustman in the docks!

"What is it—a cellar?"

"It's a sewer," said Saxon complacently. "Tessa goes there with her father."

"The Dustman takes his daughter to a place like that!"

"He says it will loosen her up," said Saxon, looking for hope in our eyes. "You see, he wants her to get married."

Saxon settled back, impudently, comfortably, in the chair. The brocade enriched him and he maliciously considered us one by one.

"To a stoker?" said Selby.

"No," said Saxon. "To me—in principle. That's why I go down there. You see, she's worried about him. We go down to see he doesn't get into trouble. I had to pull him out of a nasty fight last week. We got him out. We got him home. To her place. He hates going to his."

The notion of Saxon fighting was as startling as his dance.

"She must be very grateful to you," we said politely.

"Why do you say 'marry you, in principle'?" said Selby.

"He means," Mrs. Selby explained sharply to her husband, disliking the mockery, "the Dustman is her oldest friend, older even than Saxon is. Isn't that so, Saxon?"

"In practice, yes," said Saxon, entirely forgiving her.

"I'll go and have another look for them. They promised to come. The Dustman said it would be awfully nice to see us all again. I'll just go and see."

And he got up and trotted across the yards of hotel carpet that had a pattern of enormous roses. It seemed that their petals were caressing him on his way to the door. The door spun round and Saxon vanished.

Our wives said, "What a sad story!" and "What a bitch that girl is." But we thought: Good old Saxon. And: He's suffering for us. Selby put it crudely, saying, "That lets us off the hooks." And then our feelings changed. There was Saxon sitting like a committee on his own feelings, delegating them incurably to subcommittees, and sitting back doing nothing, relying on an amendment. He must have been doing this for the last eight years. But this led us to another feeling. *We* would never have behaved as Saxon behaved. Each of us saw that beautiful girl in our minds and thought we would have soon pulled her out of this ridiculous obsession with the Dustman and his low life. And how often we had heard of coquettes like Tessa settling down at last in their thirties with faithful bores like Saxon, men they had snubbed over and over again before that alarming age caught them out.

We kept our eyes on the main door of the hotel and were so fixed on it that we did not notice, at once, a figure crossing the dance floor at our side and looking in at us.

"Well!" we heard Tessa's slow, only too well-known voice, dwelling raffishly on the word, so that it meant "What are you up to? You didn't think you could keep me out of this." Her large solemn eyes as forcefully shortsighted as Saxon's were, put their warning innuendo to each of us in turn and the mouth of a beautiful Persian cat possessed us one by one. The spell was on us. A comfortable mew to each of our wives indicated that she had known us years before they had.

We were nearly screaming for help. It was for Thomas, the rescuer, to save us.

"Saxon has just gone out looking for your father."

She was up from her chair at once and making for the main door. She had fine legs, a fast passionate step, and Mrs. Selby said of her dress:

"It's expensive, but pink is hopeless if you're putting on weight."

But Selby, overeager for any hope that could be got out of the situation, said, "Did you see her when she came in? It was exactly like Saxon. Hunting. You know—in principle, yes, but in practice—well. She's a liaison too. I think the Dustman's loosened her up and found the man for her."

But no one paid much attention to Selby, for the swing door flashed and across the hall came the Dustman, Saxon and Tessa together.

"Look, Daddy," she said to the old man. He had not, of course, changed into a dinner jacket and his tweed jacket was done up on the wrong button. His trudging step, I now thought, was not so much a trudge as a scraping caused by the probability that he was swinging by an invisible rope hooked to the seat of his learned trousers.

"Look," she said, "all my oldest friends!"

And Saxon stood apart with his hands on his hips, watching, his legs apart, keeping goal, wistful, admiring, triumphant.

"Who's dancing?" piped the old man. And soon all of us were on the floor, the Dustman shoving Mrs. Selby along as if to her doom, and Tessa following him with her eyes all the time, as Saxon leaped into his passionate, dreadful and unavailing antics all round her. Once in a while she would note where he was, open her mouth to say something pleasant, and then coldly change her mind.

The Honeymoon

THE CEREMONY was over. We were married. The registrar who had done seventeen weddings that morning and who stood at a table between two vases of chrysanthemums, said, "It is the custom, if the parties so desire, to embrace."

Victoria, who was very small and hated anyone telling her to do anything, tipped her head back to avoid being kissed but I bent down and gave her two pecks on the brim of her hat and one, at last, on her cheek. Surprised, she kissed me. Mistrustful of our Town Hall my mother-in-law said, "They have wallpaper on the walls in these places."

We signed and then Victoria and I went out first down the long corridor and since I felt I was walking three inches above the floor I was puzzled by the marble echoes raised by my shoes. A photographer walked backwards before us. Outside, our party stood in two rows on the steps and we were photographed again, Harry—the best man—standing at the back. On the door of a warehouse across the street I saw a notice saying, DO NOT OBSTRUCT THIS ENTRANCE.

Then we drove off to my mother-in-law's house and I don't remember much more about it all, except a rather sudden unimportance, and Harry saying, when we got to the wedding-cake stage, "When she cuts, clap." The photographs were rushed round in the afternoon and it is all a blank until we went off to the station to catch the London train. There Harry did something I would never have thought him capable of; it was the sort of thing he detested: he led the confetti-throwing. It snowed on us. He flung it, in contempt, I suppose. He tried to stuff some down my neck. It was very dry and thick. He went mad, is all I can say. Something broke in me too. My teeth were wet. I suddenly hated Harry; it was a hatred stored up for two years; I went for him with my umbrella, chasing him back from the gate into the house. I think I would have half-killed him or, at any rate, made him bleed, if my father had not dragged me back to the car. As we drove off, I opened the car window and shouted, "My umbrella! My umbrella!" They had taken it from me and I could see my father propping it carefully against some shrubbery.

"The swine!" I said, brushing off the confetti and then I looked at Victoria's face and stopped. My wife, I thought. I couldn't believe it; she looked so sweet and tender as a kitten; she was pouting and blushing and when I put my arm round her waist I could feel the layers of silk moving over her soft body. How heavenly women are! For two years she had held out against marrying me; but now, in a mere three hours, she had softened and changed into mine.

When I look back on it I see the idea that I should marry Victoria was not mine alone. All her relations and friends wanted me to marry her. Harry wanted it most of all and everyone agreed with Harry that he should *not* marry her. The opposition came from Victoria. Harry was the man she wanted and Harry wanted only himself. He loved his own rich black hair, his own fawn complexion, his own romantic lips, his satanic side-glances, his clothes. He was a dandy and more than that. He loved himself as he was, as he would be and even as he had been in history. We worked in a big shoeshop in the town and when there were no customers and we had nothing to do, he used to make drawings of himself as Sir Walter Raleigh, in India ink, on old shoeboxes.

One day he said to me, eying me sideways and stroking his chin, as if he had a pointed beard on it: "One of my ancestors was executed. He was a conspirator."

* * *

At the end of my first day, when I was taken on at the shop, Harry said to me: "I've got my motor bike at the back. Let's go somewhere. I'll take you home." Victoria who worked in the cash desk must have heard him, but I didn't realize the mistake I was making.

"I believe in being in the crowd but not *of* the crowd," Harry called back to me, as I sat behind him.

The next day I saw that Victoria hated me. Harry usually took *her* home. This slight made her snap and raise her very small nose sharply, so that I got to know her nose very well, especially the tiny nostrils. It was a dogmatic, sad little nose and that is where I began to fall in love with her—from the nose downwards. But after I had gone out once or twice more with Harry, Victoria's mind was made up. She did all she could to get me the sack. She made trouble between me and the manager by making mistakes on the bills and telling me, in front of customers, that I had got prices wrong. One day a woman came in and said I had sent her one crocodile and one lizard shoe: Victoria had changed the shoes. These tricks made me laugh and when I laughed she was astonished and all the more determined. Girls always go too far. The manager was no fool. One afternoon she saw the foot of the stepladder, which was used to get the shoes from the upper shelves, sticking out beyond the corner of the stockroom door. She gave it a push—she was very small but she was very strong—thinking I was up there getting a pair of eight and a half brogues for a man who had come in with fishing rods. But it was Harry who was on the ladder. Down he fell and a whole pile of boxes with him.

"And what is all this?" the manager said, pointing to one of Harry's drawings of Sir Walter Raleigh.

"My ancestor," said Harry scornfully.

It was he who was sacked. He was very pleased.

"She's a nice girl but I can't bear her. She once threw bread at me at a dance," Harry said. "I shall go to London."

And so Victoria and I were left dumbfounded together. This changed her. She stopped quarreling with me. I walked home with her several times. I enjoyed the clatter her heels made on the pavement, the way she drove her mother out of the room, the way she spoke to dogs. I stroked her neck in the park and this made her arch her back with pleasure. She sat on my knee in my lodgings, holding me tight enough to strangle me—and started telling me how much she loved Harry, ever since school, for years.

"Harry," I said. "You mean Sir Walter Raleigh." She stiffened.

"He has proofs," she said. "I couldn't love you."

This is where her friends came in and her mother.

"Don't worry," they said. "It's all silliness. She's difficult. Be patient. Be gentle."

But Harry was in London, far away. He came back once for Easter. The three of us went to a café.

"London," said Harry, looking darkly at me, "is the most dangerous city in the world. You have to know your way about. But one can be in the crowd and yet not of it."

It was a favorite sentence of his.

"Stop saying 'one' as if you were a dummy," Victoria said. Harry looked sideways at himself in the café mirror, raised an elaborate eyebrow and smiled at himself.

Victoria picked up the remains of her ice cream and intended to throw it all at the mirror so that (she said afterwards) he could not see himself; it hit the glass but splashed over his gray suit. Later, he said to me, sarcastically, "I congratulate you. Victoria is getting over that nonsense about me. She used to throw bread before."

He was wrong. Victoria had not changed. In the next two months I lost twenty pounds in weight and had pains in the back. The manager asked me to his house to supper and his wife told my fortune. A whole hand of spades came out and I dropped the Queen on the carpet.

"You're surrounded by enemies," she said.

This was not true. I had too many friends. Within the week I got a letter from Harry telling me of a job in London at nearly twice the salary.

I was getting tired of Harry, Harry, Harry from Victoria with her arms round my neck and when I heard the news I saw the truth. I had never been in love with her. I even loved the shoe trade better than I loved her, being on my own, away from my parents, too. I got sly. I told Victoria I was leaving the town for good and going to London, that no doubt I should see Harry and I would make him realize what a wonderful girl she was. I was enthusiastic about this.

Victoria's reply exploded inside me: "When do you go? At the end of the month?" she asked. "We'll get married next week. We'll go to London for our honeymoon, that will save money."

I could not believe it. I went to London to fix up the job. She made me promise to come back, the same day. When I returned, tired out on the train that did not get in until eleven at night, Victoria was on the platform waiting for me. She rushed at me. She even grabbed me.

"I was worried to death. I'll never let you out of my sight again," she said.

I was appalled.

"I've found an hotel for us," I said.

"So have I," she said. "Isn't it wonderful?"

"Harry told me," I said.

"Harry told me too," she said. "I telephoned to him." Harry was making sure. It was he who got us married.

* * *

So there we were, married, sitting in the train going to London. I shall not forget the journey—four hours: it seemed like a fortnight. Fields, fields, people picking mushrooms, factories, telegraph poles, fields again, towns, gardens, junctions. We had a compartment to ourselves. I pulled the blinds on the corridor side after the ticket inspector had been and then I moved to kiss Victoria. She had changed into a tweed suit and she stiffened. The pout had gone from her lips. Her nose was raised.

"You haven't labeled your case," she said, looking up at the luggage rack.

"I did it this morning when you reminded me," I said, putting my arm round her.

"I can't see it," she said.

I laughed. "It's at the back," I said. And I turned the case round to show her the label hanging down.

She still did not believe me.

"Look," I said. She was small enough to lift onto the seat and I lifted her to see the label.

"It's what I thought," she accused. "You've put on the wrong label."

"I haven't," I said. I read out, "The Austin Hotel, Barnaby Street."

"We're staying at Frenns," she said. And she showed me the label on hers.

"You have made a mistake," I said. "Harry told me—the Austin."

"Frenns, he said. You know he did," she said.

"I beg your pardon, it was the Austin."

Austin, Frenns, Frenns, Austin—so we went on. She got angry.

"Mother said you were obstinate," she said.

The train slowed down beside a goods train carrying calves, which were lowing.

"Those poor things. Prisoners!" cried Victoria. "Look at them."

She turned on me accusingly. "Our honeymoon and you don't know where we're going."

"The Austin Hotel," I said. "Here's the letter confirming our reservations."

I showed her the letter. The Austin Hotel was printed at the top of the paper. Victoria was a suspicious girl. She took the paper and read it carefully from the very top edge to the bottom, twice. And then turned it over in case something was written on the other side.

"You see," I said.

"You did this behind my back," she said.

"I'll alter your labels," I said, getting out my pen.

"Don't touch them," she said, taking my pen from me. "After what he's done to me, do you think I would go to a place Harry suggested?"

"He suggested both."

"One to me, one to you," she said.

"I know why his ancestor was executed," I said. "Still he was only giving us a choice."

"A choice," she said. "You think it's funny, don't you? What choice has anyone got?"

I glanced out of the window. "A pheasant. Quick. Look," I called to her.

She turned her head. "Two," she said and sat gloomily looking at her hands in her lap. Once more I put my arm round her. "Nature is a trap," she said, moving away from me. "Leave me alone."

She closed her eyes. She could not get comfortable. Crossly she put her head on my shoulder. Suddenly a red-faced young soldier who was shouting to several others, slid our door back, gave us a look, winked at me and made a lewd noise, "Clop, clop," with his tongue and went off shouting to his friends.

"Don't touch me, I said," said Victoria.

"What is the matter?" I asked.

"Oh, stop asking me what is the matter. You whine. Talk to me. Don't ask me questions."

The soldiers were bullocking about down the corridor. Of course, when Victoria said "Talk to me," that put every idea out of my head. She was silent most of the way to London. What was on her mind? I knew what was on mine.

Villas began to thicken. The train shrieked at thousands of them. I saw a bus with the name Victoria on it. I nudged her in my excitement. She did not look. We went into tunnels and London flung smoke at us.

"We are nearly there!" I shouted with excitement.

She did not speak. She said nothing when we got out of the train at the station but it was she who said sharply to the cab driver before I could open my mouth: "The Austin Hotel."

"Where's that, miss?" said the cab driver.

"Barnaby Street," I called, over her head.

London seemed to smell of cold escaping gas and the houses looked like hundreds of dirty sparrows and the sky like a rag as we drove to the hotel.

There must have been a dozen little brown houses converted into hotels in the street where the Austin was—Linden, Stella Maris, Northern, Fitzroy, Malvern, I noticed the names. They looked friendly all together; one had blue and yellow lights round its windows; ours was next door, the brickwork painted green from the basement to the first floor. The Austin, it said. Private Hotel. Private—how nice! Victoria had said it made her sick when the manager at the shoeshop had told us that he and his wife had the bridal suite at the largest hotel in Ventnor thirty years ago.

"Did you pay the taxi driver enough? I don't like the way he's looking at us," Victoria said to me, when the driver had put our luggage out.

"He's looking at the hotel," I said.

An Irish maid came up from the basement to the door, eating something, and said, "Sign here" and "Up to the top to Number Twelve," and hearing a whistle from below, she said, "Wait till I put me bloody kettle off."

We went upstairs. It was a tidy, well-polished place, nicely painted, with a fern in a brass pot on every landing. It was wonderfully private and quiet. A girl in a dressing gown and with a comb in her hand looked out of a door on the second floor and gaped at Victoria and me.

"I thought it was Gladys, sorry," she said. Friendly people. And we heard the Irish maid say to her, as she came up at last: "It's the honeymoon couple."

My heart was banging and I felt hungry; there was a smell of steak pudding coming up the stairs, but at the top landing it had gone. The maid pushed open the door. The room had a double bed with a pretty pink cover and there was a fancy kind of net curtain at the window, with rabbits and daffodils on it.

"Ah, look at me, leaving that this morning," said the Irish girl, taking away the floor mop she had left beside the dressing table.

I waited for the door to close and then I stepped out to kiss Victoria, saying, "It's clean. It's at the front."

"We must unpack," she said, stepping back.

My father's words came back to me. "It may sound a funny thing to say but when your mother and I were first married, I was taking my shoes off, I'd never been in an hotel with your mother before . . ." well, that is what I felt like when Victoria said she must unpack. I had never seen her unpack. I'd never seen any woman unpack.

First she went all round the room to every corner and

cupboard in it, like a cat. And opened all the drawers. She unlocked her cases and out came her dresses. She spread them on the bed and straightened them, one by one. Out came the new brushes her aunt had given her. Then things for her dressing table. Then she started hanging dresses and going back to give them a pull or to change the coat hanger. Every time she walked across the room (and it must have been a hundred times), the windows shook. I had put a brown suit and a tweed jacket on a chair.

"If you're not wearing those, hang them. They'll get out of shape," she said.

I did not know where to hang them, so I hung them over the door of a cupboard.

"They don't leave you much room," she said. "What have you done with your shoes? Look what you're doing! Sweep it up."

I had taken off my jacket and one more shower of Harry's confetti went onto the floor.

"What with?" I said and went to look out of the window. An oldish man and a young woman were getting out of a taxi and came into our hotel: father and daughter, I thought. The evening was beginning and the neon lights from the Court Hotel opposite began to turn one of our walls red and made Victoria look as if she were blushing. She had finished unpacking.

"You leave your things everywhere," she said. "I am going to wash." She took off her jacket and her blouse and went to the basin. I was suddenly frightened of her, or perhaps it was of the hooks of her brassiere.

"And then we'll go and look at London," I said, exhausted, and sat on the edge of the bed. The next thing, she was asking me for her brown shoes and as I went to look for them she went to the cupboard, stepped out of her skirt and was halfway into a new dress when I looked round.

Suddenly she pulled it off and rushed to the basin.

"Go away. Quickly. I feel sick," she said.

"I'll open the window," I said. "It's stuffy in here."

She wasn't sick. I helped her to the bed.

"Go out. Go for a walk," she said.

"No," I said. "We'll go out together. We'll have a bit of air and a drink. You'll feel better."

"No," she said.

I waited. Outside the taxis were passing.

"How do you feel now?" I asked.

"Oh, do stop asking me how I feel. All right. Let us go out."

So we went out. When we got downstairs we met the landlady. She had very large blue eyes and bleached hair.

"Comfortable, dear?" she said as she went coldly and rapidly over everything Victoria had got on.

"Going to take some air," I said.

"Nothing like it," said the landlady.

Victoria must have been studying her, for when she got outside she said, "She's been drinking."

"She looked like a sofa standing up on end," I said.

Victoria did not laugh.

"Perhaps," I said, "she'd lost a caster."

Victoria did not smile.

Where we went I could not tell you. London looked heavy. There was nothing but streets of closed shops. I read out the names of them. We passed restaurants. We went to a pub but Victoria would not drink anything.

"Aren't you going to eat?" she said.

"They don't serve food here," I said.

"Oh! Then why did we come here?"

Of course, as Harry said, you've got to know London. He could have told us where to eat. I ought to have asked him.

"There's a place," she said, pointing to a lit-up cafeteria.

And on our way to it, she heard a cat miaow and we stopped in an office doorway while she stroked it. It tried to follow us.

"Go back," she said. "Go back. It will get run over. Please!" Victoria was almost in tears and we stood there coaxing the cat. Its fur was gritty. I tried to grab it and it jumped from me and raced clean across the street.

Victoria gave a shriek. Fortunately it got across safely and went into a doorway opposite and stared at us.

"Suppose it tries to get back," she said. Her nails were digging into my arm where she was holding it. Well, in the end, I had a poached egg at the cafeteria. Victoria would not touch hers. And we went back to the Austin. My heart was hammering. A radio was playing on the second floor. I went to the bathroom. When I got back to our room the light was off. I thought Victoria must be in bed, but she was not. The window was wide open and the curtain blowing far into the room. She had gone. And then I saw her. She was sitting in her nightgown at the window with both legs over the sill. I rushed over to her.

"I can't, I can't!" she cried as I caught her. I had quite a fight getting her in.

"I don't love you," she said. "I never loved you. It is Harry. I'm sorry, I'm sorry. But I can't."

She cried and she clung. "I thought I could, but I can't."

It was just like our early days but now Harry was cut off from her by our marriage.

I could not believe what I heard. I wanted her more than I can say, for her grief and tears, the ugliness of it, and the anger I felt, made her more desirable.

"I never wanted to marry you. They made me. You forced me into it."

The little twister, I thought.

"It's a pity Harry isn't here," I said bitterly.

"That's a dirty remark," she said fiercely and she stopped crying.

Well, I thought, I have heard of this happening to people but fancy it happening to me. I saw years of empty life ahead of me.

Suddenly she said, "I wonder whether that poor cat was locked out?" and we started talking about cats, her mother's cats, the cats that stalked one another on the garden walls at the back of her mother's house. She became calm.

"You are so understanding," she said. "I have done something terrible to you. That is what is so unfair."

"Get into bed. I'll go and sit over there," I said. "You'll catch cold."

She obeyed. Exhausted, I went and sat in the chair by the window.

It was a narrow, gray armchair of the furry kind and the fur pricked through my trousers and my sleeves. Do you know what she did, within five minutes? She fell asleep. The wedding night! I could hear the whistling noise from her open mouth. There was her whistle, the whipping of the cars going by, the ticking of taxis outside, the hotels, the voices of the drunks after the pubs had closed. It had seemed a quiet street and a quiet hotel, but now bedroom doors were banging, lavatories and basins were flushed, pipes jumped. Even at two in the morning people were coming in. On our floor you could hear boots coming off, throats being cleared, the high laugh of a woman once or twice and heavy bumps on mattresses as if enormous bodies, too big for the beds, had flopped on them.

I thought: I will wait. She didn't mean it, and took off my collar and tie and loosened my shoes. I was tired out. I must have dozed off. I was dreaming we were in the train and that suddenly I was being sucked out of the window by an overpowering voice that said, "I am Sir Walter Raleigh." And in a second I was fighting for my life with the manageress of the hotel who was naked and covered with grease. I woke up in terror. And then I heard shouts coming from the street. Screams were coming from the stairs of the hotel. I looked out of the window and down below in the street I saw police. They were pushing two or three women into a van. Then I saw a policeman ushering out the manageress of our hotel. She was calling back, I suppose, to the Irish maid: "Ring my solicitor. Phone him up."

Suddenly the door of our room was opened. I turned and a policeman stood there.

"Come on. Out of this," he said, ignoring me and giving the bed a shake.

"Here!" I shouted.

Victoria woke up and shouted, "Harry!"

"You keep out of this, Harry," said the policeman to me.

"What do you want? This is my wife."

"Come on, miss," said the policeman to Victoria. The cab driver had called her "miss" too.

The voice of the Irish maid came up the stairs. "It's the honeymoon couple." She got to the room. "It's the honeymoon couple," she said.

The policeman looked around the room, at my brown suit and the extra jacket hanging on the cupboard. Then he saw the confetti on the floor.

"Here's our reservation," I said, pushing the letter at him. "What's this all about? What do you mean by breaking in?"

The policeman went out to the passage.

"Here, who's this?" he called down the stairs. Someone answered and he came back. He looked at me contemptuously. "You ought to know better than to bring your wife to a place like this. Take my tip and clear out by the morning unless you want trouble."

"How dare you? My husband is the assistant manager at Walgrave's," shouted Victoria and got out of bed to fly at him, in her nightdress.

"Ma'am!" said the policeman, averting his face, "please go back to bed." And he hurried from the room.

"Why," cried Victoria to me, "did you let him insult me? Why didn't you hit him? Get dressed. I'm going to ring up the police."

"That was the police," I said.

"I'm not blind," she shouted.

"Funny places for Harry to know about," I said. "Come and look."

They were just closing the door of the police van as we looked out of the window. Then we saw people looking out of windows opposite. They were not looking at the police van. They were looking at us. We both drew our heads in and pulled the curtains across.

"This was your hotel, not Harry's," she said. "You stayed here."

"I've never stayed in London in my life," I said.

"Harry said Frenns."

Frenns, Austin, Austin, Frenns—we were off again.

"Harry told us both of them," I said. "There must be something wrong with Harry."

"What?" she defied.

"He is in the world but not of it."

She went to the chest of drawers and began taking her clothes out. "I'm going now," she said.

"Where, at three in the morning?"

"I'm going. Get my dresses. Don't drag them on the floor. Look what you've done."

She dressed. We packed everything up. We carried our

luggage downstairs. The bedroom doors were open. In the manageress's office a policeman was sitting with the Irish maid. They looked at us in silence, but afterwards I heard them laughing, the maid was peeping through the curtains as we got into the street.

We walked. I was lugging the cases and Victoria had one of hers. My arms ached as we trudged. There was no one about. We did not know where we were going.

"I wish we had Harry here," I said. "He could carry one of these. Wait."

I put the cases down and changed loads.

"And he knows, London," I said. "Come on."

"Where are we going?" Victoria said weakly.

"Where did that cat live?" I said.

We passed a small open square with a seat in it.

"This will do," I said.

"We can't stay out," she said.

At last I saw a taxi coming slowly towards us like a housefly along the black, glossy street. I hailed him. I told him to go to the station we had arrived at.

"I'll put you back on the morning train," I said. "You can have a sleep at the Station Hotel. I need a sleep myself. I'll get a couple of rooms."

And that is what we would have done but when we got there I didn't like to ask for two singles: it didn't seem respectable and I didn't like the look the nightclerk gave us. We were too tired to undress but slept in our clothes until midday the following day, Sunday.

They do a lot of shunting at these main-line stations on Sundays; the night mail comes in, the sleepers go out to the siding. As for us we got rid of Harry for good.

The Chain-Smoker

THE IMPORTANT thing was to stop Magnolia going to Venice. "That I won't have," Karvo said. "Where is Chatty? Never here when he is wanted. Drunk, I suppose. Or in bed. I bet he's at his aunt's. Get him."

At that very moment Chatterton came into the office, opening the door only about a foot and sliding in.

"Chatty!" Karvo made a sound like a wounded bull, indeed almost wept. "You've heard the news?" Karvo waved the others out of the office and Chatty sat down on the sofa opposite Karvo's enormous desk; or, rather, he folded up there like a small piece of human trellis that smoked, squeaked and coughed. He was an illness in itself.

"Yes," Chatty said. "She has heard the doctor has stopped you flying. She's heard you and Maureen are picking up the train in Paris. She rang me half an hour ago."

"Chatty, you've got to stop her. I won't have that woman in Venice," Karvo said. "You've got to keep her in London. I tried to get you last night. Where were you?"

"I was with her," said Chatty. "At the Spangle."

"I'm very grateful to you," said Karvo, calming down.

Chatty swallowed a couple of pills off the palm of his hand. "The fog got into my chest," he said. "She's still going to Court. But she doesn't know whether she will shoot you or commit suicide. What she wants to do is to commit suicide first, then shoot you and then sue the company for breach of contract. Somewhere along the line she has got to fit in a scene at some place like the Caprice in which she tears Maureen's dress off her back. She would like to see blood—not pools of it, but visible nail-stripes on Maureen's face, anywhere it will show—say, on the upper part of the back. She doesn't know whether it would be better to do this in the restaurant—I told her it had been done too often in restaurants—or in Court, but I pointed out that Maureen was not a material witness and would not be there."

Karvo paid no attention. He was looking at the script on his desk, but glancing up said considerately: "Chatty, are you all right? I can hear your chest from here. You're not going to crack up again?"

"I've been up half the night three nights running. She never wants to go to bed."

"I didn't have *that* trouble with her," Karvo grunted boastfully, looking at the script again.

"I made a mistake about Magnolia," Karvo went on. "I thought she would lift the whole story. She has the finest pair of arms I've ever seen in pictures, but she can't move them except up and down slowly like a cop holding up traffic. She can't move anything. You saw her. I thought she was Life. She's as dead as the Venus de Milo."

"It has no arms," said Chatty. "Magnolia *is* life. I told her so last night. I said, 'Magnolia, you're Life . . .' "

"You said that to her?" said Karvo suspiciously.

"Yes. She said you said she was Life. I said 'He was right. You're Life itself.' Actually, larger."

"It's no good in pictures," Karvo said.

"It's terrible out of pictures," Chatty said. "Awful in the evenings."

"You've got to stop her. I don't care how," Karvo said, shouting again.

"I know," said Chatty. "I'm having lunch with her." And he got up and used one of the telephones on Karvo's desk. "No. I know the time of the train, sweetie," he said in the murdered voice of the sick. "Bring me the Continental timetable in your own little loving hands."

"Why do you want that?" said Karvo, suspicious again.

"I was brought up on it; it's the only book I can read now without having a heart attack," said Chatty. The girl brought the book into the office and Chatty's face broke into dozens of small smiling lines, like a cracked plate, and he did two or three more coughs. The girl looked protectively at him.

"What I dream of is a beautiful sanatorium with you looking after me," he said to the girl, who said, "Oh, Mr. Chatterton, no."

Karvo shook his head.

"You ought to stop smoking, Chatty."

"I appeal to the mother in them," said Chatterton. "If I stopped coughing I'd be useless to the firm. I'll try and get Magnolia down to the farm, Tony."

"That's a good idea," said Karvo generously. "It will do you good. You need pure air."

"I'm working on the idea that her ancestors traveled in cattle trucks. I doubt if it will work."

Karvo went very red. The innuendo reflected on his tastes. He was going to make a speech, but Chatty looked at his watch, said, "I'll be late," and went.

* * *

Magnolia was not Karvo's first mistake. Art is the residue of innumerable rejections; so, in fact, is love. So is everything. Some rejections are more difficult than others. Karvo was the godhead of the organization; Chatty had had to give up years ago, after his first breakdown, but Karvo clung to him. He had drifted into becoming the oilcan of the machine, the worn-out doctor. Sooner or later, everyone from the doorman upwards was bound to turn to

Chatty: the shrunk face, the one-lung chest, the shaky hand, the sad busy eyes, the weak, grating voice that seemed to contain the dregs of all the rumors in the world, concealed a dedication to all the things the machine had forgotten to do. The very weakness of the voice contained a final assuring sense that the situation, whatever it was, had hit bottom and that he had fallen back on forces only he was in touch with. What his official job was, neither he nor anyone knew. Except that he had to put everything right.

In black moments, he would say, "I'm the company's hangman." A shrewd actress would know she was losing her part if she found herself dining at Claridge's alone with Chatty, with champagne on the table. One or two of Karvo's wives had had the disturbing experience of seeing Chatty arrive at the house with flowers and were alarmed by his tête-à-têtes. In the middle of an evening's drinking, actors would suddenly wonder why Chatty was telling them, again and again, that they were very great artists. Diners at the Spangle or the Hundred and Five would notice how a neat, sick man, darkened by sun lamp, so often seemed to be at a certain table with a girl who was leaning close to him and pouring out what was, momentarily, her heart, while he nodded and filled up her glass. They had seen some girls with elbows on the table, with tears running down their cheeks, and next to them, elbows on table too, not in tears, but wearing his wrecked expression, Chatty stroking a hand, listening, nodding, squeezing and—when a waiter passed—giving an efficient nod at the bottle. It would be replaced. Some held his arm. Others, once every half hour, he lightly kissed on the bare shoulder. He might ask to look at a ring. Or, gazing at their palms, tell their fortunes. To others he whispered a scandal: they leaned back open-mouthed and when he had finished they leaned towards him and went back satisfied to their own tale. In certain cases, the difficult ones, he might be driven almost to the edge (but never further) of his own secret. Very rarely, they laughed; occasionally simple ones would put an arm round his neck and rest a head on his shoulders, not thinking about him at all, their soft hunting eyes gazing round the restaurant and he would sit back happily, giving only an occasional glance at them. His job was done.

So now he was with Magnolia. She was a woman who easily changed size. She could inflate or contract. At the moment, not touching her smoked salmon, she was contracting. The large mouth had become no more than a slot, her large eyes a collection of flints, her flowing brows had stiffened and had the boding look of moustaches, her noble breasts were like a pair of grenades with the pins out; and those arms, usually so still and statuesque, now swiped about like Indian clubs as she talked. And Karvo said she could not move! Chatty, sitting beside her, came only up to her shoulder, and when she looked down at him, she looked as though she was planning eventually to get up and tread on him, affecting not to see he was there.

"These things never last with Karvo," he persisted, worn-out, tasting the wine and pouring her a glass. She looked at it with hatred. "A girl like that can't hold him."

"A television starlet from Walsall," she sneered. "She can't act. And she smells. Ask the cameramen. Something's happened to Karvo—what is it? You know him. His wife is at the back of this. Well, he's not going to get away with it. I'll kill her. Chatty, I'm going on that train. Why doesn't he fly?"

"The doctor stopped him."

"We always flew. He needs more than a doctor. I shall be on that train."

Her mouth widened and she started to eat. It looked as though she were eating what she had just killed.

"You know, Nolly," said Chatty, "you're a superb girl.

Shall I tell you something? I found you, didn't I? Oh, yes, I did. I saw you in *Potter's Clay* years before Karvo. It's all my fault. I made Karvo take you. I showed him what you were. I said, 'She will lift the whole show, get it right off the ground.' You'll sit there like a goddess. When you move, just as you are doing now . . ."

She was putting a piece of smoked salmon towards her mouth but stopped and put her fork back to look at him.

"There," he exclaimed, "that movement! What you did that very minute! A small thing like that: you're a lady. There's breeding in it. I'll tell you something I never told you. When you and he went off that first evening I knew something was on; I came in here and I got plastered."

She was bored. "Why?"

Chatty turned his head away. "Stop bitching. You know why."

And he turned his head back again and gazed at her and blinked. He had sunk lower on the banquette so that she now swelled enormously over him, and as she swelled, so he sank lower, reached for his glass and drained it recklessly and stared up at her through the glass he drank. She studied him with the slow astonishment of a cat that is not quite sure whether she has a mouse beside her; then with horror; then with the look of a mother who says to her baby "I could eat you," but a mother who is going to do it, and not eat, but gnaw. He put out his small brown hand and rested it on her leg and controlled his surprise at the monumental size of it.

Chatty rarely had to go as far as this; most girls—and Magnolia was one—could recognize the difference between the pass direct and a pinch that was the retraction of a careless preceding remark. With Magnolia his normal methods had failed: expressing unbelief, then sympathy, then fierce indignation at the man—he was cracking up, had lost his reason, it was "his age," etc., etc.—Chatty would then attack the other woman, mentioning false or disorganized teeth, affected voice and adding minutiae of his own: rubbing calves, perhaps, or inturned toes. He would throw in the name of some interesting man (*"not in the theatre, darling"*) and drop into a word or two of French. *Tout passe, tout casse, tout lasse*—wasted, by the way, on Magnolia who did not speak French. He would then, if they were still difficult, move on towards his own secret. He was a waif; they were both lonely waifs. Chatty's secret: that was what everyone wanted to know and they became alert at this stage. Why wasn't he married? Was he queer? Was he nothing? Mother's boy? Auntie's boy? He evaded these insinuations by talking about his farm. Ah, but what went on at that farm? Who was this woman he called Aunt Laura down at the farm? There were times when it seemed that only the desperate pass, what he called the final solution, would do.

"Darling, I want to bite that lovely shoulder. Come down to the farm with me."

They were almost agog. What orgies went on there? They would discover the secret. Discreetly he moved to enthusiastic anticlimax.

"We shall be on our own. There's only Aunt Laura there. She's deaf. Looking after her bedridden sister. Very religious. I'll show you my Hereford herd. We can cut down nettles. Aunt Laura's woman who used to come up from the village to cook is in hospital, but we'll manage. It's the simple life. Just ourselves. What d'you say?"

He had never known them not to say No. Very apologetically too. Apologizing calmed them. Then he would pay the bill, drop them in the firm's car, saying, "In the old days I used to slip away to Paris." Just the idea! But not with him, oh dear God, no! They could do better than that —and sometimes did, and when he dropped them at their flat, he had dissolved an illusion and given them a new one.

But Chatty did not offer Aunt Laura to Magnolia. He had seen that this case was too desperate; also, what would any sane woman sooner do—go to Venice or to Wiltshire? No press in Wiltshire. So when he said, "Stop bitching," and there was no answering twitch of her leg to his hand, he took a long and conquering breath.

"I know how you feel," he said. "I feel as you do. I said to Karvo, 'You don't understand Magnolia. She's virginal. There's an inner chastity, something single-hearted, when she loves she loves once and for all. I feel it, you feel it, the audience feels it. She's a one-man woman. Bucky and the Bronsinki boy—oh yes, I know about *them,* but that doesn't alter the inner truth.' "

Magnolia looked strangely at him. The idea that she had an inner nature was new to her, that it was virginal, amazed. Her mouth started to become its normal size, her brows began to curve—at the recollection, of course, of Bucky and the Bronsinki boy—and she looked with the beginning of curiosity at Chatty: she had the sensation that he was revealing an unsuspected vacancy in her life. Chatty, always sensitive to hopeful change, took his hand off her leg—a good move: Magnolia tried out a feeling of austerity, it made her feel important. Still, her refrain did not change, except in tone. There was a just detectable new note of self-sacrifice.

"I'm going on that train. I hate trains. Why doesn't he fly? Well, I'm going on it. I've got my reservation."

Was a moral nature being born? Chatty put his hand back quickly.

"We'll go together," he said. "I've got a reservation too."

"You? You have? Here," she said coarsely, "what's the bloody idea? Is this one of Karvo's bloody tricks?" A dangerous moment! Moral natures are not born suddenly. Chatty gave a violent grip of righteousness to her leg. He spoke in a righteous voice, not forgetting to put some of the ginger of the underhand in it.

"My job's at stake, too," he said out of the corner of his mouth. "I don't know about you, but I know what I'm doing. We're going together to rescue him. We've got to save that man, between us. It's worth ten thousand a year to me. But money's nothing. I don't know why I should save him—well, I do know. It's for you."

"I'm going to raise hell at the Gare de Lyon." She stuck to it. "I've got their seat numbers. I'll turn the dining car upside down. I'll . . ."

"No, darling. Listen to me. Wait till we get to Venice. The Paris press is no good to you. They'll be in Venice, anyway."

Chatty made one of his body-wrecking efforts and sent up a hard stare into Magnolia's eyes. He noted, with satisfaction, as the stare continued, that when she removed his hand from her leg she did so with a primness which must have been a new thing for her.

* * *

Months afterwards Chatty told Karvo that until the Magnolia episode, and in spite of all his experience, he had never realized what genius owes to lucky insights. The plan was clumsy and full of risks. You had to choose between evils. Better a scene at the Gare de Lyon—without the press—than a scene at Venice; the thing to avoid was something, thank God, that had not got into Magnolia's stupid head. She could easily have flown to Venice on her own and waited to trap him at the Gritti as he arrived. Why didn't she think of that?

"I tumbled on the obvious," Chatty said. "My task was to encourage this new growth of virtue in Magnolia. There is a detective in every virtuous woman—you know, 'I'm having my husband followed.' It is the idea of *following* you that has narrowed her mind."

He clinched with Magnolia quickly.

"Show me that ticket," he snapped at her. Half-bewildered, she got it out of her bag. He took it and said, "We'll scrap this part. Let me have it. We'll fly to Paris while Maureen is being sick in the Channel and pick up the train there."

Magnolia got up from the table and had a look of dawning righteousness on her face. ("She looked ready to sing 'Fight the good fight,' " Chatty said.)

"I admit," she said to Chatty, "I was wrong about you."

* * *

Chatty went back to Karvo.

"Well?" said Karvo vehemently.

"We're going *with* you. I can't stop her."

"Chatty!" shouted Karvo.

"Listen. The first principle in dealing with problems is to break them into their parts. First of all, I am restoring her virginity. I am doing that for self-protection."

"Stop being so clever. I have to think of the press. She can't come with me. That's the whole point."

Chatty began a long fit of coughing. He coughed up and down the sofa.

"There's nothing to be done about that. I've gone the whole hog with her."

Karvo looked cynically and despisingly at Chatty. Chatty understood the look.

"No, I agree, not that. Loyalty to the company does not go as far as that," said Chatty, wiping his eyes.

Karvo growled at him.

"We shall travel in the back part of the train," said Chatty.

"That won't do, I tell you," shouted Karvo. "This is serious."

"Tony, pictures have destroyed your intelligence. You're going to Venice, aren't you? You leave Paris on the Adriatique at fifteen thirty. Right? So Magnolia and I have to be on it. I have got our reservations, but by some mistake, in the office—I don't know who the girl is who looks after your reservations, but you ought to sack her—Magnolia and I are leaving Paris at seven thirty-six in the morning, on the Geneva nonstop."

"You're not going to Venice?"

"We *think* we are going to Venice. Spiritually Magnolia is traveling in the last coach on your train. Physically we shall be in Geneva."

"Why Geneva, for God's sake?" said Karvo.

"The lake, the mountains, William Tell."

"She can fly from Geneva!" said Karvo.

"I am going to be very ill," said Chatty.

"Ill?" said Karvo. "Your mind's ill. Your brain has gone soft. You've made a mess of this. I shall fly. I shall have to fly and you know what the doctor said. Come to my funeral."

"I'll be laid out in Geneva," said Chatty, "a good half day before you and Maureen get to Venice. Come to mine."

* * *

Chatty (Karvo used to say) would never have been one of the great directors; he always preferred the trees to the wood. An obscurantist. His plots were always entangled. He never thought things out. But he had two great gifts: a talent for confusing issues and, above all, for illness. This gave him the invalid's mastery of detail. When Chatty sickened he was inspired.

Before the flight to Paris he did not go to bed at all; he

was on the telephone to Magnolia and drinking hard. It made him sound sincere. Take the calls to Magnolia first:

"Magnolia. Something terrible has happened. That Miss What's-her-name in the office must have spilled the beans. Karvo's heard something. The swine's catching the *morning* train to Venice."

He waited and prayed. No. Thank God! Magnolia did not say, "There's no morning train to Venice."

"The seven thirty-six. We've got to be there. We're flying tonight. I'm changing the tickets now."

"Call it off," said Magnolia suspiciously.

"No!" shouted Chatty. "I'm getting on that train and so are you. I've got the tickets in my pocket. You're not going to let them get away with it. They're committing *adultery,* Magnolia!"

"You're drinking, Chatty."

"Of course I'm drinking," said Chatty. "I'll have the car for the airport at one fifteen. They must be in Paris already. No. I don't know where."

This decided Magnolia: that woman, in Paris!

As for illness, indispensable to the refinements of strategy: Chatty was a wreck when he got Magnolia into the plane. Only his fevered eyes seemed to be alive: they seemed to drag his body after them.

In the plane he muttered on and off during the flight. Halfway across the Channel he began fidgeting in his seat, going through his pockets and wearing Magnolia down with the words "I've forgotten my pills. I can't move without them." Magnolia was frightened by his state: the dawn gave him an awful yellow look. He collapsed into a chair at the café at the Invalides and sent a waiter to see if there was a pharmacy open and told Magnolia the man could easily make a fatal mistake. She must go with him. No pharmacies were open. Magnolia's ignorance of French brought out her aggression.

"My friend is very ill," she said in English to the waiter. He did not understand.

"My husband is dying!" she shouted.

This episode made the arrival of Chatty and Magnolia at the Gare de Lyon seem like an ambulance party rushing to hospital with three minutes to spare before the train left or the patient died. Chatty was not going to have Magnolia running loose on the platform for half an hour scrutinizing every coach or finding out they were on the Geneva train.

They sat breathless in the compartment. Chatty had a wide range of coughs, from the short, dry hack to the display that came up from the ankles and seemed to split his eyes.

"A little more air." He got up to open the window.

"Sit down," said Magnolia. She was frightened. Her strong arms drew down the heavy window of the French train.

Then she watched. When he stopped coughing at last he told a terrible story about an injection for tetanus he had been given when he was a schoolboy as the train moved off, and laughed.

"Stop laughing," she said. "You'll bring it on again."

Her face, he was pleased to see, had grown severe. A firm, almost chaste look of moral reprimand was growing on it. He got out a cigarette.

"Don't smoke," she said, and repeated with appeal: "Chatty, *please* don't smoke."

He put his cigarettes away. "You're right," he said.

"Try and sleep."

"I wish I could. People keep passing in the corridor. Do you mind if we pull down the blind?"

"I'll do it," she said, commanding.

"Magnolia," he said. "You're being extraordinarily good to me. You're a saint. I'm sorry, I seem to be making a mess of this."

"It's not your fault," she said.

"It is."

"No, it's mine," she said on a note of noble confession. But she gave a grind to her teeth. "I ought to have flown." Oh, God, thought Chatty, she's off again.

"If you had I would have gone with you," he said. "I'm going to see you through this thing. When I think of that bastard twelve coaches up the train . . ."

"Twelve?" she said, uncrossing her legs and frowning.

"You can imagine how I feel," he said. "I look at you and I see a woman he has never seen."

"Sleep," she said sternly.

"I can't," he said.

"You must."

"I've made a mess of my life. I'm sorry for a lot of things I've done. Why did I let him take you?"

Chatty closed his eyes but not completely. He had to keep an eye on her. He was not going to have her slipping out into the corridor, searching the coaches or talking to informative strangers. He was surprised to discern, though mistily through his lashes, that she was looking neither restless nor relaxed, but sat there rigidly gazing at him with apprehension. A novel combination of feelings was growing in her. As virtue was increased by her mission and by looking after him, so a new fear was born too: the fear that is native to virtue. She was traveling alone in a railway compartment with a man in a chartably disturbed state, a man who—so he said—had repressed certain feelings for years. She was in his hands. And in a foreign country too. As she watched the French meadows and the licentious woodlands go by, she wondered if he would go mad and attack her. These were pleasant sensations; they made her feel prim. What did she, what did anyone, know about Chatty? In sleep he looked very ugly.

At Dijon he opened his eyes and sneezed.

"When the sun rises the moon sneezes," he said. "Old Chinese proverb."

He laughed. She did not like that. He *was* mad! She sat back and squeezed her legs together tightly.

The ticket inspector came in.

"What did he say? He was looking at me," asked Magnolia, afterwards.

"He said he had seen you in a picture. *Disarmed.*"

Magnolia looked happy for the first time.

"I wish I spoke French like you do," she said. "Teach me some words." And taking out her mirror made up her face.

"And," said Chatty, leering, as the train clattered through the long sidings and went out of Dijon, "he was looking at the drawn blinds. The frogs never miss anything. They have imagination."

Magnolia closed her bag and was on guard.

"I can't eat," said Chatty when he heard the luncheon bell tinkle. "But I'll take you along. You must eat something."

"No," she said. "I don't want anything."

She was either not being distracted from her revenge or she was becoming increasingly the nurse. Chatty wished he knew which it was.

Hours passed sleepily and then, seeing her restive, he told her about his Aunt Laura. She used to go to Aix where the waters are good for the kidneys. The doctors could not decide whether she had two or two and a half kidneys. Many people, he said, have extra rudimentary organs. Magnolia saw herself approaching his secret.

"Two and a half! Is she really your aunt?" she said.

"I will tell you the honest truth," said Chatty.

"Yes?"

"I don't really know. We were brought up to call her Auntie. She has been like a mother to us. And yet more like a nun than a mother. Something must have happened to her—some disappointment—she gave up everything for us."

Magnolia found herself wondering how she would look as a nun.

Chatty said, "Say what you like, there is *something* about nuns. I can see it in you. All women have a nun inside them." It was pleasant to hear and made her idly double her watch on Chatty.

"Those poor nuns in Africa," she said, ready to put up a fight if he sprang at her.

Chatty was, of course, thinking of the approaching crisis. It would come when they got to Geneva. The question was whether she would see what had happened, at the station; or whether he might hold out until they saw Lake Leman. He was occupied with the fantasy that he might palm off the lake as the Mediterranean. He rejected it. He plumped for a terrible scene at the station. He would stagger off the train and simply collapse on the platform. "Get a doctor. Get an ambulance!" he would shout. He suddenly heard Magnolia say irritably, "When do we get to Venice?"

"An hour and a half, I should say."

"Don't you *know?*" said Magnolia, getting crosser.

And ruining everything, two inspectors slid back the door of the compartment, a young one and an old one. The old one had spread the news that Magnolia was on the train.

"When do we get to Venice?" she called out in English to the older one.

"Venice?" said the old man, or inspector, in English, too. "We are going to Geneva."

"Chatty!" shouted Magnolia.

"This is the Geneva train," said the younger inspector in French.

"Good Lord," said Chatty, "They've put us on the wrong train."

"Give me those tickets!" Magnolia shouted again.

The speed at which Magnolia left her religious order was something Chatty always remembered. Her face became crimson, then violet, marked by changing dabs of green; she swelled up, she rose up. She pushed Chatty aside and started on the inspectors. The older one stepped back and pushed the young one forward; the young one made a speech. She flew at Chatty, "What is he saying?"

And not waiting for an answer, she declaimed that she was due at Venice that very moment, to receive the Festival prize; that the train must be put into reverse; that a plane be brought instantly into the compartment; that the train itself must, if necessary, fly. The young inspector gazed at the fling of Magnolia's white arms from armpit to wrist, the terrifying spread of her fingers, the rise and fall of her volcanic bosom, the blue eyes that ripped him, the throat that boiled, the nostrils that went in and out like bellows, until tears of admiration formed in his young eyes. Chatty raised his eyebrows at the older inspector, who raised his eyes in profound understanding at Chatty. The lips of the young one did not speak, but they moved with unconscious, unavailing kisses.

Can't act? thought Chatty. "There ought to have been a train sequence in the film. Lift? She's lifting the train off the rails.

Of course, he reflected, Magnolia was life, not art: that is what had got Karvo and what horrified Chatty. In his quick croak he made several speeches in French, conveying that, in the present misunderstanding, the French railways were not to blame. Exchanging glances the two inspectors conveyed that the next hour and a half would be hell. They showed eagerness to share this opportunity with Chatty, even to exchange places. The desire to experience hell with Magnolia shone in the eyes of the younger man. The older one's face indicated that, in the well-known relations between men and women, it is the nuance that is always interesting. They congratulated Chatty silently on his fortune. Think—they signaled to each other—of the reconciliation! Sadly, looking restlessly at each other, they went away to the end of the coach and glanced up the corridor to see if anything was happening yet and if their moment might come. Once, the older man went up to the compartment and then hurried back to report: the blinds which had shot up in the dispute were down again. The young man sighed sadly. The reconciliation already?

No, not the reconciliation. Magnolia was crying, letting tears bowl down her cheeks—if only she could have done that on the set!—she had tried to hit Chatty twice but in the swaying of the train she had missed. He said nothing, but lighting a cigarette, fell into a run of quiet coughing. He had pulled down the blinds so that she could have a good cry undisturbed. After about fifty coughs the irritating sound made her forget to sob and reach for her handbag.

"You are a dirty swine. Karvo put you up to this," she said.

"There was no other way of getting you away from that man," he said. "I wanted you to myself."

"Don't you dare touch me," she said as he moved to the seat beside her. The fear she had amused herself with, in the early part of the journey, now became real. He was abducting her. This was a rape. Chatty innocent? Chatty ill? Chatty, the orphan bachelor shedding a tear about his Aunt Laura? Aunt Laura, my eye. He was nothing more than a dirty rapist. A new layer of virginity formed over her, icing her completely.

"Have you ever been to Geneva?" Chatty said.

"Don't insult me," said Magnolia.

"Beautiful lake," said Chatty.

No answer.

"Mont Blanc, not far," said Chatty.

No answer.

"I haven't been there for fifteen years," Chatty said. "Not since I was up at Appol in the sanatorium."

No comment.

"I left a lung up there."

"I'm getting a plane," said Magnolia.

Chatty lit another cigarette.

"That's five you've smoked in the last half hour. Look at the floor," said Magnolia. There was, Chatty noted, just a tiny bit of the nurse left in her. He tactfully picked up the cigarette stubs and put them in the ashtray and sat down again. There was nothing like a little tidying for getting a woman through a crisis.

"I've never told anyone this," he said. "I've got to tell you. Well, no, you won't be interested."

"What?" she snapped.

Chatty sighed.

"It's too painful," he said. "Some things one never gets over. Just a German girl I knew there—I mean there, Geneva."

"What German girl?" Magnolia sneered.

"Up at Appol, in the sanatorium where I was. We both were. She was very ill. It went on for months. We used to go for walks—not very far. We had one pair of lungs between us—it wasn't too bad. It was in May—flowers, you know, lambs—spring: we couldn't stand it. One morning we got into the funicular and said: "Let's go off," just like that, no luggage, just as we were. We were laughing all the way down. I got a car to drive us to Geneva. We went to an hotel, an old-fashioned one. Our room had two marble-encased washbasins side by side, very handsome ones. Two people could stand there and wash together. You could wash each other—Swiss idea of marriage, I suppose."

"Don't be disgusting," said Magnolia.

"We laughed so much at those basins," Chatty said, "that the first thing we did was to stand there, splashing water at each other. We soaked the place. We couldn't stop laughing. I was drying myself with a big towel: I'd got my head in it. Suddenly I noticed she'd stopped laughing and I pulled the towel away from my face. She was leaning over the basin. It was splashed all over with blood. It was coming out of her mouth. A hemorrhage."

Magnolia leaned back to get further away from him.

"I'd killed her," he said. "She died up at Appol two months later. I've never told anyone."

How often she had heard: "No one knows anything about Chatty."

"It wasn't your fault," she said at last.

"We were sex-mad," he said. "I never slept with her."

"Oh," said Magnolia.

"You can live without it," said Chatty.

"What was her name?"

"Greta."

A shot of jealousy hit Magnolia. The hills were turning into mountains, the fields were steeper, she strained to see if there were yet a sight of the Alps. She wanted to be high up in them.

"Where's Appol?" she said.

"High up," he said. "There's an enormous lake at Geneva. We used to walk there. I shot a picture there once before I cracked up. I've always had the idea of doing William Tell."

Magnolia's business sense woke up.

"I've never told anyone this. I never told Karvo—he's not the kind of a man who would understand. You're the only person who knows. You have sympathy. You know what it is to lose someone. Now you know why I cheated about the tickets. I wanted you to see the place and walk by the lake."

Magnolia's mind was still in Appol. How wonderful to be like Greta and die slowly, untouched, by the lake: Chatty attending her and telling Karvo the news.

Brusquely Chatty said, "Forget it. I've got us rooms at the Splendide. We'll be there in twenty minutes. We'll have a drink. The press will be there. I lined that up in London."

Magnolia came down from the high snows.

It *was* an abduction. She saw herself defending a virtue made absolute. It was a sensation she had not had since she was a girl of fifteen when she had knocked a man off his bicycle who had chased her across a common: a superb feeling.

In the taxi that took them from the railway station in Geneva to the hotel, she said to Chatty, "The first thing you do is to find out about the plane to Venice."

"Wait," said Chatty, "till you see the view. I want to show you Greta's grave."

An hour later she was standing at the window of her hotel room looking out at that view. There was no plane until the morning. She would have to hold out all night. She could hear Chatty moving in the room next door. Presently there was a knock at her door: Chatty advancing already upon her?

She called out, "You can't come in."

But the door was open and the chambermaid was there. The gentleman in Number 67 next door, the maid said, had been taken very ill; would she come at once?

Chatty was lying on his bed with his shoes off and a hole in the toe of one of his socks. He had a handkerchief to his mouth. He reached for her hand. "Greta," he said. "A doctor."

* * *

Chatty is up at Appol. He reports to Karvo on the telephone.

"Just the rest I needed. I was coming here anyway. Magnolia was an angel. She still is. What she needs is a part as a nurse. When she visits me she comes into the room on tiptoe. She's bought a dress that looks like a uniform. She's got exactly the face that goes with high necks and starch. And she is full of suffering—no, Karvo, suffering for *me*. Did I say 'nurse'? A nun, that's her part."

And two or three weeks later:

"I'm getting out soon. She wants to move me down to Geneva to an old hotel—that place with double washbasins, do you know? Remind me to tell you. It's a very morbid idea actually, but she is in that mood at the moment. It does her good to be morbid for a bit."

And later again:

"Yes. I've moved. No, *she's* got the washbasin room. I'm on the same floor though. She comes along with a nice man called Ronzini or Bronzoni or something—she met him, yes, of course, in the bar. The uniform has gone—I miss it. Well, what did I tell you? It's all right now. She's just been in to say, do I mind if Bronzoni drives her to Garda for a couple of days. Well, I don't mind, but I wonder what she has been telling that Italian. He said to me, 'She needs rest, Mr. Chatterton. You have caused her a lot of anxiety.' I have an idea she has told him she doesn't feel safe with me. No need for you to make funny remarks. I had a very trying job restoring her virginity: the sort of job that's beyond you, Karvo. You wouldn't recognize the girl who is going off to Garda for a couple of days. Exalted. I'll be back in London at the end of the month. For God's sake, send me some money. Prices are very high here."

ABOUT THE AUTHOR

V. S. Pritchett was born in England in 1900. He is a short-story writer, novelist, critic, and traveler. His short stories have appeared in collections in the United States under the titles *The Sailor and the Saint* and *When My Girl Comes Home* and as individual contributions in *The New Yorker* and *Holiday*. Among his novels are *Mr. Beluncle, Dead Man Leading,* and *The Key to My Heart*. Random House has also published *The Living Novel and Later Appreciations,* a collection of critical essays, most of which appeared originally in *The New Statesman*. He has been a lifelong contributor to this paper and is now a director. His memoir, *A Cab at the Door,* was published by Random House in 1968.

Mr. Pritchett's extensive sojourns in Europe, the Middle East, and South America have led to the writing of several books of travel, among them, recently, *The Offensive Traveller*. With photographs by Evelyn Hofer, Mr. Pritchett has written *London Perceived, Dublin: A Portrait* and *New York Perceived.*

Mr. Pritchett has visited the United States, where he gave the Christian Gauss lectures at Princeton, was Beckman Professor at the University of California in Berkeley, and has been writer in residence at Smith College.

Mr. Pritchett is married and lives in London. His critical study of George Meredith will be published by Random House in 1970.

DATE DUE

GAYLORD PRINTED IN U.S.A.